THE HEART OF A TEMPEST
THE HEARTS OF ADVENTURE SWEET ROMANCE
BOOK I

CHLOE FLOWERS

BOOK DESCRIPTION

THE HEART OF A TEMPEST

THE HEARTS OF ADVENTURE SWEET ROMANCE SERIES

BOOK 1

A LADY PLOTTING HER WAY OUT OF AN ARRANGED MARRIAGE,

A SMUGGLER WITH A CRYPTIC INVITATION TO A CLANDESTINE MEETING,

A GROUP OF PIRATES OUT FOR REVENGE.

IT'S THE PERFECT STORM.

NOTE: This is the *sexy version* of the novel The Heart of a Tempest, (Book 1 of The Hearts of Adventure Sweet Romance Series By Chloe Flowers).

She's acting a charade and he knows it. The question is-will he demand compensation for keeping her secrets?

Silly question. Of course he will. The bigger question is-will she be able to afford the cost of his silence?

From the moment he discovered her with a sword in one hand, dagger in the other sparring in a hidden meadow, smuggler and ship's captain Landon Hart has been intrigued by that independent, spirited tempest, Keelan Grey. But, he isn't prepared for the impact she has on his tightly guarded heart, or the trouble she manages to attract.

From the moment he happened upon her secret training, Keelan knew Landon Hart was going to be a storm on her horizon. With an assassin killing off members of her family one by one, and a father trying to arrange a marriage between her and a vile plantation owner, Keelan had enough on her plate without an exasperating, rakishly handsome, ship's captain getting in the way of her plots and schemes.

When Landon's own dangerous secrets collide with Keelan's, it's the perfect storm.

DISCLAIMER

This book is a work of fiction.
Names, characters, places and incidents are the product of the
author's imagination or are used fictitiously. Any resemblance to
actual people, (living or dead) events or places is entirely
coincidental.

AUTHOR'S NOTE

My son was born prematurely; he weighed 3 pounds 12 ounces. And at 18 inches long, he looked like a string bean. I spent many weeks with him in the hospital, which is where I began writing this book.

I needed a hero.

And I needed to be strong for him, so I created a strong heroine.

My son needed to be a fighter, so we named him Cade, which means little battler.

Writing about Keelan and Landon took me away from the sterile, white, beeping reality of the hospital and put me into the sultry South, with its sweet-smelling magnolia's, warm nights and delectable, mouth-watering food.

I wrote using a more modern tone and language for today's modern reader, I hope you don't mind.

I enjoyed the escape. I hope you do too.

Chloe

This book is dedicated to all the readers who wrote in and asked me to write a sweet romance version of my Pirates & Petticoats Series. I'm grateful and blessed.

CAF

I left a gift for you at the end of the book. You'll love the recipe!

The dishes Ruth served were inspired by recipes from: *An Antebellum Household Journal Including the South Carolina Receipts and Remedies of Emily Warton Sinkler,* by Anne Sinkler Whaley LeClercq. I purchased it in Charleston when touring a plantation home; it's filled with wonderful information about life in the Lowcountry, which helped in my research for this series.

Chloe

THE HEART OF A TEMPEST

THE HEARTS OF ADVENTURE SWEET ROMANCE SERIES

BOOK ONE

A CLASH OF SWORDS

CHARLESTON, South Carolina

MAY 1811

TWO FIGURES CIRCLED, each with a sword in one hand and a
dagger in the other. The first stood tall and lithe, his blade flashing, barely visible in the early morning light. His opponent,
smaller in both build and height, quickly blocked the slice.

Merchant ship captain, Landon Hart, and his best friend and
business associate, Captain Conal O'Brien, crept to the edge of
the clearing for a better view of the duel.

"We'll skirt the meadow and keep behind the cover of the trees," Landon said in a low voice. As an orphaned youth, he'd been in his fair share of unbalanced skirmishes. In more familiar surroundings, rather than among the vast plantation estates outside the city of Charleston, he would have already intervened. He and Conal had just turned down the lane to Twin Pines when they heard the collision of swords nearby.

A dense layer of dead pine needles on the forest floor muffled their steps. Soon, they were close enough to discern the whisper and hiss of the blades, followed by the strident metallic clash and *ching* as sword met sword.

Although the larger dueler had tinges of gray at his temples, he moved with a seasoned grace and nimble ease. Fluid arcs chased fleeting thrusts in seamless sequence. His sleeves were rolled to the elbows, shirt neatly tucked.

The boy's breeches were thin at the knees and stuffed into a pair of boots several sizes too large. A faded blue length of cloth wrapped his head, tied at the base of his neck where the tail hung halfway down his back. Even in the over-sized boots that threatened to trip him up with every thrust, the surprisingly agile and light-footed waif held his own.

The two duelers seemed to be alone. There were no mounts or wagons nearby, so this didn't appear to be an ambush or an attempt at a robbery. No seconds to serve as witnesses, nor a physician standing ready, so perhaps not a planned duel. But then, what was it?

Conal leaned closer, his voice soft. "Doesn't seem a fair fight. I'm going to put a stop to it." His eyebrows shot up as the boy's dagger flashed in an arc, and caught the upper shaft of his opponent's sword. The youth beat the tip away and began his own attack with his long blade.

"Wait." Landon placed a hand on Conal's arm. His friend had a knack for acting first and thinking second when it came to physical confrontations. "I don't think it's an earnest fight," Landon murmured, as he studied the movements of the duelers. "It seems to me that it's a training session of some sort. Let's see how the young one fares. I find it peculiar a grubby whelp wields such a fine weapon yet wears those poorly fitted boots."

Conal watched another moment and nodded. He leaned a shoulder against a tree trunk.

"Step away, Keelan," the older man said in a clipped British accent. He swung his sword in a swift upward flash toward the lad's chest. "You are offering too short a path to your middle. It leaves you vulnerable to my long blade."

Keelan was an Irish name. Many families from Great Britain, his included, took the crossing to America hoping to start a better life. It was interesting that an Englishman took the time to tutor an Irish lad.

In answer, Keelan slashed his sword diagonally down across his opponent's exposed stomach, deftly cutting a ten-inch swath in the older man's linen shirt.

"You mean like that, Daniel?" he retorted with a smirk. He also had a British accent on his tongue. A Brit with an Irish name, how curious.

"He's but a lad hardly weaned," Conal whispered. "His voice still has the high pitch of a child."

The two combatants paused. Daniel scowled at the tear in his shirt before lunging forward, swinging his weapon in a rapid combination while the boy tried valiantly to block the attack. The blows thundered harder, the blade hissing like an angry snake. However, it wasn't the man's skill that brought the boy down.

It was the boots.

The coarse grass snagged his heel and foiled his hasty retreat. With a loud "Oof!" Keelan went down hard on his backside, the jolt knocking the sword from his grasp.

"You are finished," Daniel said. He pointed the tip of his weapon to the boy's chest.

"Hold!" Landon shouted, stepping from the shelter of the

trees. If he was wrong about the training, another moment's delay could mean the child's life. He wouldn't stand idly and allow the outmatched lad to be harmed.

Daniel's head jerked up. When the shout distracted the man, Keelan reacted. He kicked his legs up and somersaulted backward, losing both boots in the process. The maneuver put him in a crouched position ready to fight again. Then the lad did the strangest thing.

He threw his dagger directly at them.

Landon and Conal yelped and dove to the ground as the weapon whizzed over their heads and landed in the dirt somewhere behind them.

The lad smacked the earth in frustration.

Daniel shook his head. "Your throw was not balanced." With his hand on his hip, he jabbed the air with his sword. "Your chest must point to your target before you release."

"What matters is I threw first, which yields me five points!" The boy flexed his hand and licked the inside of his thumb. "It beats the three you get for disarming me, aye, Daniel? I win today."

Daniel glanced at his wounded shirt, then over at the trees where Keelan had thrown the dagger, before he shrugged in agreement.

"An interesting game," Landon said, brushing his breeches as he got back to his feet.

Daniel turned toward them, pointing the tip of his sword at Landon's chest before stepping in front of the boy. "What is your business at Twin Pines?"

Conal stepped forward, drawing the movement of Daniel's weapon with him. "My uncle, Fynn Ahern, scheduled a meeting with Commodore Grey for this morning. I have a letter from the Commodore confirming it."

Daniel lowered his sword. "The Commodore does indeed have an appointment with a Mr. Ahern today. Where is he?"

Conal shifted. "He's dead. I'm Captain Conal O'Brien of the *Seeker*. This is my business partner, Landon Hart, captain of the *Desire*. We were Mr. Ahern's associates." Conal reached out to grasp Daniel's hand.

"I'm sorry to hear of his passing," Daniel said

"Thank you. It was unexpected," Conal replied.

Daniel returned his attention to Keelan. "Your skills have developed well. I'm proud of your progress." He deftly threw his dirk. The knife hit the same tree where, moments before, Conal had stood. It struck with a solid thunk, and the bottom half of a feather wedged into the bark, fluttered lazily to the ground. "Your impatience and lack of concentration denied you the ten points you would have earned had you actually hit the target. Instead, you're left with a meager five points and a nasty little cut." He reached down and helped the lad up. "Is it deep?"

Keelan studied it. "I don't think so. Slaney will rub marigold tincture on it and it'll be fine." He warily eyed the two strangers as he retrieved his stray boots.

Daniel put a hand to his chest and gave a slight bow. "I'm Daniel Hunter, valet to Commodore George Grey the newest owner of Twin Pines Plantation." He sheathed his sword and wiped his brow with his sleeve. Although only a couple of hours after sunrise, the air was thick and still, his shirt clingy with sweat.

Landon assessed the boy. His shoulders, though slight, were straight and haughty. Not much muscle to his arms. His wrists were thin, almost feminine, making Landon even more impressed with Keelan's dexterity. Recalling the trials of his own youth, before Conal's Uncle Fynn had taken him under his wing, he knew well the importance of besting this particular skill.

"You do well for one so young," Landon observed.

The boy shot an uneasy glance toward Daniel, grabbed an oversized boot and shoved his foot inside.

"Well, yes, er..." Daniel sent a sideways glance at the ragged figure busy snatching the second rebellious boot from the grass. The valet shrugged. "The lessons are for the child's protection. Several family members recently died under rather suspicious circumstances, so Keelan's father has decided the training should become more intense."

"Your hand with a sword is impressive, Keelan." Landon gestured toward Daniel. "It's apparent you are being given excellent instruction."

Daniel smiled and inclined his head, accepting the compliment. The boy remained mute.

Landon tried again. "My crew and I must be keen with sword, pistol and dirk, if we're to survive encounters with privateers and pirates. We all do our part to defend the ship. May I voice an observation?" he asked.

"Please do," said Daniel. He relaxed only slightly, keeping his sword in his grasp.

Landon gestured to Keelan's dagger. "Work on the short blade further. 'Tis a more valuable skill to have." The tension in the lad's shoulders tightened. There was something strange about the boy that seemed a bit...off.

The youth straightened, his face flushed. "I don't normally miss so badly," he muttered, eyeing his wounded thumb. "Can a sailor do better?"

Daniel's eyes narrowed in apparent warning, and the boy busied himself by brushing the meadow grass from his sleeves before adjusting the rag covering his head.

"I didn't mean to offend." Amused by his pluck Landon added, "But in answer to your question, aye, any of my crew can do better, else they'd be dead. Now, if you'll adjust your grip like so..." Pulling out his own dagger, he placed it in Keelan's hand, careful to avoid the cut. He moved behind and reached around to set right his hold. "Mr. Hunter is correct about facing your chest to the target. But, you must also cock the hand back, but keep the wrist firm, like this." He gripped the lad's wrist and made the adjustment. "Try it."

Keelan stood still, taut as a fiddle string, his other fist clenched at his side. Daniel took a step then stopped, as if someone else's legs were attached to his body and he wasn't sure how to move them.

"Widen your stance a bit and bring this foot forward." Landon placed his leg against the boy's thigh and kicked his boot away and forward then squeezed his shoulders and gave them a rough shake. "Relax."

Oddly, Keelan remained motionless. Was he angry for the tutelage, or embarrassed? He seemed to struggle to remain composed. Landon frowned, irritated the runt acted so ungratefully. At that age, he would have lapped up this lesson like a thirsty pup. He'd been on his own since very young, and he'd grown up fast. He learned many harsh lessons in the process. Not the least had been how to defend himself against a bigger opponent.

Landon sighed and stepped back. He half expected the child to fling the knife into the pines as hard as he could, and stomp away. Pride seemed to outweigh Keelan's anger, and he finally relaxed his shoulders. He balanced the blade in his hand, drew back, set his wrist, and threw. It hit, pinning the top half of the feather. The boy pursed his lips; whether it was in grim satisfaction or acute aggravation that the instruction had corrected his flaw, it was hard to tell.

"There, you see?" He clapped Keelan on the back. "You're a fast learner. We'd gladly welcome you as a ship's hand aboard the *Desire*."

"Thank you, captain," Keelan said. The corners of his mouth lifted a little.

Daniel cleared his throat. "You'd best get along now, and tell Slaney to inform the commodore and Mr. Grey visitors have arrived and will be at the house shortly." He grasped the lad's elbow and steered him in the direction of the house.

Keelan gave a curt nod and scuffed away. Daniel bent to retrieve the boy's fallen sword, walked to the tree and wrenched the captain's weapon from the trunk.

Landon's bemused gaze followed the child's awkward gait to the edge of the meadow. A branch snagged the head scarf just as the lad ducked under a limb. Keelan whirled with a yelp and quickly yanked at the stubborn cloth, her eyes wide in panic.

Landon froze.

Conal's jaw unhinged.

Long auburn hair cascaded over the waif's shoulders and down to her elbows. Not a boy, but a young woman.

She finally freed the scarf and crashed into the woods. Her departure hung on the breeze for a moment before away, leaving behind a stunned silence.

Landon replayed the last few moments in his mind. His arm across her chest adjusting the blade...his knee nudging the inside of her thigh to widen her stance...It's a wonder she didn't clobber him over the head with her sword.

Keelan's face hadn't been flushed with anger and restraint but instead, in acute embarrassment. Landon caught sight of the valet's scarcely extinguished frown.

"My apologies," he said, fighting to smother a grin.

Daniel nodded. He fidgeted with his belt a moment before he spoke. "It's best forgotten, if you will." He handed the dirk to the captain. "Come, let's retrieve your horses and get them to the stables. Commodore Grey and his brother are most curious as to the nature of this meeting you have requested."

CHAPTER 2

ROTTEN LUCK

O f all the horrible luck.

Keelan stumbled through the pines. She had already retrieved Daniel's dirk from the trunk and her own poorly thrown dagger, which she sheathed in irritation. Her act had been nearly perfect. Hart and Ahern had not guessed her fairer gender. She'd been outed by a tree.

Hart's words nicked at her pride. "Too bad your short blade is weak. My men can do better," she mimicked. "We fight privateers and pirates. Gah!" She placed Daniel's dagger into the back of her waistband. "I've been training with Daniel for over ten years. I should hope I could throw a bloody dirk as well as any gritty sailor," she muttered. "And now I'm talking to myself."

The heady aroma of pine surrounded her. She tore some needles from a drooping branch and rubbed them between her fingers to further release the refreshing scent, hoping to calm her nerves a bit.

She could barely contain her panic when he reached around her chest to adjust her grip on the dagger. However, what happened next almost sent her to flight like a quail from the brush.

Captain Landon Hart touched her in a place no man had ever dared. When he nudged his knee against the inside of her thigh, the outline of his leg left a lingering heat, even after he stepped away. Even more annoying, the desire to breathe momentarily abandoned her. She almost couldn't repress the overwhelming urge to kick him.

She studied her wrist. The ghost of the warm impression where his fingers had touched still lingered. Keelan frowned. In the past, enough suitors pushed their presence upon her: an arm casually brushed against her breast while fastening her cloak, a thigh pressed against hers while seated on a settee. While such errors certainly earned them her instant retreat from the room, a short route to the door, or on occasion, a stinging slap, no man had ever jumbled her thoughts the way Hart had done just now.

Her brain continued to circle back to the way he had *touched* her.

Not the dirk.

Not her grip.

Not the target.

The sensation of his touch.

When he'd reached around her chest to adjust her hold on the dagger; his arm almost skimmed her breasts. She fought to restrain her outrage, because of *course* it was outrage. Doxies played loose with favors, not a commodore's daughter. She'd almost slapped his hands from hers and bolted away.

It had been terrifying.

Perhaps the word "terrifying" was a little dramatic. Still, it wasn't proper behavior between an unmarried lady and a gentleman, and Keelan was conditioned to react accordingly. Since he had been a bit in the dark about her identity at the time, it was hard to cast the blame solely upon his shoulders.

A greater problem existed now. They discovered she was a female. If either man told her uncle...well, the consequences were dire enough to make her shiver in the dense humidity of the southern spring dawn.

Normally, she wouldn't care if he uncovered her secret pastime. However, circumstances being what they were at the moment, it was best to keep activities such as this, well...secret.

Now, that point appeared to be moot.

Pent up frustration and anger at her own clumsiness made her want to scream. Instead, she kicked a pinecone, sending it flying into the dusky underbrush.

Now all involved were in jeopardy because of her, Daniel, especially.

Acidic penalties churned in her stomach. She'd never forgive herself if Daniel was punished or released from service because of this.

Rotten, rotten luck!

After witnessing a drilling session between Keelan and Daniel, her Aunt Sarah nearly fainted from shock. Uncle Jared quietly talked with her father, and asked...well, demanded actually, that the exercises cease. For added insurance toward her compliance, Uncle Jared confiscated her boots.

Out of respect for his sister-in-law, her father acquiesced publicly, but privately encouraged Daniel to continue schooling her.

With good reason.

An assassin killed her mother, her other aunt and cousin all within a few weeks of each other, forcing her and Papa to escape to the Carolinas, fearing for their lives. Uncle Jared should be more understanding, but he coddled his wife, rather than put safe guards into place to protect her.

Keelan groaned. If the captain mentioned what he'd seen, then her uncle could flog Daniel for disobedience, and her father would use the occasion to bring up marriage. Papa believed he could secure her future by wedding her to ancient Mr. Pratt. For some reason, he was convinced that if she married and took another name, the killer wouldn't be able to find her, which was ridiculous.

The more pressing objective at the moment was silencing Hart. It was crucial she find a way to meet with him alone and persuade him to remain quiet about the scene he'd witnessed. Would he agree to keep her secret?

What kind of man was he?

Respectable, hopefully. He was a ship's captain; that had to count toward an honorable reputation, did it not? A man with influence and responsibilities? A leader of men? Surely a crew wouldn't stay with a commander they didn't trust.

Judging by their dress, both were men of significant means. With his sun-bronzed skin, and hair dark as pitch and hanging about his shoulders like a wild mane, it was easier to picture Captain Hart as a Persian or better yet, a pirate.

Maybe a Persian pirate.

He displayed the cocky arrogance of a man accustomed to taking what he pleased. His strong self-assurance was unnerving. Even the air about him vibrated with intense power and confident composure.

His russet-haired business partner, O'Brien, with his neatly trimmed mustache and beard, seemed pleasant and amiable. Quite the contrast to the smug, bold and probably terribly conceited Captain Hart.

The path broke through the trees near the stables, and she crept inside to return the boots she'd borrowed earlier from one of the slumbering grooms.

Keelan headed toward Slaney, her maid, who stood amid a flock of at least two hundred chickens and geese. The petite woman with boisterous pepper-and-salt curls and twinkling gray eyes had been with her family for as long as she could remember. Back home in Chatham, England, Mother was content to let the maid care for Keelan, and raise her.

Mother acted as if she resented a daughter's intrusion into her life and spent most days in her shop. Time with Slaney had been much more enjoyable than with her melancholy mother, who never spoke unless to criticize.

That life was gone now.

The scandal surrounding Papa's court-martial, followed by the strange deaths of her mother and aunt, disrupted the orientation of her plans like a stream of water redirected by a jagged rut carved into the earth.

Slaney, quite the opposite from Mother, teased and laughed and told exhilarating stories about pirates and giants and magic faeries. Slaney who dried Keelan's tears, wrapped her scrapes, and taught her how to draw and mix healing herbs.

Daniel taught her the significance of strength and speed in defending herself.

She chewed at her lip.

And now, she had just endangered his well-being and employment.

"This squawking and honking is enough ter wake the dead," Slaney grumbled. She scattered another handful of grain over the dirt yard, and shrieked when a bold rooster pecked at a stray kernel, on the top of her shoe.

"These are the only shoes I have, ye wicked cock! Be off with ye!"

With an insulted squawk, he flapped away in an effort to dodge Slaney's swinging foot. The sea of poultry parted briefly with his departure but soon clucked its way back into a mass of scratching and pecking fowl.

"Good morning, Slaney." Keelan said.

"A fair morning to ye, Mistress," the maid replied with a frown. Slaney clucked her tongue with disapproval, sounding much like one of the birds still milling at her feet. "Yer a sight! The whole house will soon be awake. Should Himself see ye, there will be the devil to pay, for sure. Best ye go inside and clean up, lass."

"Is Uncle Jared about yet, then?" Keelan asked, ignoring the maid's mild tirade. "There are two merchant ship captains here to meet with him and Papa."

"I'll tell him. 'Tis already almost seven o'clock, and ye know breakfast is served at half past eight."

"I'll be on time, Slaney, don't worry." A movement caught her eye, and she glanced up. Daniel and their visitors led two horses down the lane toward the stable. There was still time to have a word with Hart.

Slaney lowered her brows in an unconvincing scowl. "Well, don't get distracted this morn. Your father will want to speak to ye, and I'll not have him see ye lookin' like a common street rat."

"How is Papa?" Hopefully his color and appetite had returned with a sound night's rest.

Slaney's expression softened. "Weary. He's up and sittin' in the chair by his window. Perhaps if you sit with him, he'll eat something."

She nodded. "I will." Slaney appeared happy here in America. It was a beautiful country, to be sure, but life on a plantation was vastly different from living in England.

"I miss home," Keelan murmured.

"Ye are the daughter of a Commodore and a shopkeeper. Ye have known only the bustling life in Chatham, buying wares at the docks from ships loaded with items from exotic places." Slaney rested a hand on her arm. "It'll take time to get used to the slower pace of country life."

"I suppose you're right." Keelan stared at the pecking birds. "He'll want to talk about how an alliance with Mr. Pratt would merge the two plantations into the largest in the Lowcountry."

Slaney could only give her a sympathetic look.

"I don't want to get married."

Not yet, she thought.

And wedlock to Pratt? Not *ever*.

Marriage.

The word tasted bitter, like rancid oil, and unripened nuts.

"'Tis Pratt ye be rejecting, not marriage," Slaney said, voicing her thoughts exactly.

"After seeing how those bonds affected my parents, why would I be in a hurry to wed?" As a commodore in His Majesty's Navy, her father was gone for months at a time, leaving her mother alone and unhappy. During the short time he spent in port, Mother commanded most of it, becoming jealous of the small intervals he gifted to Keelan.

Slaney sighed. "Not all marriages are like yer parents', lass."

Still...plenty were. She reached down, withdrew a handful of corn from Slaney's bucket, then tossed it across the ground. "Why are you feeding the chickens? Isn't little Joseph supposed to do this?"

Slaney blew a wayward wisp of silver hair from her face. "You needn't worry about such matters. But if you must know, he's tending the smokehouse because they just put up a hog."

Keelan couldn't help but smile. Although Slaney tried to hide it, she had a soft spot for chickens.

The maid flung the remaining grain with the breeze and waded through the mass of birds toward the kitchen house. "I'll warm some water for yer bath. Don't tarry long, child."

Shaking away the dark musings of marriage and her ill father, Keelan turned and ran to the rear of the house, enjoying the refreshing coolness of the dew-laced grass on her bare feet. She'd never had such liberties in Chatham. One thing about residing in the Americas, the broad stroke of "Freedom" stretched well past British social conventions.

Most mornings, she sneaked in the back servants' door, to avoid any encounters with members of her extended family. While she was grateful Uncle Jared agreed to run the plantation until her father's good health returned, she must now interact more with her spoiled cousin, Doreen. Thankfully, the girl usually slept until midday.

Keelan paused. Would it be better to wait by the barn and hope to catch Captain Hart before he went into the house, or should she quickly change first?

What if she was seen dressed in boys' breeches?

She should change.

Keelan grabbed the latch and sucked in her breath at the sting that shot across her injured thumb. Fresh blood streamed along her palm and dripped off the heel of her hand. It wouldn't do to track it into the house. Remembering the marigold tincture Slaney used for cuts and bruises, she headed for the kitchen house to find the maid's herb box. It shouldn't take long to dress the cut and dash back to her room.

CHAPTER 3

A SCONE THIEF

Drat.
    The kitchen was empty.

A teakettle hung from a metal arm beside the hearth, steam still puffing from the spout. In front, and keeping warm, a platter of rice scones perched in the middle of the bench. Corn mush fried and popped in an iron skillet, the aroma infusing the air. Keelan's mouth watered and her stomach growled, pushing all other immediate issues from her mind.

An hour and a half was a long time to wait for breakfast.

Sneaking a furtive glance around the room, she liberated a warm, flakey scone. Too hungry to bother with butter or jam, she took a bite and closed her eyes as it melted in her mouth.

"Well, is 'bout time ya come visit me, Miss Keelan," Ruth said, as she emerged from the pantry.

Keelan jumped and the scone flew from her grasp. It bobbled in between her hands until she regained possession. "Ruth, you gave me a start!" She smiled at the short, plump cook and gestured guiltily at the pastry, now crumbling against her chest. "I hope you don't mind. I'm famished."

The slave gave her an odd look, but recovered quickly. "Goodness gracious, dis here's your home. You can git somethin' to eat anytime."

Her *home*. Even after several months, she still felt like a stranger. This culture was just so *different*.

The kitchen door opened and Slaney whisked inside. Kicking it shut behind her, she placed a garden basket on the table. "Wouldn't hurt ter put some meat on her bones. The lass will flutter away like a milkweed thistle in the wind one day and we'll never see her again." The basketful of herbs wafted through the room, in direct combat with the frying mush.

"All she need is a few more months of my cookin' and she'll fill right out," Ruth said with a chuckle.

Slaney gave Keelan a stern glare. "What she needs to do is get herself up to the main house and dress for breakfast," she chided, pulling a handful of herbs from her basket.

"Oh, Miss Keelan," Ruth stared at her wound. "How did you cut yo' hand?"

Keelan and Slaney exchanged glances. The house slaves likely gossiped as much as any other servants. It wasn't as if she could hide the fact she was wearing boy's clothing.

"I mishandled a dagger. Daniel is teaching me how to protect myself in case those who murdered most of my father's family in England decide to follow us here."

The slave paused, then shook her head. "I was sorry to hear 'bout dat, Miss Keelan. But dey didn't kill 'em all did dey?"

Was it only a matter of time before they did?

Keelan tried to reassure Ruth. "No. So far my father's elder brother has eluded the assassin, although several attempts on his life have been made."

Slaney inspected Keelan's hand. The woman tisked as she examined the cut, then went to the cupboard and pulled out a wooden box. She selected two small bottles and a clove of garlic.

"Let me see, lass." She held out a hand expectantly. Keelan eyed the bottle before she did as she was told. Slaney was a good healer, but there always seemed to be additional pain involved when it came to treating cuts and ailments. Slaney poured a few drops on the laceration.

Her suspicions were valid. Keelan sucked in her breath at the sting. "Ouch! What is that?" She snatched her hand away and shook it. "That burns like the devil!"

Slaney grabbed her hand firmly. "Such language from a gentle lady. Yer mum, God rest her soul, would be horrified to hear ye go on. Now sit ye still. 'Tis vinegar. That or whiskey must be used to cleanse a wound properly." Her mouth flattened. "Ye should know that, as often as I've mended ye."

Duly chastised, Keelan sat and quietly put another chunk of the stolen scone in her mouth while Slaney splashed more vinegar on the cut. The sting made her eyes water, but she didn't dare let out a peep.

Next, the maid reached for the garlic, pulled off a clove, sliced it in half, and rubbed it on the cut, eliciting another wince from Keelan. Why did everything have to *sting*?

"This will prevent infection," Slaney said. Last, she poured the marigold tincture over the injury and wrapped it in a small damp linen cloth.

"Keep it covered," she said. "'Twill guard against the pus."

"Thank you." Even though Slaney put her through mild torture with every cut and bruise, the woman meant well.

Keelan pointed to the last bit of scone. "Ruth, I would love to learn how you make these." She popped the rest into her mouth and munched happily. It was something her mother might have sold in her shop, partnered with jellies, jams and sweet biscuits.

The cook's soft, brown face broke into a pleased smile. "Come in the mornin' 'fore sunrise, an' I'll show ya in no time." She turned and pulled a plate from the shelf. "Now sit yo' self down, child. I can't stand to see ya starve to death right here in the kitchen house."

To Keelan's dismay and delight, Ruth served her fried corn

mush doused in cane syrup, a cup of tea, and another scone slathered with fresh butter and dripping with sweet, amber honey.

Mentally calculating the time it would take Daniel and the two other men to reach the stable, remove their tack, settle their horses, Keelan estimated that she had a couple of precious minutes. There would be no time to change first. She shoveled a large forkful of mush into her mouth, trying to conjure the right words to persuade the men to keep her clandestine activities to themselves.

Slaney glanced out the window. "Daniel and our visitors are near. I'd best get along and tell Mr. Grey his guests have arrived." She shot Keelan a sharp glare. "And you mistress, should go before you're caught in those...clothes."

She probably would have said 'rags'. The maid had been privy to Daniel's training for the past several months, and frequently huffed at the impropriety, prompting him to just as frequently remind her that many things were accepted in American society that weren't at home.

Keelan's fork clattered on her plate and she virtually flew out of the door. Praying Uncle Jared didn't see her before she had a chance to speak with Hart.

CHAPTER 4

A CAPTURED EAVESDROPPER

Hurry! Slaney's warning echoed in her head. Keelan took a shortcut through the garden. With the exception of her cousin Doreen, the entire household was probably awake. No time to dawdle, as Ruth would say.

She ducked beneath an arbor laden with lazy, purple wisteria blossoms. Aunt Sarah's garden created a buffet for the senses. Eight neatly trimmed squares of fragrant lavender, rosemary, and thyme hedges could barely accommodate the bright bursts of colorful flowers flaming up toward the blue South Carolina sky. The neat checkerboard of raised beds flowed down over several tiers and stopped near the glassy surface of a small pond.

The sound of Daniel's voice jolted her into motion as it filtered through the hedges. "Twin Pines is a 300-acre plantation. The main house sits at the end of the long lane you started down earlier. We've only been here a few months. The commodore's younger brother, Mr. Grey, has extensive knowledge of milling lumber and is an extremely effective overseer. He splits his time between his business in Charleston and the mill here."

"So, Mr. Grey owns warehouses at the docks and also works

the plantation? That seems a heavy burden," Captain O'Brien's Irish lilt drifted through the hedge.

"Are you meeting about the mill or the warehouses?" Daniel asked. "If it's the mill, Mr. Grey might wish to take you on a tour later. I should let the grooms know, so they have his gelding ready."

O'Brien fished out a handkerchief and wiped his brow. "Actually, we are more interested in speaking with his brother about my Uncle Fynn's request. Seems Fynn was eager to meet with him about something. We found several letters from Commodore Grey among his things, one confirming an appointment today."

Keelan sucked in a breath. A meeting with her father? Perhaps it was regarding the scandal.

Their lives changed on that stormy day when her father gave a tragic order to sink a ship he was convinced was a French privateer trying to pass as an American merchant vessel. Her father attacked it.

Unfortunately, it had not been the privateer. All souls were lost, her father court-martialed, and their family disgraced. Thieves pilfered Mother's shop.

Thankfully, Papa's closest friend had been influential enough to keep her father from prison. The speculation that now someone was killing off the rest of the Greys in England, amplified the scandal.

Papa had an older brother in Chatham and a younger one, Jared, in America. After his eldest brother's heir was found dead in a stable and his wife and Keelan's mother were killed in separate but equally suspicious carriage accidents, it became obvious someone was eliminating members of the family one by one.

The murders prompted their long time friend to smuggle Keelan and her father out of the country to protect them. He'd also financed the purchase of the plantation and bribed a ship's captain to quietly take her and Papa out of Great Britain, to the southern colonies.

Her breath froze.

Had the assassin finally tracked them here?

Was he one of the two captains?

Daniel would be on guard with the same suspicions, of that she was certain. Too much had already slipped by them, putting the entire family on edge. Daniel would be extra vigilant.

She crawled behind an iron bench. Daniel, Captain Hart, and Captain O'Brien walked along the outside of the hedge. Curious, she crept closer to peek through the bushes. Would Daniel ask the men to remain quiet about the scene they had witnessed in the meadow? If he did, it would prevent her from having to plead her case to Captain Hart, a task she dreaded doing on her own. Had they already talked of it? This garden was very private; a secluded place where they could speak in confidence.

She couldn't assume the topic had already been discussed. She considered stepping out and intercepting them as they passed. That plan would only work if the men turned left rather than right toward the front door. If she could get Daniel's attention, she could indicate she wanted to speak with them. She hurried to a gap in the shrubbery to signal him.

Daniel's voice drew closer. "Behind the Grey's house sits a kitchen house, a chicken coop, smokehouse, and a few outbuildings. In addition to crops and timber, Twin Pines also produces turpentine."

She squeezed between two bushy shrubs near a cherry tree and cautiously peered through the foliage. Daniel pointed west, his back to her. Landon stood next to him. Where was the other man? Conal O'Brien?

The valet droned on. "Beyond this garden is a small spring-fed pond, which takes up most of the meadow bottom to the east. There's another much larger lake on the plantation a few miles southwest."

Captain O'Brien stepped through the arbor.

Oh no! There was no way to escape without exposing that she'd been eavesdropping. She caught her breath sharply. This wouldn't work at all. Why would they agree to do a favor to someone who'd been spying on them?

Curse her terrible luck.

Now, she'd have to wait until they left then run to catch them before they made it to the front door.

Drat! That was impossible without being visible from her uncle's study.

She was doomed. Worse, Daniel would be punished too.

He and Captain Hart soon followed O'Brien. Keelan retreated further into the scratchy bushes behind the sweet blossoming limbs of the cherry tree. She winced as several branches poked the back of her head, legs, and arms.

"This is Mrs. Grey's pride," Daniel said, only a few yards away.

Conal stated his approval, "Tis carefully tended, for sure. Pleasin' to the eye."

Landon agreed. "Mrs. Grey has reason to be proud. The cherry blossoms are especially magnificent," he added loudly, sounding closer than the others.

Her heart jarred the walls of her chest. She crouched lower into the shadows of the shrubs next to the tree. Captain Hart was dangerously close to her hiding place. She dared not take a single breath.

"Look at this," Conal said. "The detail on this bench is as fine as any I have ever seen."

He ran his large hand over the ornate ironwork. The fragrance of a rose bush apparently caught his attention and he stepped over to sniff the flowers. He plucked a blossom, lifted it to his nose, and inhaled. Keelan's pulse pounded frantically. Although Conal stood several yards away, if he happened to glance to his left, he would discover her. She could only retreat so far into the shrubs.

Why hadn't she tried to intercept them earlier instead of just standing here pondering it?

Captain Hart coughed.

Conal jumped then grinned. "After five months at sea, 'tis a relief ta have somethin' nicer ta smell than salt water and eighty unbathed seamen."

"Come," Daniel said, laughing. "I'll take you inside to meet Mr. Grey and the commodore."

The conversation droned on after the men walked from the garden, but Keelan couldn't hear it clearly.

Drat, again.

She'd missed her opportunity.

Were they gone? She waited. After a moment, she leaned forward to glance around the branches, but froze at a sharp, painful tug on her hair. Reaching behind her head, she sought the origin of the entrapment. Her wild hair was snared. She groaned in frustration. This kind of delay was not what she needed now. She tugged, but succeeded in freeing only a few meager strands.

She tucked her chin to her chest and groped for more tangled curls. This was a fine mess. If Aunt Sarah caught sight of her now, she'd drop in a dead faint.

Again.

"Blast!" It didn't help her cause, but the curse certainly conveyed her mood at the moment. It almost made her feel better.

"That's an understandable expletive for a young girl posing as a boy, however, as a young girl masquerading as foliage, it's a bit disconcerting."

Hart!

Keelan ceased her struggle, mortified. A shadow fell over the ground at her feet, followed by black riding boots, lightly dusted from the road. She raised her gaze over fine black breeches and tapered waist. She lifted her gaze higher, and it stuttered at a white linen shirt untied at the neck, before she took in the broad shoulders, strong jaw, small scar on the chin and a straight, but haughty aquiline nose.

Captain Hart stood in front of her, his crystalline blue eyes glittering with amusement.

This was going to be trouble.

A slow smile pulled a dimple into his cheek. "You can come out now. I'm afraid you've been discovered."

CHAPTER 5

LANDON'S TERMS

P*irate.*

With his ebony hair wild about his shoulders, Keelan easily pictured Landon Hart with a brace of pistols and a scabbard, standing at the helm of a wicked pirate ship. His mouth was perfectly shaped. When his white teeth flashed, his smile was so brilliant she stopped breathing altogether.

He was beautiful.

Azure eyes took on a mischievous glint, making her wonder if he'd read her mind.

Although her mouth had gone dry, she managed to dredge up a few raspy words. "I would gladly come out, but my hair is caught."

He referred to her as a girl, which was more annoying than being caught in a bush. "I'll have you know, I'm nineteen." She clenched her jaw and fought harder to yank her hair free.

Ugh. She had the most abominable luck.

He stepped closer, bringing an aura of delicious power with him. Broad shoulders blocked out the sun. "Perhaps I can be of some assistance and liberate you from your bushy captor." He gave her a lazy grin followed by a long unsettling appraisal from head to toe and back. His molten gaze faltered at her lips and he stilled.

Hart's nearness had an annoying effect on her lungs and she found it difficult to draw a breath. There was a rakish quality in this man, to be sure. She'd learned early to be watchful of those characteristics.

As if he knew she was flustered by his proximity, he stepped closer. Heat rolled off him in waves, along with the scent of leather and sandalwood shaving soap.

He probably also knew he was ridiculously handsome. She wouldn't be the least bit surprised if he was terribly conceited and prone to more than a little deceit, as well.

Once again the word "pirate" came to mind.

She forced an even tone, despite a thudding heart, then pulled again. "No thank you. I'm sure I don't need your help." A sharper pain shot across the back of her head. "I can do it, really, Captain Hart." That was probably a lie. Why didn't he just leave her alone? Or just leave?

Either or would be fine.

She couldn't *think*.

"Nonsense." He gently grasped her wrists and pulled them away from her hair. His fingers were very warm. Well, it was also a warm morning. Sunny. Humid. Very, *very* warm.

And he was too *close*.

The scent of him mingled with leather and fresh spring air, which combined for a heady mix of male and danger and unsettled calm.

Her pulse jumped wildly under his fingers, and she was terrified at the thought he might feel it too. Tiny prickles of fire zipped under her skin where his fingers touched.

"Hmmm." He leaned over her shoulder and studied the tangled web of curls. "It would seem you have a dilemma, my sweet. There is a large amount of hair and several branches involved." He reached for his dagger. "I can easily cut you free—"

"Wait!" she squeaked. "Can't you cut the branches, instead?" She choked in a short breath, as that was all that could fit in her lungs at the moment. Why was it so hard to breathe?

The desperate desire to save her hair and the strong urge to flee warred with each other in her mind. The savage aura surrounding Landon Hart sent her nerves into a frenzied dance, and she hated she couldn't keep calm and act nonchalant. Unaffected. Bored.

Would he leave her if she demanded it?

Doubtful.

Humor warmed his eyes to a velvet blue; he was having too much fun at her expense to leave now.

He gave her a mock frown. "It'll take a great deal of effort to both disengage and keep these silken strands of copper and gold intact."

His voice dripped words like honey over scones. Thick and sugary. Her eyes drifted back to his mouth. It took a moment to remember what he'd actually said. Another before she could form an entire sentence.

"I'm confident in your skills." Hopefully she managed to conjure enough sarcasm to hide her unease. At least she didn't stutter.

It nipped at her pride no small amount, but obviously she needed his help. A chunk cut from her hair and a sliced finger would be impossible to hide. Uncle Jared was already suspicious of her tendency to rise before the sun, unlike his family, who usually slept through breakfast. One more of her incidents would likely push him past the limit of his patience.

Although he was a servant, Daniel was like a beloved uncle to her. She would do whatever she could to prevent him from being punished.

Still, no one liked to beg. Releasing a slow breath, she willed her voice to remain steady.

He was still much to close. And *hot*.

"Can you take a moment to try to untangle them?" She nudged away her pride and added, "Please."

Landon sighed dramatically and touched his fingers to his broad chest. "How can I possibly refuse such a distressed and heartfelt plea from such a comely maiden?"

A breath of tentative satisfaction escaped. She wanted desperately to believe he could be chivalrous, but her instincts were still on alert.

"However," his casual perusal skated from her eyes to the tangles and back again. "As a tradesman, my time and labor always come at a price."

It had been foolish to hope for a different response. Naïve, even. The cautious sense of relief quickly chilled. "A price?" Her voice could have coated the garden with frost, yet he seemed entirely unaffected. "What price would that be?" This was not going well.

His expression remained stoic while he scratched his chin. "The lowest on my books for freeing a young lady from a barbaric bush is..." His eyes darkened a sultry blue and again dropped to her mouth. His nostrils flared. "A kiss."

A *what*? He couldn't be serious.

She opened her mouth to rebuff him. Remind him of his place. And hers. Her first kiss would not result from a...a... barter! Or blackmail, or...

He dare *not*!

No matter what she tried to do, she couldn't form the words. She swallowed. It was as if he'd uttered a spell paralyzing her mouth and her limbs. Only her eyes worked at the moment, and she couldn't even get them to glare instead of widen.

He raised his hand and ran the outside of his knuckles along her jaw before cupping her face, causing every nerve ending beneath his palm to vibrate. He leaned forward and barely stroked her lips, feather soft, tasting. The pressure of his mouth intensified, and she lost control of her eyes, too. They closed.

His mouth, both soft and hard, consumed her sense of time and space. A tiny hum escaped from her throat. A low satisfied rumble vibrated in his chest and he dove his fingers into her hair and deepened the kiss. Her strength ebbed, as if some sort of magic transferred the energy from her body to his, and she numbly wondered if her legs would hold. He trailed kisses along her jaw, pausing near her ear. A sharp zing shot around her neck, causing an involuntary shiver to follow.

"You taste of sweet, maple syrup," he rasped, before inhaling sharply. "And smell like a spring morning."

Her lids fluttered open. Warring with a mixture of bewilderment and shocked desire, she struggled again to find her tongue.

"That...that..." *Blast it all.* She'd stuttered! Her hands were gripping his forearms and she quickly released them as if they scalded her fingers

"Was delicious," he finished for her. "Your lips drive a man mad longing for another taste." The side of his mouth quirked up, but his voice was oddly hoarse.

He was mocking her, surely. And it was nothing more than maple syrup and corn mush. And she was nothing more than a flustered maid, nearly paralyzed by something as ridiculous as her first kiss.

Stupid girl, letting a man like him get you ruffled as a spring bird.

She fought to regain her composure, which at best lay in tattered shreds at her bare, dew-drenched feet. Her body's reaction both surprised and angered her. Surprise due to the unexpected pleasure that invaded her core in a swirl of sultry satisfaction, anger stirred by that all-knowing, hooded perusal through those thick, inky lashes, and the stupid stuttering. He knew how his kiss had affected her, probably relished the sense of mastery it gave him, which only fueled her intense determination to give him some sort of dressing down.

His fingers were burning her skin through the fabric of her shirt, and for some reason, she had the front of his in her fists.

Her knuckles skimmed against the hard ridge of a rib. She let go and grasped his hands, in a vain attempt to peel his fingers from her waist, which was in *flames*.

"You have no sense of propriety," she sputtered. There. That sounded proper. And chastising. At least her voice was working again. For the most part.

"No," he agreed. "But then, I never claimed I did. Now—" He leaned close again.

"Don't you dare!" She narrowed her eyes, giving him her best death glare, unsure she'd be able to keep her dignity if he kissed her again. Not that she wanted him to kiss her again.

Of course she didn't.

Heaven knows she'd almost melted from the first one.

He chuckled and finally let go and began untangling her hair. "You've paid me well, my lady. I'm honor-bound to fulfill my duties."

She couldn't hold back a snort, not caring how unladylike it sounded. "I doubt you understand the meaning of honor," she said, convinced he was more rake than anything else. "You deserve to be slapped soundly." He truly did. "No gentleman would take such liberties, or suggest such a bargain." He definitely was no gentleman. Pointing out that fact would undoubtedly come as no surprise to the scoundrel. In fact, it wouldn't alarm her if he was proud of it.

He paused, laughter glittering in his eyes. "Liberties? I seized no liberties, only fair payment for my services."

"It gives me cause to wonder how many other ladies you have seduced into a kiss with your silver words and roguish charm," she retorted.

If it was possible, which a moment ago she would have argued it was *not*, he leaned even closer. His breath warmed her ear, his whisper from deep in his throat. "A gentleman never tells, my dear. Suffice it to say none were unwilling and not all were ladies."

"You..." Her voice betrayed her again and she barely choked out the rest of the sentence. "You really are a rake."

He gave her a wink, which stirred up those stupid butterflies again. "I will say, none were as intoxicating as you are, my love."

"I am not your—*augh!*" Her cheeks grew warmer, and she was ridiculously pleased at his compliment. He was probably well-accustomed to women falling all over themselves for a chance to enjoy his attentions. She was certainly not one of them. *Not at all*.

If he thought to place her in the same category as those weak-willed, twittering, females, he had a thing or two to learn about Keelan Grey. She certainly didn't *twitter*.

All she needed at the moment was a flippant veil of nonchalance to drape over her demeanor. If only she could more succinctly conjure that veil. Why was that so hard for her to do so in front of this man? Dragging her stare from the cobalt eyes of Landon Hart almost required more strength than she could muster. It didn't help that her attention locked on to his amazing lips, still curled into that *I know what you're thinking* smile.

He changed the topic, thank goodness. "What's a beautiful woman like you doing dressed as a street urchin and playing with blades?"

Beautiful? An odd fluttering rippled over the skin of her stomach. She clenched the muscles, demanding it stop. Her eyes jerked back to his, expecting to see them glittering with jest.

But there was no jest, only a calm interest. He lifted a brow, awaiting her answer.

She took a careful breath. Actually, he just presented an opportunity for her to talk with him about her problem. Perhaps she could still salvage the day.

She dragged her attention away from his chiseled face. "My father instructed Daniel to train me to defend myself." She fiddled with a small branch.

"It appears he's been doing it very well," he complimented, a smile in his voice. Perhaps this was a game for him, but to Daniel it was not. To *her* it was not.

She wanted to shake him until he understood how dire the situation truly was. Perhaps curling her hands into fists would prevent them from going for his neck.

Take a breath. Speak calmly.

"Since it upsets my Aunt Sarah, my uncle has forbidden me to continue the training," she went on, pretending he hadn't spoken.

He laughed softly. Now *that* was a dangerous sound; it made her toes tingle. "Ah, so I see. The prohibited exercises continue in secret now," he said.

Unnerved by the way he made the word "secret" sound so deviant, she nodded and plucked at the leaves. It seemed safer than looking directly into those eyes again.

Might as well simply say it.

Taking a deep breath she plunged ahead. What was the worse that could happen? *Ridiculous question.* "I would sincerely appreciate it if you would keep that knowledge to yourself. For *Daniel's* sake," she added quickly.

"For *Daniel's* sake?" Doubt threaded his words together, making her want to pinch him hard.

She nodded. "He'd be disciplined severely if Uncle Jared finds out we defied his orders."

"But what about your sake?" he said, eyebrows raised.

"I can deal with any repercussions which affect only me," she hissed, anger tightening her fists. He didn't understand her plea. This wasn't about her, it was about protecting Daniel. "I don't want Daniel in trouble."

His face went carefully blank. "Are you lovers?"

"What? No, of course not!"

He glanced up and appeared to ponder her request, all male arrogance in that *"I know I'm blocking out the sun"* kind of way.

What a conceited, horse's... behind.

She had to bite her lower lip to prevent herself from saying it out loud. Perhaps Aunt Sarah was right when she'd questioned whether Keelan was spending too much time in the stables. *Such language*. And the captain was still pondering.

After a couple more moments of torture, he smiled. "Your clandestine activity is safe with me."

Her quiet sigh of relief was short-lived, however, as he continued to grin, white teeth gleaming brighter than the midmorning sun, which he still blocked by the way. He had another dimple on his left cheek, which was as distracting as the one on the right.

"My terms for keeping a lady's charade a secret... are—"

"You wouldn't!" she whispered. Would he? Another one of his kisses would surely be her undoing.

Worse, what if another kiss wasn't enough to buy his silence? What if he wanted more? A strange thrill rippled up her spine, and she fought to squelch it. She'd not jeopardize her future any more than she already had. As it was, they were lucky no one had seen them. Her family would spare no time dragging Hart before a man of the cloth at gunpoint and forcing him to take her as his bride.

The thought both elated and destroyed her. She'd be the lonely wife of a man who was, in truth, married to the sea.

Just like Papa.

She could *not* let that happen.

She *would not* let that happen.

Her mother lived a miserable, lonely life while her father was at away at sea with the navy. She would not become her mother. Brittle... bitter... sad. *She* was made of sterner stuff.

She lifted her chin. "Should a member of my family witness—"

Scorching fingers circled her wrist and stilled her tongue. He pressed his lips to her palm. His wicked mouth ignited a searing sensation all the way up her arm and along the sensitive skin of her neck, leaving her too stunned to speak. The power she sensed earlier pulsed through the surrounding air, and she found herself unable to move.

Unwilling to move.

How did he *do* that?

He slowly released her hand. "I shall collect my due another day, sweet Keelan." He gave her a mocking wink. "I promise to remain mute on the topic. In addition, I am pleased to tell you I've liberated those imprisoned locks of silk from this malicious bush. You, my dear, are free."

Not yet trusting herself to speak, she stared at him. The raw hunger in those piercing blue eyes shook her almost as much as her reaction to it.

A smile spread across his face with the slowness of a sunrise. "It's indeed been my pleasure serving you." The mockery in his voice made her want to punch him. "As much as I wish to linger, regrettably I must go, though it takes all my strength as a man to do so." He gave her an exaggerated bow, bade her farewell, and left the garden.

Definitely arrogant. And conceited.

In a mute stupor, she watched him walk away. Numbly, she lifted a shaking hand to her throbbing lips, still swollen and hot, and uncurled her hand. Oddly, it was not marked, but it burned as if he had dropped a hot coal on it. The sensations both thrilled and terrified her. She inhaled and tried to steady her frayed nerves and slow her pounding heart. Even as reason had warned her to resist, her body hadn't listened. She had never been drawn to a man in this way before. It left her horrified, bewildered, and dangerously curious.

Her mother might not have been the most nurturing parent, but she made sure her daughter was well-informed about the type of men who commit their lives to the sea. Most were quite libertine in their way of life. According to Mother, they lacked moral principle and any sense of responsibility, as did the women with whom they tarried. She released a sharp breath. God forbid she turned into one of *those* women.

She'd grown up being suspicious of men like Captain Hart: wanton and promiscuous. Seducing ladies was merely a game to him and those like him. Her naiveté had probably amused him. She rolled her eyes at her stupidity as well as the shame of being among the women he had seduced into a kiss. Surely there were a lot of them, as he was so good at it.

She wouldn't fall prey to his game again. And she most certainly would *never* seek the arms of a sailor who traveled from port to port. Why would she ever choose to live her mother's life, full of longing and bitterness?

CHAPTER 6

A TEST OF SKILL

A shrill scream shattered Keelan's musings, snapping her attention to the yard. She ran from the garden, searching for the source of the alarmed cry. A young slave boy, of perhaps nine or ten years, burst from the smoke house, his shrieks ringing across the grounds. He stumbled and fell.

Keelan recognized the boy as Ruth's child, Joseph, whose chicken-feeding duty had been performed earlier by Slaney. Although crippled, he did a fine job tending the smoke house, fueling and keeping the coals smoldering while defending the meat from the dogs.

Using the fire poker as a brace, he now struggled to heave himself to his feet. Keelan ran to help. Had he been burned? Slaney had an ointment that would help.

Before she could close the distance between herself and the boy, a snarling wild dog limped out of the building, its short thick fur raised along its spine. The boy shrieked again, and in his panicked haste to retreat, lost his footing and tumbled back to the ground.

Behind her, the door to the kitchen house banged open. Ruth emerged, and began shrieking for help.

Keelan's chest constricted in panic. The dog staggered toward the boy, it's gaping mouth frothing wildly. Joseph brandished the poker in the direction of the enraged creature and swung, striking its muzzle. The animal yelped and shook its head. Its yellowed eyes locked with Joseph's terrified ones. There was no time to bridge the gap between them.

Her dagger! Keelan slid to a stop, snatched out her dirk and threw.

And missed.

Daniel's voice echoed in her head telling her she rushed the throw, her chest didn't point to the target. Her wrist wasn't cocked correctly (Hart's voice). She didn't keep it firm (Hart's voice, again).

The movement or maybe sound of the wayward blade striking the packed dirt diverted the dog's attention from the boy to her. A violent jolt shot through her limbs, and for a second she was paralyzed. Joseph still sat, frozen in terror, defenseless on the ground.

The rabid dog swiveled its head back to the boy. The image of it attacking the child spurred Keelan into action. She clapped her hands and shouted, again gaining the beast's attention. It turned and took a step toward her and lowered its head. A low, insidious growl emanated from deep within its throat.

At least if it came after her, she could run and hopefully make it to the kitchen house before the dog. It would give the child time to scramble to his feet and lock himself in the smokehouse. It was then she remembered Daniel's dagger she'd wedged between her waistband and belt.

She grabbed it and paused long enough to take careful aim, imitating the grip Captain Hart had taught her, then stiffened her arm and let it fly. The knife pierced the matted coat behind the animal's shoulder. It snarled and snapped its jaws at the hilt as it fell, twisting and writhing less than four feet from where Joseph sprawled, wide-eyed, on the ground.

One look at the thrashing, wild, dog told Landon the animal was diseased and dangerous. Even wounded, its bite could kill. If Keelan got too near... He doubted the proud young woman would heed an order to go no closer, so he picked up his pace. Just as she threw the second dagger, he sprinted past her, grabbed the boy, then swung him up over his shoulder, and carried him further from the creature before depositing him back on the ground.

She slipped past and knelt by the young boy's side. His shaking hands still clutched the poker; tears streamed down his face as he dragged in shallow, ragged breaths. His eyes were filled with shock and fear, and he stared at Keelan as if she had sprouted three heads.

"Are you hurt, Joseph?" she asked softly, helping him to his feet. She kept hold of the boy's arm and gently brushed a spot of soot from his nose.

Joseph shook his head, his wary gaze locked on her flushed face. Two other slave boys crept up to Keelan's side.

"Good God, Miss Keelan, you pierced the monster's heart!"

Landon nodded in appreciation. "An impressive throw." It was. He could have done no better, although he wouldn't have missed the first time.

The boys' eyes brightened in awe. "How'd you learn to do dat, Miss Keelan?"

With an impish glint in her eyes, she responded gesturing to Landon, "Captain Hart taught me this morning." She tossed him a smug smirk.

The chit was smart. She just put him in Daniel's place. When gossip traveled about the plantation, his name would be associated with the incident.

One of the boys leaned forward and said in a raspy whisper, "Ain't no one goin' to believe dis."

"Ain't nobody...goin' to hear...'bout it," a stout black woman panted, stopping for breath beside Keelan. She pointed her meat mallet at the boys. "As far as anyone knows, I kilt this devil." She shuffled over to the dying creature and brought the mallet down on its skull with a sickening crack.

Keelan cringed and turned away. For all her bravado, she didn't have the strongest stomach. Would she faint at the sight of blood? Somehow he didn't expect it, but women were an unpredictable lot.

The woman spoke again. "Miss Keelan did a brave thing. Don't you be getting her in trouble with her papa and uncle by blabbin' about it. Understand?"

"Yes'm," the chastised boys answered in unison.

She wrung her hands as she turned to face Landon. "Please, sir, I don't want no problems for Miss Keelan."

Landon inclined his head. "Rest assured. I won't retell this tale. It will be our secret."

He slid a knowing glance at Keelan. There would be a price, though. She narrowed her eyes, obviously reading his expression perfectly. He couldn't keep from grinning. He suspected she didn't believe he'd stay silent, which made the situation more entertaining. It would be fun to tease her a bit more, enough to win another of her fiery kisses. Or maybe two.

"Don't worry about me, Ruth." Keelan patted the woman's arm.

Ruth bent over and tugged the dirk free, then wiped the blade on her stained apron. "Miss Keelan, I'll git this knife back to you soon as I boil it clean again." She flung her arm at the two older boys. "Now take dis mad animal down past the creek and bury it deep." She shooed them away. "Go on, now."

The braver of the two scuttled over and nudged the mud-caked, wild dog with his toe. Satisfied it was indeed dead, the boys grasped its hind legs and hauled the carcass away.

Ruth, grabbed her son with the fierceness of a mother bear, and crushed him to her bosom. Joseph let out a jagged sob. Tears slid down Ruth's cheeks as she and her son swayed together in the dirt yard.

Keelan's face softened. With what? Tenderness? Yes, but there was something else. His chest clenched as he realized what he was watching.

Longing.

Her reaction stirred his curiosity. Which did she long for? A child to love or a mother that loved her?

She shifted and caught him staring. Her face became shuttered, once again masking that raw corner of her soul.

The slamming of the front door jolted everyone into action.

"You'd better leave," he advised. "I'll take responsibility for the events here."

Keelan gave him a hesitant, but grateful nod and whirled toward the garden path. Her gaze sliced to a first floor window and she took in a sharp breath. Her mouth parted briefly before snapping shut. He turned in time to see a hand release the curtain. He'd not readily give away her secret, but if someone else had seen the commotion, his promised silence might no longer matter.

Keelan ran to the servant's door, like a forest sprite in bare feet. He shook his head in wonderment. She'd tweaked his interest, for sure.

He'd find a way to see her again.

CHAPTER 7

A MARRIAGE DILEMMA

Keelan tiptoed up to her quarters, where Slaney had a bath waiting in the next chamber. She disrobed, hiding her waif's garments in an old trunk. A blissful sigh of contentment escaped her lips as she sank into the water. Warm, but not too hot. She sniffed. Fragrant. A linen pouch of lavender, hyssop, and basil floated in the water, steeping. A tincture of the same combination sat in a small bottle by her bed.

"Rub it on yer skin, and it'll keep ye from becoming a tasty meal for the wee buggers at night," Slaney had earlier explained.

Keelan reached for a small pat of scented soap and frowned as she pondered the secret observer in her father's study. She worked up a lather and scrubbed her head and face vigorously.

Her hands froze as a thought hit.

Of course.

Her father, Captain O'Brien, and Uncle Jared might have been waiting to discuss business. She groaned. The spy could have been any one of them. Her shoulders tensed. She would find out soon enough.

Bright, blue eyes interrupted her thoughts. Hart's slow, easy smile had sent her heart tripping, even though he'd claimed an advantage over her while she was in distress, the black-hearted scoundrel. He'd kissed her on the lips. Were all kisses that...*invasive?* Thrilling?

Chiseled cheekbones and an ebony mane completed the picture in her mind. She ought to berate herself for letting such meanderings carry her to a place she would never go, but any woman would be helpless to control herself from mooning over that man, at least a little.

This is nothing more than a passing infatuation.

Hart would not linger long here. Soon, his ship would take him to far off ports, where other more willing young maids would fill his arms and his desires.

Her skin tingled at the memory of his warm body moving near when he had reached around her to set right her grip. Everything about him was memorable, from his face to the hard muscles on his arms, flat stomach, and the pressure of his mouth while they kissed. She leaned her head against the back rim. She would now hold every future suitor against the standard Landon Hart's kiss established. She almost felt sorry for them; they'd never meet the mark.

Not that she'd ever admit that to Hart.

Slaney had always said that the sensations of lust differed vastly from those of love. She wasn't sure how to tell those two emotions apart, but Keelan recognized a rake when she met one. He was definitely not the type who would offer devotion and an honor-bound oath, which truly was the only thing that could save her from Pratt.

She doubted Hart needed to give promises of love and marriage. There were certainly many women who'd gift their bodies for his pleasure, regardless.

She straightened. Her father might argue, but her hand (as well as her virginity) was hers to keep or hers to give; she would relinquish them only for love and honor, no less. A man like Hart had no reason to provide either.

Not that she cared. Neither did Pratt for that matter, yet her father was more than willing to push her to the old man.

Still...the situation Hart currently controlled sent her stomach churning. Just how did he plan to "collect his due another day?" More importantly, what would he demand?

A small clock on the mantle chimed the eighth hour. Keelan expelled a lungful of air. She could change nothing by sitting in the cool water and worrying about her reckless behavior. As tempting as it was to permit the fingers of procrastination to grasp her limbs and pull her deeper into the bath, she forced herself to rise.

A soft knock on the bedroom door was followed by Slaney's light step. "'Tis me, myself, Mistress. Ruth made some Indian corn porridge for ye ter take to yer Da.'"

The cheerful maid popped her head into the bathing room and handed Keelan a towel. "Come, I'll help ye with yer dress and yer hair." Slaney crossed to the tallboy and began to sift through Keelan's undergarments. "Will ye wear the blue gown to the ball? 'Tis yer most flattering, ye know. I pressed the ribbons yesterday in the event ye may need them."

"I suppose the blue one will be fine." Keelan briskly toweled her arms. Cousin Doreen's upcoming ball was the talk of the Lowcountry. Dr. Everett Garrison, of course, would attend the affair. Circling another dance floor with him would surely be putting her feet at risk of irreparable damage, she was quite certain of it.

Remembering the most recent party she'd attended with him, she mumbled, "I am not looking forward to Dr. Garrison trodding upon my toes like a mule on hot coals."

At Slaney's disapproving frown, Keelan bit her lip and reached for the light chemise Slaney had retrieved from the tallboy. Dr.

Garrison had wiggled quite comfortably into the good graces of most of the women in the manor. Slaney was no exception.

"Dr. Garrison is a kind man, child. Where would yer Da' be now without the medicines he provides?" Cocking a jaunty brow, she admonished, "It wouldn't hurt fer ye to show a little more gratitude toward him."

Yes, they were lucky he traveled with them to Twin Pines after Papa became ill on the journey from London to Charleston.

Slaney was right; she should act more grateful. Still, it would be difficult. Whenever she and the doctor were in the same room together, she could sense him watching her every movement. It made her neck tingle and her chest twist uncomfortably.

Slaney stooped and gathered the discarded towels. "We're in America now. Things are different here. Although Dr. Garrison is a wee bit clumsy and shy, he's kind. He's been a close friend to your Da' and tended to his melancholy when yer mum died." The maid reached for the vial on Keelan's bed table, poured a few drops of oil into her palm and rubbed Keelan's arms. With any luck, those flying insects would avoid her tonight.

Dr. Garrison, in a ceaseless effort to find the cause of her father's illness, spent many evenings in the study poring over his medical journals and writing letters to colleagues in London and Richmond. A tall, awkward man with gentle brown eyes and a quick smile, he easily charmed his way into the hearts of all the women in the household.

Except Keelan (although it wasn't due to a lack of trying).

"Papa, in truth, doesn't seem to care that Dr. Garrison is interested in courting me. You realize he is pressing for me to wed Mr. Pratt, instead."

Just saying that name made her nauseous.

Slaney's mouth flattened and she gestured for her to step into her gown.

Keelan cocked her head, sensing the maid's disquiet. "What's raised your ire, Slaney?" The maid's eyebrows shot up and Keelan laughed. "You've been with me since I was a babe. I can tell when you're annoyed."

Slaney flicked her hand impatiently. "I'd just like ye to find better than old man Pratt."

"A goat would be better."

Slaney giggled as she began to fasten the buttons. "Another reason that mayhap you should consider Dr. Garrison's attentions."

To show his gratitude, her father had serendipitously offered to provide the doctor with a portion of their much-needed funds to establish his office in Charleston. Her father had done this without her opinion on the matter. She would have advised against it, since they had precious little left from selling her mother's shop in Chatham.

Keelan couldn't precisely determine why she objected to Dr. Garrison when everyone else seemed to find him so alluring. But there was something... Some vague, indefinable thing about him, beyond his jolting movements, his manner, the way he looked at her, that made her uneasy. He was always polite and kind, yes.

Maybe that was what bothered her.

He was *too* polite, too ingratiating, and too eager to win the favor of her and her father.

Whatever it was, she was never at ease around him.

Uncle Jared had even offered Dr. Garrison a room in his town-house on Meeting Street, to give the him time to establish his practice before investing in a residence of his own. However, as her father's condition worsened, the doctor made fewer trips to his Charleston office, then chose to stay with the family at Twin Pines to tend his benefactor. Which seemed loyal and kind...on the outside.

She turned to face the open balcony doors and stared at the long magnolia-lined lane as Slaney quietly began to button the back of her gown. Her room was on the upper corner of the house, giving her the luxury of a view from the north and east sides. A movement caught her attention and she peered through the magnolia branches toward the garden.

To her surprise, Doreen and Dr. Garrison were walking across the far yard toward the kitchen house, little Joseph limping between them. When the boy stumbled, Everett stopped and hoisted him up onto his shoulder. The boy squealed while Dr. Garrison jostled him up, down and sideways, as if he would dump the child at any moment. Doreen let one of her rare smiles escape as she walked along with them.

The doctor lowered the boy to the ground as Ruth opened the door. After speaking with her for a moment, Dr. Garrison patted Joseph on the shoulder. Apparently, the child was no worse from the harrowing ordeal with the rabid dog. He offered his arm to Doreen, and the two of them headed back toward the house. It was the first time Keelan had seen her up and about before noon.

As kind-hearted as the doctor was, Keelan didn't want to marry him. She didn't want to marry Pratt for financial reasons, either. She pinched the bridge of her nose. She'd do her duty as a good daughter, but it wouldn't keep her from trying to find a more pleasing route to the altar. She also didn't want to disappoint her ailing father. If only she could devise a way to please him without having to spend the rest of her life miserable.

She still held to the dream. Her mind drifted to Hart's kiss in the garden. Why couldn't she fall in love with a man who ignited her body on fire and whose kisses left her breathless?

She wanted a man willing to lay his heart bare, pledge to her his undying faith and devotion, and gently accept hers in his hands to cherish and protect until the end of his time.

But if her uncle and father had their way, she would wed a man for convenience.

If that was to be the case, she'd rather not marry at all.

Again, her mind wandered to a muscular man with wild, black hair and eyes the color of a cloudless sky. His fingers were vibrant yet tender, and the outside of his thigh hard against the hers. His lips were sweet and passionate, and...

Stop being foolish.

She'd witnessed the effect her father's long tours at sea had on her mother. The loneliness, which accompanied his absence, had turned Mother into a quiet, withdrawn shadow.

Always sad. Always waiting.

Keelan whirled from the window and sat down. Reaching for a small dish full of pins, she busied her hands. She selected one and held it as Slaney brushed her long, russet locks. The maid remained oddly silent she as reached over and plucked the pin from her fingers.

"I did not mean to sound ungrateful before," Keelan finally said. "Indeed, Dr. Garrison has been most comforting to my father. He's a very kind man and genuinely cares about us. I believe he fancies me, and I don't want to offend him. I only wish I could find a kind way to tell him I'm not interested in his attentions."

Slaney paused behind her and Keelan envisioned the maid's stern countenance. Thinned lips. Frowning eyes.

"Then you'd best find the words and ply them to his ears soon, lass. Men can't stand women who play with them like a sated cat toys with a mouse. It makes them irritable."

She turned to Slaney. "I am not some shameless trollop who flirts with men simply for sport."

"Of course yer not!" Slaney confirmed in a protective tone then continued, softly chiding, "But ye have made no attempt to tell the man his efforts are in vain, either."

"That's not..." The denial faltered on her lips. She put the dish down and tossed the extra pins into it, a twinge of guilt twirling in her stomach. "You're right. He's trying hard to help Papa. I can't stand the thought of hurting his feelings by telling him I don't welcome his affections. Although he's a sincere and compassionate man, I can't love him."

"Oft times love comes later, lass." Slaney placed her hand on her shoulder and gave it a motherly squeeze. "Yer head is full of girlish dreams of a knight in silver armor coming to sweep ye away to his castle in the clouds. But, if ye set yer standards at that lofty height, ye might find no one capable of making the climb."

CHAPTER 8

A PLEA FOR TIME

"He has the personality of a doorknob." Keelan paced to the bedroom window. "Mr. Pratt's an old sniffling, drooling beast of a man and I do not wish to marry him, Papa. Please don't ask this of me."

Her father's mouth twitched before he narrowed his right eye at her. His morning nap renewed some of his strength. He had wasted no time bringing up the topic of Pratt's marriage proposal.

"Keelan, don't be selfish. Think of what this union could do for our family. My old friend spent a fortune to purchase this property and transport the two of us here. The money from the sale of your mother's shop is almost gone. We can't afford much more of a delay." He clutched the bed sheets and stared at his white knuckles, leaving the rest unsaid.

If they lost Twin Pines, they would have nothing left, not even enough to invest in rent for a store. Her stomach churned. She wanted to be a dutiful daughter and do her duty, but to sacrifice her life to become a miserable aging slave owner's wife made her dismally queasy.

She turned to face the window in an attempt to hide her growing vexation at her father and bit back the accusation burning on her tongue. If he hadn't sunk that ship, she'd be running their merchant trade, instead of living in another country, arguing against a business merger requiring her to wed.

Her father's voice dropped, exposing his wounded pride. "Mr. Pratt owns land nearly twice the size of Twin Pines and combined, the property would become the largest in the Lowcountry."

Uncle Jared moved his family to South Carolina a couple years earlier, and offered to live here and help run the plantation until she and her father became comfortable with the task. Thank goodness for that. Neither she nor her father were prepared for the differences in conducting estate business. They knew nothing of turpentine manufacturing and even less about maintaining slaves, which placed them nowhere near an area of satisfied comfort.

Although Uncle Jared did his best, Twin Pines faced the new harvest with dwindling funds and increasing uncertainty. They still didn't have a solid budget for generating future profit needed to pay their creditors.

"Papa, you are asking me to sacrifice happiness for wealth." If their places were reversed, *he* surely wouldn't want to marry Pratt.

"If you have wealth, then you will have happiness. Daughter, I am ill. I would like to have you settled before I die. Don't begrudge an old man satisfaction on this issue."

If her father did nothing exemplary the rest of his days, one could always say that he excelled at smothering a person with guilt. She turned from the window to face him. "I can settle myself comfortably without relying on a husband."

Especially one older than my own father.

She put her fists on her hips. "I handled all the ledgers for Mother for many years. I know I could run a place in town that would be as successful, maybe more so." She forced some of the exasperation from her voice. Losing her temper would accomplish nothing.

She moved to sit on the edge of her father's bed. "Think, Papa." She couldn't keep the excitement from her voice. "Barrels of exotic spices and brightly colored fabrics from the southern climes, beautiful carvings...I'd sell them not only to the people of Charleston but also to merchants we know in London."

It was unconventional for a woman to own and run a business, so the shop had been in her father's name. But her *mother* made it successful. With her father away at sea for months at a time, it not only brought in a steady income, but also kept her mother almost too busy to be lonely. Her father sold it, of course, after her mother was killed. Rather than using the money to open a similar one in the city, he chose to invest in land. And in Dr. Garrison.

She didn't like the situation. She couldn't put a finger on the reason why, but it was as if the plantation fit like a shoe that was two sizes too uncomfortable.

"You have a quick mind with numbers, that's for sure," her father agreed. "That is why I need you to keep the plantation ledgers in top form."

Keelan fidgeted with a loose curl near her ear. "I dislike accounting for people as one would for livestock. It doesn't sit well with me."

The sound of him shifting in his bed made her alter her attention and reach for the water pitcher and glass. Her heart lurched at the sight of his shrinking frame. His skin had melted onto his bones. The sickness had attacked him on the journey here and continued to weaken him as the months passed. Even the continuous efforts of Dr. Garrison hadn't helped.

"Is the new medication from Richmond easing your pain any?" She poured a cup of water for him and pressed it into his hand.

"Nay. I hate the way it twists in my stomach, but the doctor said it takes time to work. I must trust he knows the way of this sickness." He sipped the water and gave the glass back to her. "Hold out your hand, Keelan."

Her father held a red ribbon on which was strung a gold ring. A signet ring.

"What's this?" She allowed him to drop it into her palm.

"This is yours. I want you to have it now."

She peered closer. An interesting gift for her father to buy her. Without trying it on, she could tell it was way too big. Not wanting to hurt his feelings by pointing that out, she smiled brightly at him. "Thank you. It's beautiful."

"Yes, well it's an important heirloom. It has a special story attached to it," he said.

"Oh? What story?" She tied the ribbon around her neck and let it fall into the crevice between her breasts.

"Well, you see...er, it once belonged..." He paused and stared up at the ceiling for a moment then batted his hand. "Never mind. I'll tell you about it another time. You're probably hungry and eager to eat some breakfast."

He'd been having trouble remembering things lately and would occasionally lose his line of thought. Not wanting to embarrass him by pressing for more information, she simply nodded. "Another time, then. I can't wait to hear the tale." She smiled and patted his hand, gaining a slight grunt of satisfaction from him.

Her father's illness also added a more urgent impetus to his decisions, thus the topic of marriage arose with increased frequency. She closed her eyes and took a deep, calming breath.

Time.

She needed to develop a valid plan to support her cause. That required careful planning and that required *time*.

"Papa, perhaps if we delay making a decision about Mr. Pratt for a while longer, a better resolution will present itself after the ball," she asked hopefully, keeping her voice soft.

Soothing.

Her father lowered his bushy brows. "If you're thinking you'll be able to persuade your uncle to financially back an enterprise for you, I'm afraid you'll be disappointed. He agrees with me. It's time for you to settle down and start a family."

She clenched the arm of her chair. "A shop in Charleston could generate enough profit for us to live comfortably. I'd be very, very happy and you never know, perhaps I'd meet a gentleman there who will make a suitable husband."

She tilted her head and smiled as her father harrumphed yet again. "You know how much I enjoyed being in town. I've always preferred city life to the country. I enjoy the more social aspects of being closer to the throngs of populace. Please, Papa."

Her father sighed heavily and leaned his head back, closing his eyelids. "Your mother could always bend me to her will the same way as you do now. You have her eyes, you know. Sparkling emeralds of light."

His voice slurred. Was the new medication finally taking hold?

"And fiery curls that glowed like burnished copper at dusk," he whispered.

Keelan smiled, although she was perplexed. "Mother's hair was pale brown. I appear to be the only one in the family with the anomaly of auburn hair."

Her father's lids twitched as if he was making a feeble effort to open them. "Nay! In her youth, your mother had hair like yours." He heaved a long sigh. "Losing her was the cruelest punishment God could have dealt me. So many years of longing and grief have left me...broken and bitter."

The medicine was sending her father adrift from reality. Her mother had been dead less than two years. He made it sound like it had been decades.

There had never been much warmth between her parents. Their relationship had always seemed distantly formal, at best. As a child, Keelan prayed for brothers and sisters, with the hope it would create a warmer family circle. They were all three left bereft.

Although she dreaded abandoning England for a southern

plantation in the American south, her spirits had been buoyed by the thought of living with her cousin, Doreen. She'd had hopes of the two of them becoming close, like sisters.

Doreen had been sweet enough at first, but when gentlemen callers began asking to see only Keelan, her cousin's mood had soured. Now they barely spoke.

Perhaps it was just a dream to one day have a large loving family. But it was her dream, nonetheless. Her father's current desire to see her wed to Pratt conflicted directly with that goal, making her determined to find a way to satisfy her father without throwing her life away in the process.

There was a better solution out there somewhere, and she would find it.

Papa's face relaxed in slumber. Sighing, she stood, leaned over to kiss his forehead, and tiptoed from the room. She shut the bedroom door and headed for the stair. The faint clink of china told her the morning meal had already been served. She descended to the first floor and neared the dining room entry, pausing when she came within range of the conversation.

"What brings you to our gentle city, sir?" her aunt asked.

Keelan froze as a newly familiar voice responded. "I have cargo to deliver to our other buyers. Additionally, we had a serious skirmish with pirates, leaving our ship in need of repair. It requires us to move the rest of our goods into one of your husband's warehouses for a few weeks."

"Pirates! Oh my!" Aunt Sarah exclaimed, "Captain Hart, how did you ever get away unscathed?"

A low chuckle sent a shiver across Keelan's shoulders.

"It sounds much more adventurous than it really was, Mrs. Grey."

CHAPTER 9

A MYSTERY UNSOLVED

F ynn Ahern's intentions remained a mystery, leaving Landon and Conal at a loss as to the reasons for the meeting. Yet, at the mention of Fynn's name, Landon could have sworn something flickered in the commodore's eyes.

Surprise? Anger? Panic?

Although the commodore denied any knowledge of Fynn, Landon didn't believe him. The man was lying. He could tell by the set of Conal's shoulders that his friend hadn't been convinced of the commodore's sincerity, either.

There was nothing more to be said after that, so he and Conal met with Jared Grey, the commodore's younger brother, to finalize arrangements for them to rent temporary warehouse space. They would be in Charleston for a few weeks while their ships were in dry dock. Plenty of time to further explore the mystery of Uncle Fynn's interest in the commodore.

But all in all, the day hadn't been a total waste of time.

There was Keelan, the spirited young lady he'd met; her vivacity, as well as her curves, which she'd hidden so well while sparring, but revealed more intimately while kissing, were tantalizing. Alluring.

The most humorous part was that he'd earned another kiss by agreeing to remain quiet and not tell her uncle about her activities, when he had absolutely no idea who her uncle was. Not that it mattered. He had no reason to mention her antics to anyone anyway. Besides, he was a bit chagrined to have been so deceived himself.

He should have guessed her fairer gender, if nothing else by the slender fingers and fine wrists. But, she played her part well. He saw what she wanted him to see...a young boy yet to sprout his first whisker.

He turned his attention back to Mrs. Grey, who'd been asking him about pirates. Thankfully, Conal had been paying attention and answered for him.

"Well, to better outrun them, we had to lighten the ship, by dumping most of our fresh water and provisions. Thankfully, we were only a day's sail from port, so our needs weren't dire."

A small movement by the doorway caught Landon's attention. The edge of a skirt. An eavesdropper? Grey noticed it as well.

"Well, come in, girl!" he barked. "'Tis bad manners to hang by the keyhole. Come meet our guests."

Landon prepared to greet the girl Jared Grey called into the room and shoved his chair back to stand along with the rest of the men, expecting Grey's young daughter. Every child gets caught at least once with their eye to a keyhole, spying on the adults inside.

But it was no little girl who entered.

Breakfast had just become much more interesting.

"Good morning, Uncle. My apologies. I was surprised to hear unfamiliar voices. I didn't know we had guests for breakfast."

Mrs. Grey blushed. "Oh, Keelan, forgive me! I became so enthralled in Captain Hart's tales, I completely forgot to send Tillie up to tell you. Come, my dear and meet two most *fascinating* gentlemen. They were just about to tell us a scandalous tale of pirates!"

Keelan bent to kiss Mrs. Grey's cheek then straightened and gazed casually about the room.

The girl had transformed from the nervous, saucy chit in the garden to a calmly composed, graceful young lady. He'd witnessed her calm during the frightening episode with the dog, but the demeanor she displayed now went beyond that. By the tilt of her chin and the graceful curve of her neck, she could have passed as an aristocrat's daughter, a young lady of the *ton*.

The simple light green gown fit her perfectly; those curves he touched while kissing her were much more evident now. Even knowing earlier that she wasn't a boy hadn't helped his imagination to picture her dressed like a woman.

At least not *this* woman.

How long it would take to crack that chilly, regal shell of hers?

Mr. Grey broke the brief moment of silence. "Gentlemen, allow me to introduce my niece, Miss Keelan Grey. She is the daughter of former Commodore George Grey, my elder brother."

UGH.

Keelan wasn't sure which was worse, Dr. Garrison and his eager smile of adoration, or the hulking form of Landon Hart, who even now looked at her with a raised eyebrow and a lascivious grin. Both he and O'Brien practically filled the room with their bulk, dwarfing her uncle and making Dr. Garrison look like a willowy stork.

Wide shouldered and tall, O'Brien was thicker, all muscle and brawn. Hart was sleeker, like a panther, coiled and alert. He flashed animal white teeth in a ferocious smile when she stepped into the room. Although her composure was more fragile than a thin layer of porcelain, she'd never let the arrogant sea captain discover how his presence rattled her. She bit the inside of her cheek and willed those stupid fluttering butterflies to settle.

She should have expected Uncle Jared to invite his guests to breakfast. She pressed her lips into a thin line; she'd been too distracted by this morning's events to think ahead clearly, which was unlike her.

Uncle Jared continued, "Keelan, I present to you Captain Hart and his business partner, Captain O'Brien."

O'Brien, being the closer, reached her first and bowed grandly. "Tis a pleasure to make your acquaintance, Miss Grey." His kind, emerald eyes twinkled with her secret.

She returned Captain O'Brien's greeting with a curtsy and a small smile before she turned to Hart. Since Captain Hart's back faced the rest of the room, no one but Keelan saw his appraisal moving in slow admiration down the length of her body, making her feel as if she were standing in nothing but her shift. His eyes took on a brightness that betrayed the wayward meandering of his thoughts, which was disconcerting to say the least. The kiss in the garden was something she'd been trying very hard to forget, although unsuccessfully. Well, perhaps she didn't really try that hard, but being in the same room with the captain made the exorcism downright futile altogether.

"Miss Grey." Landon's deep voice resonated with warmth and mirth while he bowed and extended his right hand, grinning mischievously. He was intentionally baiting her.

He knew of her wound yet awaited her to place her hand upon his. Keelan clenched the fist hidden in her skirt. She glared at him and with every fiber of her being, wished his outstretched appendage would fall off.

Along with another appendage...or two.

He raised a brow, then had the audacity to wink. *Wink*!

Of course, to refuse to offer her hand would be embarrassing and rude. If her aunt and uncle noticed her injury, how would she explain it? Seeing no other option, she complied. "Pleasure, Captain Hart." She tried to give him a tight smile, but her face felt frozen.

He placed his knuckles beneath her palm as a rest, heat radiating up her arm like a fire races across oil-soaked fabric. He bent to brush his lips across her fingertips. "Believe me when I tell you," he murmured, his voice husky, "the pleasure is truly mine." He glanced at the wrap on her thumb and placed a gentle kiss on the injured digit.

Barely keeping herself from flinching, a blush splashed over her cheeks. She snatched her hand back and hoped the glare she gave him would give him cause to behave better. Although, given what she already knew about the man, it was probably a vain hope, indeed. She steeled herself for an onslaught of Captain Hart's ornery charm.

Dr. Garrison hopped forward and clutched her recently released fingers. "Flowers pale next to Miss Grey." He squeezed her hand, including her wounded thumb, making her flinch openly this time.

"Goodness, Miss Grey." Dr. Garrison said, looking down, "What happened to your thumb?"

She glanced down and shrugged with what she hoped was a casual air. She hated to lie. Mainly because she was awful at it.

"I was in the kitchen house this morning." That part was true. "I'm afraid I was rather clumsy in the way I handled a knife." Also true. "But Slaney has treated it and it's much better."

Still true. She released a tense breath.

"Slaney is very good with her herbs." Aunt Sarah nodded and turned her attention to her tea.

The doctor led Keelan to a seat next to his, and she could barely suppress a despondent groan.

Captain Hart sat directly across the table. Her breath stilled as his gaze traveled leisurely down the length of her neck and paused. She could only surmise he was ogling the more feminine curves her current garments exposed, compared to the loose fitting shirt and breeches from earlier this morning. The heat of a pink flush crept down her neck and bloomed across her chest and she fought the urge to cross her arms over it. She lowered her brows at him as his gaze returned to capture hers. Smiling, he nodded in return.

Annoying man. She wished his approval didn't please her, but it did. Accepting a cup of tea, Keelan quietly sipped as she fought for calm and tried to ignore the voice in her head reminding her that one comment from him could land her and Daniel in serious trouble faster than one of those butterflies assaulting her stomach could blink.

Everett's head swiveled from Captain Hart's direction to her and back again. His eyes narrowed slightly. In fact, if she hadn't been looking right at him, she wouldn't have noticed how his cheek twitched. Had he caught the look she and the captain exchanged?

Aunt Sarah leaned forward in her chair. "Tell me, Captain Hart. Do you often have to deal with pirates in your travels?"

Thankfully, Hart turned his attention to her aunt. "Occasionally. We have to be diligent. We keep constant watch for pirates as well as privateers. This last encounter had been with a particular group, which crossed our path in the past."

The steely tone in Captain Hart's voice made Keelan pause in mid-sip. Hart and the pirates had a history, then.

"I'm ready to return and give those pirates their just due," O'Brien growled, breaking off a chunk of scone. At the perplexed looks from the rest of the table, he explained. "The cannon shot that blew away the mizzen topsail and yardarm of my uncle's ship sent splinters and shards raining down on the crew. Killed my uncle. May those pirates rot in..." Captain O'Brien's eyes suddenly widened in horror, his face reddening. "Beggin' your pardons Mrs. Grey, Miss Grey."

Hart added, "Captain O'Brien's uncle captained the third ship in our small fleet."

Dr. Garrison interrupted, his words sounding sharper than

usual, "'Tis a cruel end to meet. I, too, have lost family to the sea. You have my sympathies, sir."

The doctor's comment attracted Keelan's attention. Curious, Dr. Garrison had never mentioned that before. Perhaps that's why she'd seen him staring vacantly at the wooden model of Papa's ship, which sat on the desk in the study. Maybe he'd been thinking of loved ones lost at sea.

Simon, Ruth's husband, refilled her cup and she nodded her thanks, then reached for the cream. Normally, she preferred her tea without the cream's cooling effect, but the warmer spring temperatures in South Carolina demanded she adjust her preferences. Adapting to drinking tea at a more tepid temperature hadn't taken long.

Hart continued, "Fynn took me in hand when I had nothing and taught me everything I know about the sea. His loss has weighed heavily upon us all."

"You have our sincerest condolences, gentlemen," Uncle Jared said, laying down his fork.

Captain O'Brien leaned forward. "The main reason we initially accepted cargo bound for Charleston was to give my uncle an opportunity to meet with the commodore. Uncle Fynn wouldn't say why, other than he wanted to be certain of his facts before he divulged his theories. We'd hoped Commodore Grey would be able to tell us, but he didn't recall ever meeting Fynn Ahern."

Uncle Jared's face went blank. He shook his head as if it was on a wooden post. "Fynn Ahern. I don't recognize the name either." He picked up his fork again, speared a piece of ham, and went to work cutting it into small squares, keeping his head down as he sawed through his meat.

O'Brien sent Hart a slight shrug, but watched Uncle Jared closely.

He was *lying*. Her uncle's shoulders tightened. Was he wondering if O'Brien's uncle had sought out her father because of the sinking of that merchant ship? Had it been one of his? Had

Fynn Ahern lost a loved one? If so, it was likely he tracked down Commodore Grey for retribution.

"I'm sorry for your loss, Captain O'Brien," Aunt Sarah said. "I beg your forgiveness at the indelicate nature of my earlier question."

"No apology necessary, Mrs. Grey," O'Brien said. "Were it not for the skills of Captain Hart, none of us would have escaped those pirates' greedy claws at all."

Hart shook his head in humble disagreement as he reached for his napkin. "It's the speed of the *Desire* that saved our skins, Captain O'Brien. That and a crew who knows every breath she takes."

"Aye to that," O'Brien responded, slapping his thick thigh. "Would that I could find a lass who handles as well, I'd marry her and leave the sea forever!" His laughter spread, and she had to admire the way he set aside his pain to lighten the mood. His face had a familiar gentleness about it, like a well-used quilt. The same couldn't be said about his friend, Hart, who didn't bother masking his deviant thoughts. There was no gentleness in Hart's face. It was all hard angles and predatory planes.

Captain Hart continued. "Conal's uncle ran the trade routes from Cartagena to Boston and back for years. Cartagenian pirates and privateers are thick along the southern route, especially in the gulf region. It's not unusual to encounter them."

"It's Gampo, that bloody second of Lafitte's who will see the broad side of my ship's guns one day," O'Brien said in an angry voice. "Or the sharp end of me saber." Again he apologized. "I beg your pardon again for me language. But I mean to avenge me uncle's death. 'Tis no less than the pirate deserves."

Captain Hart gave a sharp nod, the hunger in his eyes told her he would relish the opportunity to take such a plan of action. A cold quiver skittered down Keelan's spine, making her wonder exactly how dangerous Captain Landon Hart could actually be.

CHAPTER 10

PIRATES AND PETTICOATS

Uncle Jared scooped several spoonfuls of potatoes to his plate. "Gampo. It sounds as if you have quite a history with him."

Hart let out a cool chuckle. "Because we have slipped through his fingers so many times, I think we've become as much of a crumb in his craw as he has in ours."

"Why didn't you plow a hole in her hull and sink her?" Dr. Garrison's expression was uncharacteristically harsh, bordering on bloodthirsty.

Conal O'Brien lowered his brows, his face registering surprise. "Well, that would have made us murderers, wouldn't it?"

"But it would have been justified," Dr. Garrison argued. "An eye for an eye." He reached over and stabbed a piece of ham. "He should pay for it," he muttered.

"It would have made them *pirates*," Keelan bit back a smile. Hart glanced up and caught her in a heated blue gaze. A mischievous glint in his eyes told her she wasn't far from the truth. She couldn't help wondering how Hart could deal with a pirate such as Jean Lafitte's second in command, and still maintain his code of ethics. If he even *had* one.

A conundrum to be sure.

"There are other ways to mete out justice," Hart said, as if reading her thoughts.

What other ways were there? Perhaps Hart's code of ethics merely stopped short of murder. Maybe all else was fair game.

O'Brien shifted in his seat. "Their captain is a pirate to be certain, but often times, pirates take prisoners and slaves and force them to do their bidding. You can never be certain *all* hands are willing."

Ruth bustled in, placed a fresh pot of tea on the sideboard, and removed the empty pot and meat platter, tossing Simon a quick smile.

Aunt Sarah spoke, her brow furrowed. "Ruth, how is Joseph doing? I heard he had a fright this morning."

Keelan froze. Afraid her expression would betray her unsettled nerves, she pushed around a bit of shirred egg on her plate and surreptitiously watched Ruth's reaction.

Ruth dipped her head. "He doing fine now, ma'am." She glanced at Keelan then gestured at Hart. "I'm grateful for dis kind gentleman's help."

"I'm glad I was there to assist." Hart actually spoke with a hint of modesty, prompting Keelan's brows to jump in surprise. He responded with the tiniest narrowing of his eyes, although they held a hint of humor.

O'Brien swallowed a bite of fruit and nodded. "From the study window, I saw the knife strike the creature. It was a very good throw."

Keelan almost melted with relief. *Thank goodness!* She let out a grateful sigh. It wasn't Uncle Jared, it was Captain O'Brien at the window.

Dr. Garrison cleared his throat and folded his napkin into a precise rectangle and placed it on his lap. "I examined the boy prior to breakfast, to make sure he wasn't bitten by that rabid creature. He was unharmed."

"Thank you, Dr. Garrison," Aunt Sarah gushed. "We're so lucky to have you with us today."

Simon took the hot pot and filled Keelan's cup, along with the others at the table.

Uncle Jared placed a spoonful of the fruit on his plate. "What hear you, Captain Hart, of the possibility of war between the United States and England?"

"War!" Aunt Sarah exclaimed, putting down her fork. "I thought the United States remained neutral with regard to the conflict between France and England. Has that changed?"

The United States may have remained neutral, but by the gossip at the Chatham shipyards, the British had other plans. Keelan watched the captains closely, wondering if they would confirm what she'd heard months ago.

Hart spread jam on his scone. "It appears neither France nor England is willing to trade with a country who will not declare its absolute allegiance. It is only a matter of time before we are forced to choose sides."

Jared leaned in. "Will you have to adjust your trade route?"

Hart gave a slight shrug, "Possibly. Our primary mission is to avoid the British navy and the French privateers." He glanced at Keelan and the corner of his mouth tipped up. "And other pirates."

Other pirates? Was he teasing her or was that a subtle hint?

Sarah pressed her hand to her throat. "Are you saying the British navy will attack unprovoked?"

Captain O'Brien shook his head. "Not attack, exactly. The English still think of us as British citizens, not Americans. They continue to illegally search our ships and impress American seamen into service for the British Royal navy. Privateers are given letters of marque from the king, giving them authority to take possession of enemy merchant ships in exchange for a share of the prize. It makes for dangerous waters."

Uncle Jared grunted in agreement. "Disrupt a country's trade and you weaken the resources needed to fight," He tapped his finger on the table as he spoke. "Congress can no longer remain reticent. They will have to act soon. I believe it's only a matter of time before we're all pulled into war." Her uncle sighed and shook his head. "Though we cannot afford it, since this country is still building its forces. It doesn't yet have a strong navy to protect the coast."

Hart cocked his head and placed his elbows on the table, lacing his fingers. "The United States has several frigates on the seas. Commodore Hall, of the *USS Glory,* is a good friend of mine."

Uncle Jared looked hard at Hart. "This war will not be fought solely on the seas."

"That's certainly true, Mr. Grey," Captain Hart agreed. His gaze locked on Keelan as she bit into a scone. "We all might be asked to do our part. Why, who knows, perhaps women will have to be instructed to bear arms as well."

Aunt Sarah immediately responded to Hart. "What a silly thing to demand. There are better ways for women to help in times of war."

The twang of Keelan's nerves fraying like taunt twine was almost audible. She tried to swallow, but the scone had turned to dust, throwing her into a violent fit of coughing.

"Are you all right, Miss Keelan?" Dr. Garrison asked, patting her back.

Aunt Sarah gave her a concerned glance. "Dear me! Simon! Bring some milk at once."

Attempting to wash down the offending morsel with a gulp of tea, Keelan instantly regretted the action when the scalding liquid hit the back of her throat and threw her into a worse fit of coughing and sputtering. She did her best to ignore the two captains who attempted to hide their amused smiles behind their own cups.

Insufferable ingrates.

"War and weapons are no place for women or children," Uncle Jared stated after she had finally regained control of her breathing, oblivious to the cause of her discomfort. "It's a man's duty to protect his own and be noble enough to never engage the fairer gender in battle."

Keelan reached for the cream pitcher, and poured a liberal amount into her teacup, while staring hard at Landon Hart, wishing he were the one mute from a scalded tongue.

Dr. Garrison was watching Captain Hart intently. His gaze shifted to her then back to Hart a second time. She needed to maintain better control of her emotions. To have Dr. Garrison watching her this closely was always worrisome. If he started asking questions, there was no guarantee she'd be able to provide an answer without lying.

And as everyone in her family knew, she was a *horrible* liar.

But Hart seemed unaware of or unconcerned with her internal battles. Probably both. He countered Uncle Jared's comment with a question. "You say it's a man's duty to be noble enough to avoid engaging the fairer gender. But what if the fairer gender fires the first shot?" Landon Hart asked, a wicked gleam in his eyes. "What then?"

Uncle Jared paused and gave the captain a puzzled frown. "To what do you refer, Captain?"

Keelan gripped her napkin tightly. Her heart ricocheted against the walls of her chest, its vibration pounding in her ears.

I'm a naïve fool.

She should have suspected he wouldn't keep his word. Regardless of his promises, and her honest payment, he was a scoundrel. A black-hearted man with no scruples or honor.

He was a seaman.

Surely, even a pirate would be less nefarious!

Afraid her expression betrayed her emotions, she stared at her clenched fists. A sickening sense of dread pulsed in her stomach.

If Daniel suffered a punishment because of Landon Hart's broken promise, she would seek her own vengeance.

And although Hart seemed to harbor no moral compass when it came to keeping his word, he was about to learn that Keelan Grey *always* kept hers.

Landon chuckled, placed his elbow on the table, and rested his chin in his hand. "There are tales of a lady pirate who dressed like a man. For a while, even her husband's crew did not know her fairer gender."

A lady pirate?

Keelan let out a long slow breath and managed to narrow her eyes at Hart. In return, she received a merry wink. *Dratted man.* Taking a smaller sip of tea, she tried to hide her agitation. So, he enjoyed watching her squirm in her chair. She wished she could turn about the conversation in a way that would make him squirm, too, but couldn't think of anything that wouldn't also put herself in the same position.

To Keelan's surprise, her very proper aunt's eyes widened before her excited intake of breath drew the captain's attention. "How scandalous! Please tell us more about her."

"Her name was Anne Bonny," he answered. "She handled a blade and pistol as well as any man. Eventually she was captured and sentenced to hang in Jamaica."

"Oh, dear," Aunt Sarah sighed. "How very sad."

"However," Hart continued, "she was with child at the time and received several stays of execution. Until one day, she vanished from the gaol."

"Vanished! Where did she go?" Aunt Sarah leaned forward. "She escaped, didn't she! How?"

The captain shrugged massive shoulders. "It is alleged that a group of loyal friends crept ashore in the dark of the new moon to rescue her."

Unable to help herself, Keelan asked, "And what of her

husband?" The story seemed incredibly romantic to her, but why would her husband not lead his men?

"Calico Jack Rackham had been captured the same time as Anne. No reason existed to stay *his* execution." Hart tilted his head, studying her.

That was a bit disappointing. She could easily envision a handsome dark-haired pirate, proudly standing at the bow of his grand ship with his legs braced wide and arms folded across his expansive chest, as he sailed into danger to rescue his love.

"Pity," Aunt Sarah murmured, apparently as disappointed as Keelan. "What of the child?"

Captain Hart's brows furrowed. "She and her son disappeared. I've heard different rumors that she changed her name, or married and started a new life in Virginia. Other tales place her in New Orleans. She was never heard of again."

To meet a woman such as Anne Bonny would be thrilling. Imagine, a lady pirate, as lethal with a sword as any man, and also keen with a pistol. Keelan was less skilled with a firearm. Tomorrow, she'd ask Daniel to teach her.

Without shifting to look, she could almost feel the doctor's gaze. Ignoring the chill slithering across the back of her neck was almost impossible.

"How long are you at port Captain Hart?" Dr. Garrison changed the subject.

Keelan straightened in her seat, drawing another curious perusal from her aunt. Trying to appear unconcerned, she pretended to focus on rearranging her napkin over her lap. When Captain Hart didn't immediately answer, she chanced a glance in his direction.

Landon Hart sat back in his chair, as if waiting for her to look at him. "A few weeks." He shifted his gaze to Keelan. "At least."

Oh, dear.

"Well, then," Aunt Sarah said. "You must allow us to offer you the full hospitality of Twin Pines. We would love the pleasure of your company. And you too, Captain O'Brien."

No! Keelan's lungs froze. She would not be able to abide seeing Hart and his bloody, rakish grin on a daily basis.

"That is a most gracious offer, Mrs. Grey. I can only imagine the full extent of what Twin Pines has to offer." The handsome captain smiled. Dimples dimpled. Crystalline eyes glittered. Aunt Sarah had no chance against such an onslaught of charm and magnetism.

Keelan was doomed.

She fingered the handle of her cup, which prompted Simon to refill it before slipping out of the room with the empty teapot. She eyed the cup like a snake waiting to strike. No more hot tea for her this morning.

"Unfortunately," Landon continued, "my ship demands close supervision, and most of my business duties remain in Charleston. Therefore, I have already secured lodging arrangements. However, I sincerely appreciate your warm and gracious offer, Mrs. Grey."

Thank goodness she'd be spared the torture of the captain's presence in the house for days and days. But as her stomach climbed up into place, Aunt Sarah sent it spinning away yet again like a child's top on a polished floor.

"As compensation for our disappointment, you and Captain O'Brien must accept an invitation to our ball next Friday," her aunt countered.

"We'd be honored." Hart responded with a polite dip of his head.

Aunt Sarah clapped. "Wonderful!" She passed a dish of potatoes to the captain. "Do try these, Captain Hart. Mr. Grey had them shipped from Philadelphia. He absolutely loves them. Keelan dear, you've barely eaten a bite. Are you well?"

"I'm fine, Aunt Sarah." She met Hart's amused gaze. "I seem to have lost my appetite this morning."

He remained stoic except for a mischievous twitch of his mouth.

Conal O'Brien leaned forward. "Miss Keelan, have you any kinsmen in Ireland, or perhaps Scotland?" The captain's deep forest eyes studied her intently.

It wasn't really an odd question. Not many British had hair like hers. "No. My parents' families are both quite well-recorded."

"Tis hard to believe a lass with your hair and eyes dinna have roots in Ireland or Scotland." Conal O'Brien pursed his lips as he stared at her a moment longer.

"I'm a bit of an anomaly, I suppose. I'm the only one in my immediate family gifted with auburn hair." She shrugged, an attempt to remain nonchalant. Even a fool would jump to the next question, or assumption. *Any chance your mother strayed? Took an auburn-haired lover?*

Not only was it an unusual auburn shade, it was wild and chose to curl on a whim. No matter where she went, she had to withstand the surreptitious stares. Her hair drew people's attention as if it was a character separate from her yet still connected, like an extroverted twin.

Best to depart before any more questions were broached.

"I'm going up to sit with my father for a while." She nodded to each of the other three men who had risen from their seats. "Dr. Garrison, I will speak with you later, and gentlemen, it was a pleasure to meet you both." She tilted her head. "Captain Hart, I understand Charleston has excellent shipwrights. I hope you are able to complete your business here quickly."

And continue on your way as soon as possible.

Hart returned to her a charming smile. "Why, thank you for your concern, Miss Grey. I don't anticipate delays. However, in the interim, I shall enjoy my visit. It seems the Charleston area has an abundance of wonderful sights. I might decide to extend my stay in order to take them all in."

Simon appeared at the doorway of the breakfast room. Uncle Jared motioned him inside. "What is it, Simon?"

"Mr. Pratt's in the parlor and's asked me to tell you he wishes a word."

"Perhaps Pratt would enjoy some breakfast." Uncle Jared reached for another scone. "Send him in."

With a respectful nod, Simon disappeared. Keelan couldn't stop her teeth from clenching together. Mr. Pratt wasn't simply passing through. He probably intended to talk to Papa about proposing.

Propose! Ugh.

Well, she wasn't staying to find out.

CHAPTER 11

A FLIGHT OBSTRUCTED

T*ime to go.*

Jumping to her feet, Keelan darted to the sideboard where she picked up her father's breakfast tray.

Dr. Garrison pushed away from the table. "Allow me to carry that for you, Miss Grey." He tossed his napkin down, successfully knocking over his tea. "Oh, quite sorry," he cried, horrified, as he clumsily righted it then dabbed at the spill with his napkin. When the stain simply spread, he abandoned his efforts and stood, tipping his chair over in his haste.

With an exasperated grunt, Uncle Jared extended his arm and pulled the chair upright again. Garrison gave him a quick, embarrassed smile.

Keelan briefly caught the intrigued look Captain Hart exchanged with O'Brien before he turned his attention back to her. He smiled one of those dazzling smiles that probably made every woman on the planet swoon. "It was a pleasure making your acquaintance, Miss Grey. I shall speak with you again at the ball. I would be honored if you would reserve a dance for me."

A dance with him? That would be dangerous.

And exciting.

But mostly dangerous.

Better to avoid that temptation. Keeping her expression as blank as possible, she nodded. "Of course, Captain. Until then, good day." There. She'd lied effectively, which did a lot to boost her confidence. Nothing good would come from dancing with Captain Hart. Later, she'd determine how to avoid it.

However, her attention at the moment must stay focused on the most dire objective: her mission to stay out of Pratt's sight.

Dr. Garrison followed Keelan as she attempted a hasty escape up the stairs. "Miss Keelan, *please* allow me to carry the tray." He pulled himself up by the banister rail, barely able to keep within three steps of her. She was, after all, *most* determined to avoid Pratt.

"I can manage, Dr. Garrison," she said with forced cheer while continuing her climb. If only he would leave her alone and let her dash upstairs. If no one was watching, she could hike up her skirts and take the stairs two at a time, even with the tray. The porridge didn't slosh, thank goodness. With Garrison nearby, she was forced to climb the steps in a more genteel manner.

"Please, I must insist." He took the steps two at a time, and placed his hands on the tray next to hers. "And I do wish you would call me Everett."

Of course he insists. Keelan sighed and allowed him to take it from her while doing her best to avoid rolling her eyes when he jostled the dishes as he took possession, spilling most of the cream. Freed from the encumbrance of the tray, she quickened her pace up the stairs.

Almost there.

"Well, good morning, Miss Grey." The reedy voice rasped over the plastered wall like dry leaves, making her breakfast churn in her stomach.

She looked longingly at the last three steps.

Turning, she managed a stiff nod. "Good morning, Mr. Pratt."

He stood in the hall, one hand clasping a limp handkerchief and the other a sturdy cane, bearing his bulk.

"Would you care to join me in the breakfast room?" He dabbed his mouth and gave her a closed-lip smile.

"Thank you for the invitation." She gripped the banister. Perhaps the reason he didn't show his teeth when he smiled was because he didn't have many. Maybe he had none. "However, I have already eaten and am taking my father his meal."

Pratt's eyes hardened, but the thin line of his mouth remained slightly upturned. "Allow the kind Dr. Garrison to deliver the tray to your father, my dear. Join me. I insist."

Why must men always *insist*? A murky sensation clamped over her shoulders as she walked back down the steps, feeling much like a doomed prisoner plodding to the gallows. Pratt waited patiently and held out his arm for her. She slowly looped her hand around his elbow to rest on his forearm and did her best to fight off a nauseous shudder that threatened, although she feared nothing would be able to pull her from the foul mood in which she now found herself. And to have Hart witness this awful moment made everything worse.

Pratt strutted into the breakfast room much like a bandy rooster in the yard.

Uncle Jared jumped up and shook Pratt's hand. "Pratt! Welcome! Won't you join us for breakfast?" The pleasant smile on his face faltered a bit when he met Keelan's glare.

"I'd be honored." Pratt pulled out the chair Keelan had recently vacated. "Here, my dear." Then he lowered his bulk into the seat beside her. Once again, she had to face the amused countenance of Captain Hart, which wasn't quite as bothersome as the presence of the man seated next to her. Well, maybe it was. She was caught between a snake and a panther.

When Hart quirked a brow in silent question, she threw him a glower through her lashes that should have withered a watermelon. He rewarded her with a slight widening of his crystalline eyes, to which she could only pretend to ignore. Along with the smirk, damn him.

Introductions were soon made, and Simon placed a full plate of food in front of Mr. Pratt, who shoved a heaping spoonful of shirred eggs into his mouth before he spoke. "I have considered the proposal you and the commodore presented to me." He nudged Keelan with his shoulder and winked at her.

Small bits of egg tumbled from his mouth with the words "proposal" and "presented," The urge to gag was overpowering. The only thing keeping her from bolting from the room in hysterics was her father's earlier promise to delay any decisions until after Doreen's ball. That didn't give her a lot of time; she'd have to come up with a reliable plan. At the moment, the most appealing consisted of packing a small satchel and running away.

It was a solid option.

Certainly, Landon Hart was heartily amused. She cast a fast glance at him. Instead of amusement, however, a shocked look flashed across his face before it was replaced by one of pity. As if he were thinking, *Rotten luck for her.*

She pressed her lips together. It *was* rotten luck, but she didn't need his pity. A hiding place somewhere on his ship however, would be very helpful.

Pratt continued. "You'll be happy to know I have decided to accept it, and I shall have papers drawn up that will merge Great Oaks with Twin Pines as soon as the nuptials are completed."

Nuptials *completed?*

Uncle Jared shifted uneasily in his seat, avoiding eye contact with her. "Ahh...well, then, I shall relay that to my brother."

She stared pointedly at her uncle. "You should know that Papa has decided to postpone making any firm decisions until after Doreen's ball next Friday."

"You don't say?" Pratt perked up a bit. "He seemed most eager at the time of our prior conversation."

Don't panic. There's still time.

The gusting sound of a tornado filled Keelan's head, for a moment blocking out all other conversation. She had to devise a way to avoid all this. She hoped to marry someday, but she wanted it to be a man of her choosing.

Someone she loved.

Someone who loved her.

Her hands curled into fists. She would *not* marry Pratt. There had been a greedy gleam in his eyes when he spoke of the *merger*. It was apparent he wanted the land badly. Her father expected her to be an obedient daughter, and she'd always tried hard to be so. But she would indeed run away before she'd *ever* marry Pratt.

Or...she could find a way to use Twin Pines as leverage for what she wanted.

Keelan jumped at a sudden pressure on her thigh. Her breath caught in her throat as she realized Pratt had put his hand on her leg. She frantically searched for a fork but none were within reach, since Simon had cleared her place when she left earlier. More rotten luck.

Hart handed the large fruit bowl across the table to Pratt, forcing the man to remove his groping hand to take it. "Mr. Pratt won't you try the brandied fruit? It's the best I've ever tasted."

"Thank you, Captain Hart. Don't mind if I do, as long as it isn't too chewy. I lost another tooth this morning so I have to be careful." Pratt busied himself scooping several spoonfuls of fruit on his half empty plate.

Keelan let out a relieved breath and chanced a glance at Hart, who gave her a sympathetic smirk. She choked back a snort of laughter. Captain Hart had a quick-mind, to be sure. If he wasn't such a rake, she'd actually admire his tactics. She pushed her chair back and rose.

"Please excuse me, gentlemen."

As the other men stood, she managed to spin away before Pratt could push up from the table and reach for her hand.

"Join me in the parlor later, dear," Aunt Sarah called as she whisked from the room. "I'll be working on my needlepoint and would love some company until Doreen joins me."

"I would love to, Aunt Sarah," Keelan called with as much enthusiasm as she could muster, which was minimal, considering her loathing for needlepoint. At least she would be free of Pratt's groping, and Hart's mocking but smoldering looks.

And his perfect smile, which made her stomach flutter and dip, (blast him, again).

CHAPTER 12

A PROPOSAL

Things were not going as Everett Garrison had planned.
He walked to the window of the old man's chamber and ran a hand through his hair. The events of the day had, so far, *not* been to his liking.

Pratt's visit was unexpected.

The merchant captains' visit was also unexpected as was the alarming interaction between Keelan and Hart. There was no mistaking it.

"What has you so agitated, Dr. Garrison, that you must pace a trench in the floor boards?" Commodore Grey paused, his spoon halfway to his mouth.

Everett clasped his hands behind his back and spun on his heel. "I'm very concerned with Mr. Pratt's pursuit of your daughter's hand."

"You don't say." The fool swallowed a bite of the Indian porridge then dug in for another.

Now that the topic had been opened, he must move forward with care. After witnessing the subtle exchanges between Captain Hart and Miss Keelan during breakfast, he'd come to the conclusion it was time to act. It was obvious those two shared an attraction or interest. He couldn't allow it to continue.

Then there was old man Pratt. He was another massive obstacle to overcome, due to the man's wealth.

Most distressing.

Acidic anger roiled in his stomach and it was a struggle to keep his tone calm, logical and authoritative. "Sir, over the past couple of years, we've developed a strong acquaintance." He'd rehearsed this speech a dozen times in his head. It was imperative he sound practical.

The old man nodded. "Yes, I certainly agree. The tenderness you showed my injured wife was what spurred me to seek your help with my melancholy after her death."

Everett frowned. "I still regret the damage was too severe for me to save her."

The commodore lowered his spoon and sighed. "I know young man. I'm appreciative nonetheless, which is another reason I wanted to assist you in settling here in America, knowing it was a goal of yours." He reached for his tea, a slight tremor in his hand.

The effects of the medication.

"Yes, sir, and I am eternally grateful for your financial backing. It's allowed me to secure a Charleston office and begin my medical practice with enormous success." Even as he said the words, they reeked of bitterness and pain. All the money in the world would not bring a loved one back from the dead.

"Glad to hear it, Garrison."

He fingered his watch chain. "I have also had the honor of befriending your daughter. I have grown quite fond of her and, like you, desire for her happiness. I understand a father's aspiration to make sure his only child is properly married, but my casual observation of Miss Keelan and Mr. Pratt together tends to give me pause."

Grey's eyebrows fell. "How so?"

Careful here.

"Well, sir, she almost fled from the room when Simon announced Pratt's arrival, and she seemed most distressed when he caught sight of her and insisted she join him." He tried to appear sympathetic. "I don't believe she fancies a union in the slightest."

The miserable recreant let out a beleaguered sigh. "I know. She said as much. Working in her mother's shop made her too ambitious and too independent. Living on a plantation out in the country hasn't helped." His eyes were sad and weary. "I'm dying. I can sense it. I can taste it, the rotten, bitter flavor of age and decay." His gaze travelled to the window and his voice softened. "I want to see Keelan suitably cared for before I die, Dr. Garrison. That is my wish."

Everett nodded and gave the commodore a compassionate smile. "I understand. Therefore, I propose an alternative."

Grey turned his attention back to him and raised a shaggy brow. "Go on."

"I have been building a successful practice over the past year. Word of mouth of my expertise contributed substantially to that end. Your daughter favors a civilized life in town." His palms began to sweat and he rubbed them on his trousers. "I could give that to her." He stepped closer to the commodore's bedside and laced his voice with as much empathy as he could muster.

"Commodore Grey, I would be honored if you would grant me permission to ask for your daughter's hand. As I said earlier, I'm fond of her and would be most diligent in seeing to her happiness and care. She would be able to live comfortably and we could open a store, if she desires to do so." He watched the man closely.

The commodore wiped his mouth with a napkin then pushed away his tray. "Dr. Garrison, I will be blunt." He grasped the edge of his blanket and pulled it up. "At this stage of my life, a sense of decorum commands less power over my tongue anyway. You must understand that Keelan's future is my primary concern. If she marries Pratt, he would see her well-cared for in the event of his death, because she would possess something tangible in the end—land. A lot of it."

Everett ground his teeth. This conversation wasn't progressing in the direction he wanted.

The commodore continued, "However, in the case of *your* death, there'd be nothing she could use to provide relevant income." He held up a hand to cut off Everett's protest. "Be assured, Garrison, I'd prefer she marry a young buck like you rather than an old stag like Pratt. But her long-term welfare is of the utmost importance to me."

Everett tilted his chin down and pursed his lips, fighting a scowl. "I understand, sir. But I would implore you to recall your daughter's intelligence and experience in trade. I have complete faith that an enterprise run by her would soon surpass those of other merchants."

The wretched man scrutinized him for a long moment. The tension in Everett's shoulders eased a tiny bit when he broke eye contact and stared down at his gnarled fists.

"You made a sound point, Dr. Garrison. I shall consider your proposal, but Keelan must agree to it first. Only then will my younger brother and I further discuss the possibility."

CHAPTER 13

A PIRATE FOR HIRE

Gampo was late.

For the tenth time, Everett scanned the dimly lit pub as he fingered the handle of his mug. It was early in the afternoon; too early for the place to be noisy with men half in their cups, but late enough for several patrons to mill about, enabling him to blend in with the back wall.

Two men, about his height, but probably forty pounds fleshier, trailed by a short, thick tar, snaked their way past the bar and headed in his direction, the one in front obviously the leader. The planes of his muscular shoulders and commanding jaw had the other customers allowing him ample berth. He and his men pulled out chairs and sat at the table next to him.

A tavern wench sauntered up and gave the men a slow, sultry smile, her eyes moving from each with a half-lidded gaze. "What'll ye be havin' fine fellows?"

The one with several fresh jagged scratches and cuts on his cheeks and arms gave her a lusty leer as he flipped her a coin, which he eyed with interest as she slipped it down her bodice. "Bring ale and a trencher of fruits, meats, and cheese, fine lass."

"And bread," the short one added.

She nodded before she swung toward the bar, tossing a quick grin over her shoulder. He gave her a jaunty wink before turning his attention to Everett. "A man shouldn't drink alone, especially since the day's still young."

Everett tipped his head in recognition of the code words the man spoke. "You'll be Gampo?"

"Keep yer voice down, man," the thick one growled.

Gampo's cool, lethal smile did not reach his eyes. He touched his hat. "'Tis I. And you'll be the one requiring my services?" A slight accent wove its way between his words.

"I am," Everett responded with what he prayed was an authoritative tone.

Gampo gestured to the two men. "Crowe and Pike, my quarter-master and bo'sun."

Everett nodded a greeting. "It's my understanding that a merchant shipping company formerly run by Mr. Ahern has been an enigma for you in the past."

Gampo quirked an aristocratically shaped eyebrow. "Formerly run?"

"Apparently, Mr. Ahern died during your last engagement." Everett watched the man closely.

Gampo sat back in his chair. "That's the true word? More's the pity." He rubbed his chin for a moment before he continued, "Sí, they caused considerable pain to the marrow over the years." He brushed a strand of ebony hair from his eyes. "What's about it?"

Everett took a shaky gulp while the server distributed three frothy ales to Gampo and his two companions. She bent a little lower while she deposited Gampo's before him, which from his grin, he enjoyed tremendously.

She left and the men turned their attention back to him.

Everett grimaced. "I, too, harbor a vexation with the same company, more particularly Captain Hart. I believe we can be of equal service to each other." He folded his hands. The pirates would never turn down the low hanging fruit he was about to offer.

Gampo pulled a gleaming dagger from his belt and pierced a dried peach slice. "What's in your head about it?" He tore the fruit from the knife with his teeth, and chewed slowly.

Everett shifted in his seat, eyeing Gampo's dagger. "Well...er, I possess knowledge of Hart's plans. His ships are in for repairs, he'll be moving cargo soon for safe keeping."

Gampo reclined in his chair. "And what makes you think I've a mind to care? My argument's with Ahern, not Hart."

He glanced from Gampo to the other two tars, who were eyeing him warily from behind their mugs. "I heard that they've done some damage to your vessel on several occasions. I'm thinking you'd like some compensation to use toward the costs of repairs. And such."

"And such." Gampo repeated, leaning back. His voice dropped. "By the devil's twisted tail, are you tossin' the notion of stealin' his ship's holdings? Or mayhap his ship from dry dock?" He raised dark menacing brows.

Everett took a moment to gather his nerves. "No, well, yes. In a manner of speaking." If he thought his hand wouldn't shake, he'd lift his mug and attempt a nonchalant swallow. "I can't help you with the second ship. But my proposal is to give you information as to the day, time, and trail of the goods as they are transported from the pier, giving your men an opportunity to lie in wait and relieve them of it. I know the precise place."

He slid a map he'd drawn earlier closer to the men and jabbed it. "The *precise* place, Captain."

Gampo rested his elbows on the table and laced his fingers . "Let's hear it, man."

Everett hunched over the parchment, tracing tiny lines, feeling more confident. "Here is a narrow alley they'll use as a cut-through. There are three recessed doorways as well as an iron stair. It won't be hard to stay hidden in the darkness of the predawn hours. And, I will offer you access to a nearby vacant building where the products can be stored for a time."

He paused, holding his breath. Had he talked too fast? Did he come across as too nervous? The biggest problem would be if Gampo decided to steal his plan and use it for his own means, leaving him out. He must make himself indispensable enough for them to warrant his presence. The impassive expressions on the faces of the three brigands had his stomach churning. Everett dug in his jacket pocket for the key and put it on the edge of the map, but close enough he could grab it back.

The walls in Twin Pines were thin, and it had been easy to eavesdrop on the conversation between Jared Grey, Hart, and O'Brien regarding warehouse rental and transportation. Grey owned several storage properties in Charleston, a few almost empty, due to the time he had to spend at the plantation. There had been only the small matter of unlocking the drawer and borrowing a key from Grey's desk.

Gampo draped his arm lazily across the back of the unoccupied chair next to him. Yet his body stayed tense and coiled. "And what see you as to your part in this plot?"

Everett pulled the items back near his half empty mug, praying the pirates didn't notice his fingers tremor. He tapped the map. "Along with half the money we get from selling the goods, I need you to apprehend a woman who may not...*realize* that it's in her best interest to leave her current environment. In exchange, I've prepared the base work, found the ideal location, created this map. I know the time of day that will make this stratagem successful."

Pike shoved a piece of meat in his craw then followed it with a chunk of bread. "'Tis give and take with our lot," he said as he chewed. "Share and share." He glared hard at Everett as he swallowed.

Gampo's smile barely slit his face. "'Tis the law of the coast. Right mates?"

The two men nodded. Crowe took a long draught of his stout and wiped his mouth with his sleeve before he spoke. "The capt'n and quarter-master gets two shares, the bo'sun and gunner a share an' a half, and officers one an' a quarter. Rest of the crew gets one." He ripped a hunk from the loaf. "That makes ye one of the rest, unless yer one of the other. Which yer not."

Everett's mouth went dry. This venture wouldn't be as profitable as he anticipated. However, the pirates' theft would keep Hart away from Twin Pines thus away from Keelan. If the man was kept busy searching for stolen goods, Everett could continue with his plan to seduce the girl. The best part was that it would cost him nothing.

"Fine, then." Everett pushed the paper and key back toward Gampo. "Share and share. Do we have an agreement?"

Gampo sliced a glance at his men. Crowe gave a nod and Pike simply shrugged. "On my faith, we have an accord but mark this." Gampo's blade impaled a sausage from the platter. He wiggled the steel tip free from the wooden trencher before raising the sausage to his mouth. He held it there, suspended. Steely eyes locked on to Everett's. "If we're crossed or foul-advised, may I guzzle a bowl of fire and brimstone with the devil if I don't have yer gizzards for breakfast the next day."

CHAPTER 14

A SCHEME

Captain Hart. Would he keep her secrets?

For the next couple of days, Keelan awoke each morning more tense and worried than the day before. Although there were times when her father could rise and move about with less discomfort, his health continued its slow decline. His stomach rebelled against almost everything but a thin broth, and sometimes even that didn't stay with him. Concerned, Dr. Garrison had even traveled to Charleston to purchase a new medicine, hoping it would work better.

To stay busy, Keelan spent the waning morning hours in the kitchen house, learning Ruth's recipes before sitting with the ledgers in her uncle's office in the afternoon. In addition to the plantation books, Uncle Jared had recently asked her to keep his business' records as well. Those activities consumed much of her day, but the distraction pleased her. The most precious time occurred in the minutes following the dawning of each day.

In the small meadow, when she was surrounded by the vibrant scents of late spring, Keelan's burdens fluttered away with the breeze. There, in the subtle light of the Southern morning, she moved through her exercises, thankful for the freedom of movement the boy's garments provided. Only the hiss and swish of blades cut the tranquil silence surrounding the field hidden in the forest. The escape was rejuvenating, short as it was.

But in the evening after she slid between the cool sheets of her bed, several nagging concerns blocked the path to slumber.

Had the assassin traced them to Charleston?

How can her father's wellness be restored?

Captain Hart. Too many thoughts about him.

There had been no mention by her uncle of her early training with Daniel. She could only assume the Hart kept his promise of silence. But what of the payment? When would he demand it? Her stomach made an odd little hitch. What would it be?

She clenched her jaw, not accustomed to this wobbly sense of vulnerability. Hart's absence should make her feel more secure. Instead, it caused her to glance over her shoulder several times a day.

Tonight, she opened the doors to the small balcony from her bedchamber and listened to the cicadas while she unpinned her hair. Their song reminded her of a stick clattering along the slats of a wooden fence. Although it was dusk, a moist film clung to her skin.

Which would be worse...to shutter her room against the insects and suffocate in the stagnant air, or leave them open for the occasional puff of breeze then pray the veil-like sparver draping over her bed would protect her from tiny flying teeth?

She removed the last pin. Her hair fell past her shoulders and blanketed her back. Slaney always said to tame Keelan's tresses was like "trying to still a flame." She walked to the small vanity and dropped the pins into the dish. Pulling her hair to the side, she quickly braided it.

With a sigh, she plopped into bed. Tree frogs joined the chorus of cicadas, creating a woodland cacophony of chirps and twitters, among the undercurrent of humming and clacking.

"What a bloody racket," she muttered. "I'll never understand how the other creatures sleep." She closed the curtains around her bed then extinguished the candle at the bedside.

Sleep did not come.

Her mind skipped from thought to thought like a bee buzzing from flower to flower. Too hot to breathe, Keelan climbed out of bed and pulled on a dressing gown. Perhaps her father was still up. She decided to sit with him a while, awake or not.

She crept in bare feet, careful to avoid the creaky boards a third of the way down the hall. The doors were recessed in small alcoves along the hallway. Loud snores emanated from behind Cousin Doreen's, and Keelan suppressed a snort as she slipped past. Outside her father's room, she paused.

The murmur of voices indicated someone else was inside. Curious, she stooped close to the keyhole.

"I would like to see Keelan properly cared for, before I die, Jared."

"Don't talk like that, George," Uncle Jared responded. The hesitation in her uncle's voice drifted under the door.

Her father gave an exasperated huff. "We both know my health is not improving. If anything, I am worse."

"George, as Keelan's guardian, I assure you, I will take excellent care of her," Uncle Jared said. "She's almost twenty. She should wed after harvest season. Pratt is a keen businessman and tripled his family's estates and coffers since he accepted control thirty some years ago. When he dies, Keelan would be one of the largest plantation owners in the state."

Silence.

Keelan winced. The silence meant her father was contemplating Uncle Jared's words. From the duration of the pause, nothing had yet come to his mind that would provide a valid argument against what his younger brother proposed.

Uncle Jared coughed. "Dr. Garrison is interested, but he possesses no experience running a turpentine mill."

"I know," Papa's gravelly voice replied. "He talked to me this morning and asked for her hand in marriage."

An involuntary gasp escaped her lips.

"And did you consent?" Jared asked with the same trepidation that swirled in Keelan's gut.

"I told him I would consider it. I'd almost rather Keelan chose him, since I fear her preferences do not lie with Pratt or country life."

Keelan moved in closer toward the door. He finally acknowledged her desires. It was a small step, but a positive one.

"George," her uncle retorted, "that daughter of yours has sent every young buck in three counties home with their tails twixt their legs. There's a very small pool of fish from which to choose in these parts." Uncle Jared's footfalls paced the floor. "Her husband should be of the ilk who can handle Twin Pines in her best interest. Pratt would see it better done. I cannot continue to split my time between my Charleston business and here for much longer. It's only a matter of time before one of the two begins to show signs of neglect."

Papa hesitated before spoke, "Well, it would be a tremendous comfort to me if she is married and settled soon."

"What about Ahern?"

"Ahern's dead."

Keelan flattened her lips. He *did* lie. Both did. She curled her fists until her nails put tiny half moons into her palms.

Her father sighed. "You're right, Pratt's the better choice. However, I promised Keelan she had until after the ball to make her decision. I doubt another solution will present itself, but I gave her my word. I would much prefer she concur with the decision than object to it."

She leaned back in despair, then froze as the floorboards creaked.

"I will—" Uncle Jared paused. "Did you hear something?"

She clapped her hand over her mouth, whirled and flew down

corridor. The opening click of her father's chamber latch had her ducking into the alcove of Doreen's room. Breathless, she pressed flat into the shadows as the door opened. She dared not move. The dim light fanned out onto the floor. A shadow fell across the floorboards, remaining for several long seconds before it disappeared back into the room. The door shut. When her heartbeat slowed to a more normal pace, she peeked down the corridor. Seeing it vacant, she tiptoed back to her room.

Keelan flopped down on the bed. The sound of her father's feeble, saddened voice tugged at her heart. The past twelve months had been miserable. Her mother's death was so sudden, then Papa's vigor seemed to fail without warning as well. Someone had gone to elaborate lengths to snuff out members of her father's kin in a lethal and gory manner. Only Uncle Jared's family remained whole.

What part did Fynn Ahern play in all this?

She curled into herself. Tears seeped to her pillow. For so many years, she'd prayed for her father to come home, and make more of his time available to her. Now that he was near, it seemed cruel that his tenure was to be so short. Father's death would leave her truly alone.

She swiped the tears from her cheeks. She would not let Uncle Jared destroy her life by demanding she wed a man she didn't love. She desired the opportunity to be independent and pick her own husband, should she decide to marry. She was in America, after all. As Slaney told her, things were different here.

She would *not* create a household mirroring the one in which she grew up. Her resolve locked, she rolled to her back and stared at the ceiling.

She would take the time to study the ledgers first thing tomorrow morning. A willowy idea started to take root in the fertile loam of her mind. As she pondered the situation, a plan began to sprout and blossom. What if she could use Dr. Garrison's interests to her advantage?

CHAPTER 15

A BETROTHAL

"I will marry you, Dr. Garrison, if my father approves." Keelan fought to keep her voice bright. This plan seemed less crazy and frightening when she was going over it in her bed last night.

If she agreed to marry Garrison, her father would likely give his blessing. He and Uncle Jared would need an alternative plan to finance the plantation. At least that's what she hoped. After reviewing the ledgers, she felt confident she could devise a proposition that all would find agreeable, and may actually succeed in convincing them to allow her to follow her dream. If not, Garrison was far more tolerable than Pratt. She could do worse.

Like marrying Pratt.

Regardless, she would do everything she could to delay the nuptials.

She and Dr. Garrison were seated on the iron bench in Aunt Sarah's garden, near an arbor draped in pale, lavender wisteria blossoms. Hidden from the house by a large magnolia tree, the bench would have been the perfect place for a tryst, or a marriage proposal from the man of her dreams. She fought back a snort.

"Please, Keelan, darling, call me Everett." He reached for her hand. The vision of a chicken's foot came to mind as his cold fingers grasped her own. He tugged her closer. "Your father and uncle can make the announcement at the ball. I should like to marry as soon as possible."

Keelan fought the panic surging in her chest. *Too soon!*

What could she do to prevent his push for an immediate wedding? Fake sickness? Require a special gown be made? That would only buy her a few weeks. She needed more time. "But what about your family?" She finally blurted. "Surely you'll want time to—"

Garrison interrupted. "Not an issue. I don't have a family to accommodate." The frigid flat tone of his voice made Keelan pause. "Not anymore," he added.

Poor man. "I'm sorry. I didn't know." She waited for him to elaborate, but he kept strangely silent. Perhaps the topic was too unpleasant for him to openly discuss. Or too new.

"I can see no reason to delay our wedding." Everett smiled stiffly. "Can you?"

Time to take a different tack. Something on which Aunt Sarah would agree. A social faux pas, perhaps.

Clutching her throat in horror, she choked, "I fear people will talk if we rush into a marriage. They will think I have been... *compromised*." She pressed her palms dramatically to her cheeks, hoping her ruse fooled him. "I couldn't bear the humiliation."

His eyes widened. "Good Lord! That never occurred to me! I would never want to mar my reputation as an honorable gentleman." He reached for her hand and added, "And of course, I would never want to put you through any such embarrassment either, my dear."

Perhaps if she suggested a specific date, he would stop pressing her. "Let's marry on Christmas Day." That might give her enough time. *Might*.

Everett smiled. "Perfect! Plenty of time to spread the word, plan the ceremony, and avoid the gossip mongers." He grasped Keelan's elbow and tugged again, pulling her closer.

She swallowed hard. Good Lord, he was going to kiss her! She clenched her teeth and instinctively turned her head.

"Come, dear Keelan, no one can see us," he whispered. "The bench is completely hidden from view. Grant me a drop of sweet honey from your lips, so I may know what treasures await me in our marriage bed."

His clumsy attempt at poetic prose nearly unlatched the door behind which she had locked away her hysteria, impulsive nature, and reckless tongue. Well, maybe not her impulsive nature.

She squeezed her eyelids shut as his face loomed nearer. Everett's lips pressed to hers in a firm pucker. She could almost feel his teeth behind them. As he pulled away she sighed, relieved it was over.

The doctor gave a contented hum. "My heart is blissfully happy also, my love. Your sigh of rapture warms my soul. I gaze into your eyes, which sparkle like emeralds, and I see such devotion, it makes me weak in the knees."

She blinked, then bit the inside of her cheek. Although she fought to keep her composure, panic-laden laughter welled in her chest like a bottle of shaken ale. Time to flee. *Now.*

She quickly stood. "My dear Everett, you are so eloquent with words." It was all she could do to keep her expression soft. Stoic. Calm. Think doleful thoughts. Recite Ruth's recipe for scones silently in her head...something, *anything* to keep from losing control.

She felt like a butterfly cupped in the hands of a toddler. "I must run this instant and speak with my father. I shall see you at dinner this evening." She hopped up and stepped away from the bench, in case he planned another kiss. Or worse, more nauseating endearments.

"Well, of...of course," he stuttered, smiling sheepishly. "Until tonight then." He reached for her hand, missed, and gave a feeble wave instead.

Moments later, still shaking and biting back nearly hysterical laughter, Keelan closed her bedroom door and leaned against it. God, what had she done? She'd feared Everett would see through her charade, but he did not.

The course was set.

Dr. Garrison believed she wanted to marry him. He'd likely never forgive her deception. Her desperation had climbed to its zenith; she could think of no other way to escape Pratt and plantation life.

Except to run away, which was still a viable option.

Now an avalanche had started, but if she didn't find a way to get out of its path, she'd find herself buried alive.

CHAPTER 16

A THEFT

Keelan Grey was a *distraction*.

It would be best for Landon if he could push her out of his mind entirely. He had business to attend to in Charleston, the outcome of which could affect the lives of other folks in a most drastic manner.

A wide, damp band of sweat crept around the rim and up the sides of his hat. He wiped his brow again. He'd rented storage space from Jared Grey and wasted no time arranging the transfer of the *Seeker's* cargo. To avoid working long in the heat, they started moving it before sunrise. The last few loads departed the docks, just as the sun rose high enough to add more uncomfortable warmth to the humidity. He was ready to head to a nearby tavern to enjoy a mug of coffee and a small feast with Conal.

He reined his horse down the street where the warehouse stood. Conal took off his hat and waved. Landon returned the salute and spurred his mount to a trot up to the doorway.

"The shipwright started the repairs on the *Seeker*." He dismounted from Orion's back. "The *Desire*'s waiting in dry dock. As we suspected, her damage is more severe. After losing Fynn and most of his goods, we can't default on any more obligations. Whichever vessel is seaworthy first, will sail to the next point of delivery and attempt to keep the trade schedule. Is everything secured here?"

Conal dropped his hat back on his head and nodded, "Aye. I'm just waitin' for the last of it to get here, then I'll lock the door and post the sentries."

Landon whirled to face his friend, a tightening in his chest. That meant there was a problem.

"It all left the dock a couple of hours ago," he responded testily. "They should have arrived and been unloaded by now. Blast it all, those wagons carried those bolts of Chinese silks." Their customer paid handsomely in advance for them.

"Perhaps they lost their way," Conal suggested uncertainly. "Who accompanied the last group?"

Landon's paused to think. "Billy was the only member of the crew riding with the last load." His consternation increased and uneasiness churned in his gut. "The rest were locals, so it's unlikely they got lost. I just traveled the same route they would have followed."

He clenched his jaw and inhaled deeply. The boy had left, excited to see his aunt, who lived on the northern fringes of the city. A kindhearted lad who worked hard for his share, he always seemed eager to show that he was more man, than galley boy. No doubt something had gone wrong, and Landon's concern deepened even more.

"I'll rally some of the men for a search," Conal said.

Landon nodded. He made it a point to take a personal interest in his crew's well-being and livelihood, allowing him to assemble a fiercely loyal group of lads, and his allegiance to them was just as committed. "Choose your men with care," he warned. "If there is foul play involved, you'll need someone in fighting form to guard your back."

Conal rubbed his neck. "It won't be easy, though. I let most of them go on leave. They're likely by now either half in their cups or easing their lust." He gave Landon a wry smile. "And neither puts them in a proper condition to fight."

Hart reached for the door. "Do what you can. I'll retrace my path. We'll need to check the inventory list against the master to determine what's missing."

"I've the list right here." Conal dug a piece of paper from his pocket and handed it to him.

Landon skimmed the list then put it in his saddlebag. "Mr. Grey should know of other warehouse properties in Charleston besides his own. He might provide advice regarding who might be able to plan and fund a theft like this."

Conal scratched his chin. "They'd have to both provide a hiding place and pay for the dockworkers. Most anyone of significant wealth will be attending Grey's ball."

Landon agreed, his plans following an identical line. "It might be worth my time to inquire later today. We can better prepare to ask the right people the right questions at the ball, in the event we don't locate Billy or the cargo."

Conal cast a sideways glance at Landon. "A visit would also give you ample opportunity to take in more...appealing sights as well, aye?"

He grunted in response. The man had an uncanny knack for reading his mind. He'd just been thinking how pleasant it would be to see that fiery young vixen again. "Don't you have work to do?" he muttered loud enough for his friend to hear.

Conal chuckled and headed toward the stables. "I couldn't help but notice the regard you took in the lass. Especially since you've never given a woman more consideration past a casual dalliance since—"

"No need to elaborate." He cut him off, then shrugged a shoulder. "I can't afford the luxury of anything more than a casual dalliance. Like you, I have a business to run."

Although, there was a time when he rushed back to port from

his travels to a wife and a hearth. There was a time when he believed love and marriage between two people was unbreakable. Unfortunately, leaving a beautiful woman home alone while he spent months at sea was a fool's decision.

Conal raised his voice as he walked away. "Well, the lass has spirit. I like her."

He snapped his head around to glare at his friend's back, strangely irritated. "You don't need the distraction, either."

Conal kept walking, but his words carried back to Landon. "I dinna say I was lookin' for one."

Landon adjusted his saddlebags and tightened the girth strap. Truth be told, he couldn't get the chit out of his mind. It was maddening.

Even if he did visit, what then? She was likely by now, betrothed to Pratt, and the rules of polite society demanded he not interfere. Still, he was never one to care much about polite society and their mandates. The only ones commanding his full consideration were those which influenced either his income or his life span. That's it.

There was much more to the lady than her obvious beauty and the adventurous side he and Conal witnessed in the early morning mist. She had both a quick mind and rapid reflexes. Sleek and stealthy.

She was brave. The incident with the dog proved it. But it was the look on her face when she observed the interaction between mother and child that gave him pause. For a brief moment, she dropped that shield of indifference, and her expression revealed a yearning like he had never seen before.

Yes, his curiosity had definitely stirred.

He demanded a kiss in the garden with the good-natured intention of igniting in her a similar shock to the one she gave them earlier. To tease her, to see if he could crumple her confident demeanor a little, and expose a bit more of her true nature. He had expected her to turn her head, argue with him or lash out.

It was her reaction to his kiss that had almost brought him to his knees. Her lips had become soft and pliant beneath his, then began responding to his movements and pressure. She had accepted his kiss in surprise, but he also sensed pleasure and passion. She'd plunged her fingers into his hair, then moved down over his shoulders to grip his forearms. What had started as a boyish prank to antagonize and taunt had ended in a swirling eddy of dense ardor and roiling desire, well beyond basic, physical reactions.

He shook his head in bewilderment. Last night, she prowled through his mind like a sultry green-eyed tigress. When he tried to convince himself he had no sincere interest in the girl beyond indifferent curiosity, his heart continued to muddle his thinking. The night before, she came to him in his dreams as the waif lunging and sparring, laughing as she removed her scarf... smiling as she slipped out of sight. What noises would she make if he kissed the tender skin on the side of her neck?

"I said: GIVE MISS GREY MY KINDEST REGARDS."

Conal's shout dispersed the images like a falling boulder to the glassy surface of a lake.

His friend sat astride a roan and had two guns jammed in his belt and several ropes attached to the saddle. A bag of coins jingled at his waist. He was grinning like a bloody fool.

Landon scowled. He gave his friend a curt nod and swung up on his horse as smoothly as he could manage, while trying to ignore Conal's chuckles. The witch! Even his daydreams betrayed his common sense.

"After I recheck the wagon's course, I'll stop and inform the sheriff that a boy has gone missing with the last wagon," Landon stated curtly. "Afterwards, I'll ride out to Twin Pines to speak with Mr. Grey. I expect to be back before nightfall."

"I'll meet you at The Whistling Pig Tavern on the wharf," Conal said as he turned to depart.

"Have the men start from that point and fan out. Finding Billy is their primary duty," Landon replied.

Conal's brows furrowed. He nodded, then trotted away. Landon nudged his mount back toward the docks, a knot of worry constricting his chest. He wanted to be hopeful, but something told him Conal's search would be unsuccessful.

CHAPTER 17

A STORM APPROACHES

A storm was coming.

In more ways than one. The lunch hour approached, but the events of the day destroyed Keelan's appetite. She had to postpone her plan to discuss her tentative acceptance of Everett Garrison's marriage proposal with her father, because he was sleeping. She hated the effects the medicine had on him.

Keelan fidgeted with her hair; the curtains billowed, inviting her to join the freedom of the breeze outside. As if beckoning, a whinny rent the air from the stables, followed by the angry pounding of a hoof against the stall boards. Her uncle's stallion, Shamrock's Prince, was showing his vexation at being separated from his harem of mares, grazing in the lower pasture.

She brightened. A brisk ride would clear her head and ease her soul a bit. Although she preferred riding in a carriage, she needed to expel additional energy today. Daniel taught her how to handle a mount when she was quite young. There were certain skills the man believed all women should master, even if a cause never arose to put them to use.

Perhaps her father was secretly behind Daniel's tutelage.

Perhaps the commodore had always wanted a son.

A lively stroll through the city would have been more satisfying, but no matter. She would make do with what availed her. She hurried to her room to don her riding habit. Her mind elsewhere, she jumped when a shadow fell across her path.

"Late for another caller?" Her cousin did not attempt to disguise her disdain.

"No, Doreen, there is no caller," Keelan spoke through clenched teeth. Her cousin's spiteful tone grated on her nerves.

"I'm nearly shocked to the point of fainting," Doreen answered, examining a fingernail. "Every eligible bachelor, and even several non-eligible and non-bachelors have found a reason to pay a call on Twin Pines since you arrived." She slid her gaze to Keelan. "Yet, after a few minutes of droll conversation, or a cup of tea, you simply thank them and then depart, leaving me to walk the irate, dejected man to the door. By then, they barely notice my presence at all."

It wasn't difficult to see through Doreen's vindictive words. Maybe she lashed out because she felt undeserving of a gentleman's attention. Maybe she was just jealous.

"Doreen," She softened her voice. "I'm older. You're only sixteen. Your time will come."

"By that time, no potential husband will want to return." Doreen's voice sounded small and hurt. She raised her chin. "Ladies of the Lowcountry know how to comport themselves. However, I'm not surprised at your behavior, since your upbringing appears to have been somewhat stunted."

Keelan was determined to control her ire and not cause a scene so close to her father's bedroom door. She refused to let Doreen bait her. "Please let me pass. I'm going for a ride."

Doreen cocked her head. "Your mother's dead. Your father's dying. With no one to monitor your deportment, it's no wonder you act like a rude, uneducated wharf rat. What will become of you when Uncle George dies? A wedding, I think. To Mr. Pratt, I hear."

Keelan squelched the prick of tears at the cold harshness those words brought and brushed past her cousin. As she closed her door, the faint notes of Doreen's humming drifted down the corridor. That girl needed a pastime.

She changed quickly and was heading for the front door when she heard a sudden crash in the study. Wasn't Papa in his room? Perhaps he awoke and decided to read over the ledgers she'd finished. In his weakened state, he would have a hard time navigating around the furniture. She dashed down the hall, fearing father had fallen, or worse.

She rounded the corner to find Dr. Garrison staring at the shattered remains of her father's model ship, scattered on the floor. She paused, startled by his appearance. The doctor's lips were nothing more than a thin slash separating his nose from his chin. He stood rigid as a wooden post, fists at his sides.

"Dr. Garrison?" There was something about his posture that made interrupting him seem like a bad idea. Frightening, even. Stepping into the room, she kept her voice calm, soft. "Are you all right?"

He jerked as if physically prodded. A tattered piece of paper fluttered to the floor behind him. "I... yes. I... " His eyes returned to the broken model. "It seems I have caused your father's ship to break."

"Think no more about it," she said as she inched toward him. "Accidents do happen. My father of all people would understand that."

His nostrils flared in response, but whatever his thoughts, he didn't speak them out loud. He sank to his knees and began picking up the pieces, leaving her to stare at his back for a moment, trying to decipher his mood and find the right words to help lighten it.

The paper he'd dropped when she entered caught her eye and she picked it up. It was soft from frequent handling, the edges slightly rounded, the creases like hinges. The fold on the lower third was in tatters and it flapped open, revealing an elegant script and the faint scent of roses. It said:

... and I look forward to our wedding day with a joyful heart.

Yours Always,

Rachel

Her new fiancee's past was a mystery to her, although he'd informed her he had no family. He'd been educated in London and was born in the United States, but that was all she knew about the man.

The doctor finished collecting up the fragments and placed them on the desk. He turned toward her, and his eyes widened when he noticed the note in her hands.

"This was on the floor behind you," she hastened to explain, already feeling guilty at having read part of a very personal note, even if it was accidental. She handed it to him, the bottom flapping back open. "Is it yours?"

"It's torn!" he cried hoarsely, accepting it with both hands and cradling it like a broken-winged bird.

"I... I'm sorry," she replied. "When I picked it up, I didn't realize it was in such a fragile condition."

He gently closed the missive along its creased folds and tucked it into his inner coat pocket. They stood for a moment, not speaking. The doctor cleared his throat, breaking the awkward silence.

"I... yes, the letter's mine," he said, finally making eye contact with her.

The anguish in his expression made her press a hand against her chest. "I can tell it's precious to you." What else should she say to her fiancé?

What else don't I know about you?

She desperately wanted to say those words but didn't dare.

She should feel jealous, at least a tiny bit, but she didn't. In fact, the understanding that he was probably still in love with another woman oddly comforted her.

"Rachel is...was...my fiancée a few years ago." His voice was thick with emotion. "She died tragically."

How awful for the doctor; he had obviously been in love with Rachel. "I'm so sorry for your loss."

"Thank you." His voice sounded detached from his body, as if it came from a ghost standing next to him. "Well." He shoved his hands into his pockets. "I should check on your father. If you will excuse me..."

"Yes, of course." She stepped aside and let him go. A husband like him would never make her giddy with happiness, but now her chest tightened and her stomach swirled in a sickening spiral. His melancholy spirit surrounded her and poked hard at her apprehension. She'd been certain she could suffer this marriage, now she wasn't as sure.

Good Lord, what had she done?

CHAPTER 18

A WILD DECISION

K eelan needed to do something bold to expend the nervous energy pulsing through her body.

The interactions with Dr. Garrison and her spoiled cousin, combined with the heavy still air of late morning, pulled at her spirits as she left the house. Normally, she'd have asked Slaney to join her, but today she wanted to be alone to sort out her life. She hoped a ride across the farm would buoy her mood, although in the back of her mind she pondered the idea of just riding away and never returning.

She turned in the direction of the barn. In exchange for overseeing the plantation business, her father had granted Uncle Jared use of a substantial tract of land, where he built an impressive stable filled with some of the finest stock in Charleston. They would someday be part of Doreen's dowry.

She paused at the small paddock nearby. Several brood mares stood under the immense oak tree on the far side. She whistled softly.

One of the round-bellied creatures turned her head and perused her for a moment before turning to plod toward her. The mare lifted her nose over the fence and nuzzled Keelan's sleeve.

"Good afternoon, Juliet, my love," she crooned as she stroked the sleek blue-gray neck. "I wish you were able come with me today, but alas, in your delicate condition, 'tis best you reserve your strength."

A voice spoke near her elbow. "She should be droppin' her foal any day now, Miss Keelan."

She turned to find one of the young stable hands staring at the gentle mare. The boy had a nasty welt across his cheek. She inspected the mark, narrowing her eyes.

"Thomas, what happened to your face?"

He stared at his bare feet. "It ain't nothin,' Miss Keelan. Only a scratch."

Unconvinced, but unsure what to say, she returned her attention to the mare. "Juliet is moving slowly today. I don't think she's very comfortable." She gazed worriedly over the mare's bulging sides.

"Don' you worry none, Miss Keelan. Seamus say she lookin' fine, so she is. He been at dis a long time, so he knows things."

Keelan smiled brightly. "I shall place my trust in Seamus then. Since I cannot ride my favorite palfrey, would you please saddle Camilla for me?"

The boy glanced away. "I can't do dat, Miss. She not here. Miss Doreen told me to turn her out in the lower valley."

Undaunted, she shrugged. "I understand." Juliet nudged her arm again, and Keelan rubbed her muzzle gently. "Would you please saddle Uncle Jared's gelding?"

Thomas shook his head. "Mastah Jared rode him this mornin' down to da mill."

She sighed and gestured toward the barn and adjoining pasture. "It doesn't matter, Thomas, you may prepare any one of the other mares."

The boy dug his toe into the dust. "Sorry, Miss Keelan, I can't."

She stopped stroking the horse. "Why not?" she asked.

He mumbled, "Miss Doreen said she'd flog my hide if I let you ride any of her daddy's mares."

Keelan bristled. So Doreen was responsible for the ugly welt. It was within her rights to override her cousin's order, but she wouldn't dare place Thomas in a position that would tempt Doreen's rage.

"Miss Keelan?"

She tried to mask her agitation. Juliet gave up on Keelan and nuzzled Thomas's sleeve. He absently reached into his pocket, pulled out a crust of bread. She delicately accepted the treat from the groom's palm.

"I'm awfully sorry, Miss Keelan. The only ones Miss Doreen say I can saddle for you is Ole Poke, or..." he swallowed.

"Or?" Keelan questioned. She raised her eyebrows suspiciously. There was only one other option.

The groom darted a glance toward the thumping sounds emanating from the rear of the barn. "Or Shamrock's Prince. Mister Jared's stud."

She clenched her jaw and scanned the pasture for Old Poke. He stood lazily in the shade of a large, gnarly tree. The aged mule casually flipped his tail in a half-hearted attempt to shoo the flies from his backside. She shuddered.

No. She might as well sit on a pile of bouncing rocks.

Old Poke was an option she refused to consider. He was no more desirable than the past suitors her cousin escorted to the door.

Keelan frowned. No doubt, Doreen only included Sham on the short list of available mounts because she didn't believe Keelan would dare attempt to ride the beast. It nettled her sorely to think of Doreen's pale, pampered face spying on her from the window.

Gloating.

Keelan set her mouth in grim determination. She'd not give

her cousin today's amusement by riding a lumpy old mule. Decision made, she tried to ignore Sham's impatient kicking. The rhythmic pounding against the boards echoed her heart ramming her ribs.

"Now, Miss Keelan," Thomas said nervously while he peered up at her, expression wary. "Lemme hustle up and saddle Old Poke for you to take on a nice easy, stroll around the plantation. He'll be fine for a spell at a slow pace. Besides, Ruth's bones say we got a big storm a comin'. You might want to stay close by."

"Humph!" Keelan couldn't restrain a snort. If she abandoned the ride and returned to the house, the humiliation of conceding the afternoon to Doreen would be unbearable. She turned and bestowed a radiant smile on the groom.

"Would you please saddle Sham for me?"

Thomas' forehead creased. "Please, Miss Keelan...dat horse is well-trained, but he's a strong 'un. You could git real hurt if he gits a mind to take the bit in his teeth and run."

Laughing lightly, more carefree than she truly felt, she waved his remarks aside. "I'll be fine, Thomas. I've been riding since I was ten years old." Just not recently. And never a stallion. And rarely without a carriage attached.

The young groom expelled his breath in a soft whoosh before ambling to the stable, as if his pace might change her mind. It was several m minutes before he led the prancing steed from the barn. He steered the horse to the hitching post farthest away from the brood mares, but the strong-willed stud had other plans. While arching his noble neck and raising his tail like a banner, he trotted toward the pasture, dragging poor Thomas along like a ribbon in the wind. After a few mumbled curses and more than a few stumbles, he finally regained his footing enough to give an irritated yank on the lead, abruptly gaining the stallion's attention.

"Whoa, there, Sham!" he said, annoyed.

The mares paused from grazing as the stallion pranced. Keelan sucked in her breath. Even on this overcast day, Sham's chestnut coat rippled like liquid copper.

Thomas secured the horse and moved to help Keelan mount.

"Sometimes I think the devil hisself sired this cantankerous, mule-headed horse," he muttered, rubbing his trampled foot.

Biting back a smile, she cautiously reached up to caress the velvety nose. "Now, Sham, my good man, do be a gentleman today and provide a well-mannered seat for me."

The horse nuzzled her empty hand then stomped a long foreleg in impatient irritation.

Pausing near the stirrup, she tilted her head up to Sham's back, two hands taller than the top of her head and took a slow breath. She could do this. He was just a horse.

A very tall horse.

Swallowing hard, she tried to ignore the trepidation flapping wildly in the hollow of her stomach.

The slave stood rigid as Keelan adjusted her feet in the stirrups. Taking the reins in her hands, she finally exhaled. Successfully riding a horse depended on the confidence of the rider. Confidence came with experience, experience came with repetition.

As for repetition, she rode a lot as a child, but not recently. She'd had plenty of experience riding her gelded pony in England. Big horses the size of Sham...well there was a first time for everything, was there not?

She relaxed her shoulders. Horses always seemed to sense the demeanor of their riders. Just another sunny day on a horse. She peered up at the distant clusters of clouds. Sunny for a time, anyway.

Daniel had taught her skill and trust control a steed. Hopefully she had the skill. She was a little thin on trust with this huge beast.

She carefully reined the horse toward the lane. The stallion's muscles quivered beneath her like threads of contained fire. The opportunity to stretch his long legs was near at hand, and he broke into an impatient trot then a restless, short-gaited canter. Keelan tightened the reins and spoke in what she hoped was a calm, authoritative tone. "Whoa, sir! Allow me to prepare my seat and hands."

The horse complied, showing his eagerness to fly only by swishing his tail in short, jittery swings.

Keelan fidgeted. She wanted to go for a gallop. Did she possess the strength to slow the stallion if he became stubborn?

Confidence. Yes, she could.

She allowed him to trot again then pulled him back to a walk. He was well trained, for sure. Repeating the exercise a few more times had her more relaxed and confidant.

Much better.

As they approached the house, she glanced at the upper windows, noticing the curtains at Doreen's window flutter briefly.

"You will not have satisfaction today, cousin," Keelan muttered.

Seconds later, Doreen burst out of the front door, startling Keelan and sending Sham into a startled sidestep that almost unseated her. It took every bit of her concentration to prevent the horse from bolting. An angry admonition on her lips, she turned toward her foolish cousin, but Doreen's gaze focused on a lone horseman approaching from the main road. Keelan didn't need to wait for him to get closer. From the broad shoulders and straight back to the shiny black boots, it was obvious the rider was that arrogant rake, Captain Landon Hart.

She groaned. What brought the man all the way out here today?

I'll collect my due another day, sweet Keelan.

The earlier wiggles of trepidation hatched into a swarm of butterflies that flitted from her stomach to her toes and back. She shook her head. She was making more out of their encounter than she should, certainly.

"Good morning!" Doreen's voice cut through the humid air. "Welcome to Twin Pines!" If the girl knew what a scoundrel he was, she wouldn't be waving and smiling as he approached.

He tipped his hat at Doreen. "A fine morning it is, Miss. And thank you for the kind welcome. Landon Hart, at your service." He turned to Keelan; his white teeth gleamed against his sun-darkened face. "Miss Grey you look radiant today. It's a pleasure to see you again."

Doreen's smile faded. The glare she threw at Keelan could have burned a hole through a rock. Hart appeared not to notice as he focused solely on the horse and *her*. Keelan fought to keep her expression neutral, not to mention Sham calm, as the man moved his gaze from her perky green hat down to her hem and back up again. The urge to turn her heel into Sham's side and flee almost overpowered her sense of decorum and common sense in general. She may be a tad impetuous, but she was not stupid. Instead, she returned the greeting as politely as she could manage. Slight tip of the head. No smile.

"Good morning, Captain Hart. What brings you back to Twin Pines so soon?" Dare she hope it was simply business?

"Back?" Doreen said, confused.

Keelan rolled her eyes. If the girl got out of bed before lunch, she'd know more.

Hart's expression sobered. "I'm afraid there's been a theft of some of our goods, and I've come to seek your uncle's advice." He dismounted and loosened the saddle's girth strap to allow his horse to cool down.

Keelan stiffened. "Are you accusing my uncle of stealing your cargo?" she asked. That would be a bold accusation.

He shook his head, his mouth set in a flat line. "Not at all. Our shipment was being moved to one his warehouses farther from the waterfront. At some point, some of the wagons disappeared, and a young boy is now missing. I merely need to take advantage of his knowledge of the area, so our search has a better chance of yielding results."

Keelan frowned, concerned for the boy. "Have you alerted the sheriff?"

"Yes, and my entire crew is combing the city of Charleston."

A search party of that size should be able to find the child. Hart sauntered over and ran a hand along Sham's neck and shoulder. He gave a long low appreciative whistle. "A very handsome steed."

Doreen chirped from the porch. "He's my father's. The plantation might belong to Keelan's, but the horses belong to mine— her uncle. The man to whom you wish to speak." She raised her chin and gave him a condescending smile.

"Is it any wonder why the girl has no suitors?" Keelan mumbled under her breath as she adjusted the reins. She caught an amused grin from Hart, and couldn't help but smile back. His eyes sparkled with humor and for a second, she couldn't break eye contact. Maybe she didn't want to.

His responding wink made those annoying butterflies dive to her knees, and she almost had to remind herself to breathe. She hated the way her belly misbehaved when he was near. It would help if he wasn't so handsome. He was likely thinking about the secrets he kept for her. She welcomed the annoyance that last thought brought with it. It was less frightening than the strange pull, which tugged at her earlier.

"Do you ride this stallion often?" The captain's tone was casual, but the humor had left his eyes. "He seems quite spirited for a lady."

She patted Sham's neck. "Although this is our first outing together," Keelan almost spoke without sounding breathless, "I have complete confidence that we will get along fine." Her last few words came out sharper than she intended, but the captain was undaunted, and continued to question her equestrian skills.

His deep blue eyes reflected the concern in his voice. "Don't you think you might better enjoy riding a more gentle mount? One that would offer you a more relaxed experience?"

Yes.

Keelan gave Doreen a pointed stare, which was returned with a sly smile. "Unfortunately, there are none nearby." She nodded toward the bank of clouds in the distance. "We might get some rain later, and I wanted to be back before it began, so I don't plan to be gone long."

"If you linger until my business with Mr. Grey is concluded, I would be happy to escort you." Landon ran his long tanned fingers through Sham's coppery mane as he talked. Keelan followed them, remembering the touch of his hands in her hair not too many days ago. It was only the sound of her cousin's voice that broke her concentration.

"I'm sure Keelan is eager to be on her way," she said.

It appeared only Keelan heard the snide undertone, as Landon continued to gaze at her while still stroking his fingers through the mane.

Doreen persisted. "Come inside, Captain Hart, and I'll have Ruth make you some tea while I have Simon fetch my father."

Keelan wasn't sure why it irked her that Doreen did her best to pull the captain's attention away, but she found herself wanting to stifle the attempt. "You can escort me as far as the mill," she said to Landon. "I was told my uncle rode his gelding there earlier. You'll be able to discuss your concerns with him immediately, rather than await him here. You said a young boy is missing, so it appears your need to see him is most urgent."

Hart flashed her an easy grin, returned to his mount and swiftly tightened the girth strap. He tipped his hat to Doreen and settled into the saddle. "Thank you for the hospitality, Miss. A pleasant afternoon to you."

Doreen's jaw clenched through the stiff smile she gave to the captain. "I hope to see you again soon, Captain." She gave Keelan a stony glance before she twirled, snatched the door open, and stomped inside the house.

Sham pranced sideways. She spoke to the horse in what was hopefully an authoritative tone to quiet him. He settled down a bit, but still snorted his impatience in response to her tightening the reins. How she wanted to loosen them and let the beast stretch his legs!

She chanced a quick glance toward Landon. Perhaps her handling of her mount eased his concerns. Especially, since he'd probably have something annoying to say if she told him her current thoughts, such as: *How fast could such a powerful animal run?*

To Shams great disappointment, they walked. A tangy scent of pine and earth wafted from the wood. This particular lane meandered through the entire plantation, connecting the homestead to the fields, mill, slave cabins, and farmland. It was broad enough for Twin Pine's lumber wagons to haul timber from the surrounding forests to the mill, making a ride through the countryside mostly free of strangers and other riders, as well as peaceful.

Stern gray clouds mottled the bright blue sky, giving them some respite from the hot June sun. Landon glanced up. "It appears we will indeed have some foul weather before the day is done."

She followed his gaze. "At breakfast, Ruth predicted rain and Uncle Jared concurred. He'd originally planned to go into Charleston but decided to wait another day or so, to avoid miring the carriage in the mud near the lower creek crossing again." She shifted in her seat to balance her weight a bit better. "That's why he's working at the mill office today."

"'Tis my good fortune then," Landon said.

At Keelan's curious look, he elaborated, "Otherwise I wouldn't have the opportunity to enjoy such pleasant sights." His crystalline gaze never wavered from hers.

He was *flirting* with her. The completely innocent expression on his face didn't fool her in the slightest. He turned his head and looked down the lane lined with oaks, Spanish moss dripping off their branches like a tattered veils.

No quirking eyebrow, no wink, no ornery grin.

He was up to something.

Keelan loosened the reins, and Sham quickly stepped up to a perky trot.

"I'm in no hurry," Landon said, urging his mount next to hers. "In fact, a slower pace allows me to savor your company longer."

She smirked. As much as she'd like to entertain him and respond with some witty cut, she knew better than to encourage him. "Has it occurred to you I might not wish to extend our time together? It seems to me the more we interact, the more trouble I seem to encounter."

"You wound me deeply." Hart's smile was anything but wounded.

Actually, the blue heat in his gaze spoke to a different affect. The warmth pulsing around her neck and chest was certainly due to restrictiveness of her riding habit, not the close proximity of Captain Hart. Truthfully, if she were alone she would have traded comfort for propriety and removed her hat and jacket and tied them to the back of her sidesaddle.

Perhaps later.

She couldn't bite back the smile as she imagined how refreshing it would be to have the breeze comb her hair. There was something deliciously exhilarating about a breathtaking gallop. Now that the thought had invaded her mind, the more appealing a gallop became. She chanced a sly glance at Hart. She loved competition. He must too. What man did not? Other than Dr. Garrison.

"What is your horse's name, Captain?"

He reached down and gave his mount a firm pat on the side of the neck. "This is Orion."

The horse was as tall and elegant as Sham, except he was the darkest black she'd ever seen. "He's beautiful. Is he very fast?"

He gave her a humble shrug. "He's swift enough. According to your uncle, Orion's from excellent stock. I bought him at Mr. Grey's suggestion. He said he was as fine as any he owned."

"Hmm." She perused the horse. "Let's see, shall we?" She patted Sham's neck and crooned, "Now then my handsome steed, lets give the wind a sporting chase." She slid a glance his way. "On the count of three, Captain?"

Surprise blanked his face before he flattened his lips. "I'd prefer not."

"One..." she said.

His eyebrows plunged down. "Miss Grey, I strongly advise—"

"Two..."

The next words were a low growl. "I will not—"

"Three!"

She relaxed her grip on the reins and took a fistful of mane for added stability. The stallion needed no further urging. His muscles bunched beneath her as he leapt forward, eager to stretch his legs. She barely registered the angry shout behind her. Soon, they were flying with joyful abandon down the lane. She laughed in giddy delight while Sham's strides beat a steady rhythm on the turf. It wasn't long, however, before she heard Orion's hoof beats getting louder.

Small clods of earth flew up in their wake as they burst out of the woods and raced along the outskirts of one of the fields. A small group of slaves paused in their labors and watched their flight as they thundered past.

Although Sham worked up a lather on his neck and flanks, his breathing wasn't labored. In fact, he still strained against the bit. How fast would he go if she let him set the pace? She pulled the reins, but the horse did not respond. She pulled back again, harder this time, and tried to ignore the panicked band tightening around her chest.

She threw all her weight back in the saddle and added a shouted command, then another. She expelled a breath she didn't realize she was holding when Sham hitched his gait, allowing her to eventually slow him to an easy canter as they neared the mill.

Thank goodness.

A triumphant laugh exploded from her chest when she succeeded reining in the animal. "Come now, Sham. I need to catch my breath, even if you do not!"

After a few prancing steps of half-hearted rebellion, the horse heeded her instruction and slowed to a reluctant walk. Hart reined in beside her, and shot her a thunderous glare.

"What's wrong, Captain?" she quipped breathlessly, "Not used to being outrun by a woman?"

"Little fool!" His tone was harsh. He reached over and grabbed Sham's bridle. The horse threw up his head, nostrils flaring. The close proximity of Hart's mount agitated the beast, but Landon held the bridle and gave Sham a firm command. When he finally settled, she was once again the recipient of his heated gaze.

"You're just upset that you lost," she countered, trying to divert his anger. It actually *was* foolish. She wasn't sure what she'd have done if she hadn't been able to slow the horse. She bit her lower lip. Her heart was still slamming a staccato in her chest, betraying her act of bravado. She was grateful the captain couldn't hear it, or he'd guess how close she'd been to losing control.

"Your horse could have hit a rut in the trail and gone down with you on him!" Captain Hart's face was dark as a storm. "You could have broken your pretty little neck," he said fiercely.

Pretty little neck?

"Well, he didn't, as you can well see." She adjusted her reins to avoid looking at him. She had to admit that while the ride was exhilarating, it had also been mildly terrifying. Well, maybe a tad more than mildly.

"I'm not some helpless little chit," she added, in case he was thinking so.

"Oh, you have proven that to the point of redundancy," Hart ground out. His eyes practically sparked with blue fire. "It's the reckless nature of your decisions I find most infuriating. Approaching rabid dogs. Riding at a full gallop on a dangerous mount you obviously can't control—"

"Well, that really should be none of you concern, should it?" she snapped back, annoyed at her cowardice.

Stand up to the man. He has no power over you.

Despite lifting her chin and easing back her shoulders, it was hard to keep from shrinking away like a chastised child, even though in hindsight, it was indeed reckless. Perhaps even stupid. His glare scraped her pride like a gravel path to a bare knee just the same.

His kiss had set her on fire, she had to be honest about that. But one kiss would not wilt her. One secret would not control her. "I can take care of myself. Go find some small-minded strumpet from whom to charm kisses. I'll not be a pretty piece for you to use while your boat is being repaired. I'm not looking for a...a...liaison." Mother would be proud of her for saying that.

An odd expression fluttered across Captain Hart's face and for once, he had no retort.

She nodded toward the mill ahead, her confidence almost refilled. Except there'd be no more gallops for her today. "You'll find Uncle Jared in the office."

He released her, his expression blank, voice flat. "It would be best if you returned to the stables before the rain starts."

Yes, it would be.

"I will when I'm ready," she replied, not about to concede anything at the moment. The thrill left her empowered, strong. She had sole control of her next decision. "I'd like to follow the trail ahead a bit further, first." She reined Sham away before Hart could grab the reins again. "Good day, Captain Hart."

Sham jumped to a quick trot as soon as she relaxed her grip. She allowed the horse to progress into a slow canter as they moved on down the lane. Resisting the urge to check the captain's reaction, she hoped she appeared more confident than she actually felt.

CHAPTER 19

A SCANDALOUS DIP

L andon Hart was *dangerous*.

She may not be well-experienced in the ways of men, but she was sharp-witted. Something told her that Hart's charm had been well-honed on young women like her. It made her even more bent on resisting him. At least, that would be the smart thing to do.

The thick air pressed Keelan's clothing against her skin like a damp blanket. A trickle of perspiration carved a pathway down the side of her face and along her jaw, before continuing down her neck. Once she rode beyond the sight of the mill, she doffed both her waistcoat and bonnet and tied them to the back of her saddle. Propriety be hanged in this heat. She was thankful Slaney pinned her hair high up off her nape this morning.

That merchant captain was entirely too flirtatious. *Stop thinking about him*. She wasn't sure how to shield herself from his charm, which was a huge predicament. Something about him made her temperature rise, and when that happened, she didn't trust herself to make unerring choices.

When she was a girl, and needed to clear her mind or ponder the solution to a problem, she always took to a horse, dragging along whatever household servant she persuaded to join her. In town, she went by carriage, but when they stayed at the country house, she rode. Which was only occasionally.

This ride did not differ from the ones in the past, except for one tiny thing.

A chaperone. And she was on a giant horse, not a pony.

Fine. Two things.

She shook her head in self-chastisement. Again, a rash decision on her part had her teetering on the precipice of disaster. When would she learn? If she'd paused long enough to think her actions through, she would've brought Slaney. Perhaps she inherited this particular personality flaw from Papa, who was eccentric in his own right. She frowned as her musings turned toward her father.

His prognosis was terrible, and the thought of losing him dropped a cold ache in her heart. As much as she wanted to squeeze her eyes closed and wish the trepidation away, she could not.

She gripped the reins a little tighter. To stand idly by and avoid preparing for her future would sentence her to years of dull misery with Everett.

The only bright spot was that at least she might avoid old man Pratt now. It was obvious he overindulged in food and wine by his stature, and his bulbous red nose. Since servants and slaves tended to gossip amongst themselves, Slaney had provided Keelan with several lurid stories of strange sounds emanating from the master's bedroom at night. Becoming Pratt's bride churned up a wave of nausea.

She'd run away first. She'd—

Her shoulders fell. No, a devoted daughter would stay by her sire's bedside. Duty and self-preservation tugged her in divergent directions. She couldn't have one without forfeiting the other. Papa's health still declined, although he was lucid enough to plan her future from his sickbed.

If her recent scheme worked, she was likely rid of Pratt, thanks to Dr. Garrison.

If her father and uncle agreed with her proposal, she would break the betrothal. She brushed away the guilt that accompanied that last thought. She truly didn't want to hurt the doctor.

In love. Ugh.

Unbidden, Landon Hart's chiseled face intruded into her mind again. "Stop," she groaned to herself. If only she could show Captain Hart that she wasn't some boyish twit intent on playing games in a meadow. She wanted him to recognize her as a woman, confident and capable. She squared her shoulders.

And totally in control of her destiny. And her mount. Mostly.

She blew a stray curl from her cheek and gave a resigned sigh. Except it would demand she play the same game with Hart as he played with her. And it was a *game,* that was certain. Obviously Hart's attentions were based on nothing other than his desire to seduce her.

Even if his intentions were honorable, happiness with a sea captain as a husband would elude her. What woman could stand being abandoned for months at a time, never knowing when, or if, her husband would return, especially one with a vendetta against a pirate?

"Augh!" Swatting the air in front of her as if batting away the image, she muttered, "Leave me be!"

Her stomach grumbled loudly, and she regretted not bringing something to eat. Although the sun remained hidden behind the leaden gray clouds, she estimated it was past noon. Thomas had kindly strapped a canteen to her saddle, and she retrieved it and sipped until it was gone.

Sham flicked his ears forward and back, taking in the surrounding countryside. The stallion hesitated, sampled the wind, and spun around to scan the lane behind them.

"What do you hear, my fine steed?" she murmured. Absently stroking his glistening neck, she tried to peer into the trees.

Nothing.

"Are you seeing ghosts, sir?" A slight breeze shifted the upper branches of the towering pines on each side of the path. "I fear you'd be worthless in a fight. 'Tis fortuitous you have such a swift stride. At least you can outrun your foes."

She reined him back around and they continued along the wide trail. They passed three shanties in various states of dilapidation. One still had most of its roof, but the other two were little more than piles of clapboards, shingles, and sandstone. A sudden scurrying within the weeds near one structure startled Sham; he shied away to the side, while keeping a wary eye on the monster in the grass.

"It's likely a rabbit, you big coward." Keelan smiled. "Honestly, for such a grand creature, you really should be braver."

As the soil changed from red clay to sand, Sham's ears twitched, and he sniffed the air again, then huffed. He stopped and pranced a few obstinate paces to the left.

This was unfamiliar territory for her. How far had they traveled from the mill? It was probably best she head back. Surely Hart's business with Uncle Jared should be concluded by now and the merchant captain on his way back to Charleston. Glancing up at the sky, the bank of clouds still crouched on the horizon signaling a storm, but not for a while.

Curious, she allowed the stallion to follow his nose.

"I imagine you'll soon have us both miles away, all because you've discovered the scent of a dainty little filly," she mumbled dryly. A few moments later, they emerged out of the forest to the border of an immense lake.

"Ohhhh!" she breathed. "How beautiful." She gaped at the pristine scene before her. So *this* was the largest lake on the plantation. It was much bigger than she'd imagined.

The balmy breeze rustled through tall pines near the water's edge, making the wispy boughs sway lazily. A purple-tinged haze meandered between the rippling surface of the lake and the solemn sky. Cypress trees stretched gnarled roots toward the water and hunched close to the shore like a cluster of hags sharing a secret. Spanish moss hung from the branches in long, graceful ringlets.

Sham plunged forward. When he reached knee-depth, he lowered his head.

"You were thirsty, too." Keelan stroked his neck. They were standing at the point of a small inlet. Without traveling the entire shoreline, it was impossible to determine how many other thin fingers of land extended into the waters.

A splash shattered her reverie. Water doused her ankles and thighs. She hardly had time to catch her breath before another current of water walloped her full on the chest.

Keelan blinked through the rivulets streaming down her face as the ornery beast lifted his front hoof above the water and slammed it down with determined force a third time.

"You brute!" she coughed, hauling back on the reins and forcing him into a hasty retreat. "If you wanted your belly cooled down, you needed only take two steps forward!" Water splattered her clothes. "You have soaked me to the skin!"

The horse did not act the least bit chagrined and walked forward to take a few more swallows.

How was she going to explain a wet riding habit? Her aunt and uncle would discern how far from the main house she'd wandered. There would be no avoiding her uncle's ire now. Unless she dried before she returned. Keelan licked her lips and gazed at the bright, fresh water as it rippled and twinkled. She plucked at her dampened collar. It had been itchy with perspiration before Sham had soaked it. The cooler water was quite refreshing. It would be lovely to... She glanced around. She was very much alone.

As usual, she made up her mind in a blink. The anticipation of crisp water against her overheated skin made her almost laugh aloud. She nudged Sham to the grassy clearing, hopped down, loosened the girth a little, and reached for her new hat and coat.

They were both gone!

She stared for a moment at the empty straps and shook her head, perplexed. She would have to keep a keen eye while retracing her path home. Hopefully, she would find the wayward garments along the route, no worse for wear.

Keelan hobbled Sham and secured the reins where he wouldn't step on them. With a quick pat on the rump, she sent the horse sauntering toward a tuft of sweet grass.

It took an exasperating amount of time to wiggle out of her skirt and drape it over a craggy boulder. Her chemisette soon followed.

Keelan paused. She might not be able to re-lace her corset. Ah well, she might as well enjoy herself now, and deal with the clothing issue later. Corsets were evil articles of clothing to begin with. She'd like to burn this particular torture device. It pinched ridges into her skin. Perhaps she'd toss it into the lake.

She pulled off her shift. The sun-warmed heat of the stone would dry her clothes before she needed them again. She kicked off her boots, and barely contained her excitement as she approached the sandy edge. This was going to feel *marvelous*.

She stepped into the water and grinned. She wiggled her toes and waded further. *Sublime*. Moaning, she immersed to her neck then froze. Wearing a sopping garment under her clothes might be more than a little uncomfortable.

However, no lady of the Lowcountry would dare bathe outside completely...naked. She snorted. No lady of the Lowcountry would snort or dare to strip down to her shift for a dip in a lake.

Scandalous.

The corners of her mouth tipped up.

But then, she was not a "Lady of the Lowcountry," was she?

It was more a matter of practicality than morality.

Rising out of the water, she wrenched the garment over her head. At least half the pins Slaney used in her hair this morning had fallen out during the ride after she removed her hat. The coiffure ruined, she pulled the remaining pins out and tossed them near the dripping chemise.

Chances were, she was already mired in trouble. First and foremost, she took out her uncle's prized stud without permission. Second, she left with no escort. Third, she'd never get her riding habit on correctly and she unless she found a way to sneak into the house unseen, there'd be no way to hide that she'd removed it.

Doubtless there were more reasons, but they didn't carry the weight of the first three. She'd probably be forbidden to ride ever again, have to sit with Aunt Sarah in the front room and work on needlepoint, or banished to her room. Maybe all three.

Maybe Papa and Uncle Jared would forbid her to attend the ball. They'd be doing her a favor if they did.

She eased back into the silky depths. She was free for the moment and it was *thrilling*. The water moved over her naked limbs in tender, soothing strokes, like an angel's caress. If she weren't in such an exuberant state of bliss, she might have felt absolutely wicked. Taking a deep breath, she dipped beneath, careful to remain at a depth where her feet still touched. She expelled a lungful of bubbles before she popped back up, breaking the sparkling shell of the lake's surface.

A partially submerged rock a few paces away coaxed her a little deeper. The water was almost up to her neck. She grasped the boulder and leaned on a narrow ledge. It made a perfect hand rest. Lying back, Keelan held on and fluttered her legs from the bottom to float. The sky was darker to the east, but patches of blue still peeked through. She wanted to arrive home before her uncle and the rain, so she would not tarry overlong. Closing her eyes, she inhaled and released a contented, relaxed sigh. A bird warbled nearby and his mate soon answered. The sun had emerged from hiding; it warmed her skin. Cool air flickered over her body, and gooseflesh pricked with its breath. The faint, soft thread of jasmine danced on the wind and mingled with the sharp tang of pine and heady scent of earth and water.

Her rumination drifted along as well. She pictured a pair of twinkling, azure eyes and an amused smirk. Her brow wrinkled as her mother's warning echoed in her head.

"There's no settling down for a man of the water. He'll pledge his troth to you to be sure, but his lady is the sea, and she ever beckons him home. In time, he'll leave you for her charms. They always do."

Slaney said as much earlier today.

Certain that many women had been lured to Hart's bed by his rakish good looks and charming wit, it would be best to forget about the impression left by his hand on her wrist and his thigh against her own. Forget about the enticing feather of his lips on her palm. Forget about the gravelly sound of his voice.

Her own flesh burned with the memory of the fire that whipped under her skin when his fingers clasped her arms. *Gah!* Even when absent, he tormented her!

Best to divert her attention to a safer place, like how she could persuade Slaney to run away with her if her sire still tried to push her to marry Pratt after she told him about Dr. Garrison's proposal.

A loud snort, and the clomp of a horse's hoof, interrupted her daydreams. Sham returned for another drink, which was convenient. It meant she would not have to go far to find him when she was ready to head back home. She sighed. She should get out and start struggling with her garments. Heaven knows how long she was going to have to fight to get them back on.

Lazily opening her eyelids, she turned her head toward the bank. There, not a stone's throw away, stood an enormous black stallion. It stomped again and pawed the ground with an impatient foreleg.

Orion.

Oh, no.

On the animal's back, leg casually thrown over the saddle horn, was the very person she had been in the process of banishing from her thoughts.

Landon Hart's magnetic gaze captured her own, and a slow, lazy grin spread across his tanned face. Her bonnet sat at a cocky angle on his head, and he touched the cap in a spry salute.

With an alarmed shriek, Keelan flung her arms across her chest.

And sank.

She couldn't touch the bottom.

Where was the bottom?

She clawed and kicked. Where was the *surface?*

Thrashing wildly, terror seized her body in a deadly crush as her mouth and nose filled with water.

CHAPTER 20

A WATER SPRITE

The ominous sky had urged Landon to seek out Keelan. And something else he was uncomfortable admitting, even to himself. When her stallion didn't slow as they approached the mill, his stomach shot straight down to his boots and he couldn't breathe. He'd prayed that God would protect her even as he gave chase. No way she could survive a fall at that speed. It was a long time before that terror-filled moment passed. He had to take a few moments to collect his emotions before seeking Grey. It wouldn't do to punch a hole in the man's office door, although the release of frustration that woman invited would almost have been worth it.

A wall of dark purple-gray clouds moved westward. A gale was not only probable, it was certain. Still, she shouldn't be out alone, regardless. Containing her ride to the plantation land did not mean she stayed out of harm's way. People traversed across Twin Pines when the situation warranted. He was vaguely familiar with the layout of the property thanks to the owners of The Whistling Pig. They'd described it well. He also learned that fleeing slaves occasionally used the abandoned cabins near the lake.

The lady's bonnet grabbed his attention first, and fearing she'd fallen or had been thrown from her horse, he spent several terrifying minutes looking for her broken body in the brush. Worse, he had to continue the search, since the bonnet could have fallen off at any point during the ride. It was a relief when he found her coat. That's not something that could easily fly off unless she'd removed it. At least he found her trail, which prompted him to increase the pace.

He shook his head in wonder as he recalled the prim and proper-looking woman he rode with this morning. Who was the real Keelan Grey? The composed young lady with a quick wit and tongue to match, or the boy-waif who enjoyed sparring in the early morning?

Perhaps she was neither.

Perhaps she was both.

A many-faceted image tiptoed into his mind. Keelan crouching like a tigress, the set of her mouth and stark focus in the meadow as she blocked Daniel's attack, her glee when she scored first. The corners of her mouth twitching upward, challenging him to a race. Her face flushed and eyes bright with exhilaration and victory.

There. That was the real Keelan.

What would she be like on the open ocean with its unpredictable moods and ruthless privateers?

Orion lifted his head and perked his ears as they neared the lake. Pausing at the edge of the trees, he perused the tranquil and secluded area. There were many places where a person might hide.

Sham grazed near the shore; no sign of the impetuous young vixen who'd challenged him to a gallop earlier. He clenched his jaw; it had been a mistake allowing her to journey on alone. If something had happened to her...

A slight ripple attracted his attention and when he scanned the lake, he almost fell off his horse.

Floating offshore near a gigantic boulder floated the willowy form of Keelan Grey.

And she was completely *naked*.

Now, *there* was a sight to behold.

So he did.

One hand casually rested on a boulder, the other fanned the water at her side. Her hair swirled around her like a liquid flame. A vision like this certainly called for a more leisurely perusal. Her face, pert nose, kissable lips and the smooth creamy skin of her neck made his mouth go dry.

She kicked her legs up, treating him to a pair of ivory thighs. He shook his head in both amazed disbelief and breathless admiration.

Keelan Grey was a woman who acted as if she didn't care if she conformed to polite society or not. She went her own way. He liked that about her.

He now faced a dilemma, however. It was doubtful he could alert her of his presence without causing her acute embarrassment. Perhaps he should simply wait and allow her to finish with her bath. He studied at the sky and frowned. If she dallied much longer, they'd be hard-pressed to beat the storm to Twin Pines.

Reaching behind his saddle, he retrieved her bonnet and plopped it on his head. Throwing his leg over the horn, he decided to enjoy the view for a moment more.

Apparently, Orion wasn't as easily entertained, and he stomped his hoof in boredom. The noise startled her, and she opened her eyes and turned her head toward him.

And shrieked.

Then sank.

The water bubbled. Realization hit him like a hoof to the chest.

The chit can't swim!

He jumped down and started to run, then paused to yank off a boot. He glanced up. Her head popped above the surface. He relaxed slightly. Until she gurgled in a breath and sank again.

Blast it. Why did she enter the water if she couldn't swim?

Hopping on one foot, he pulled the other boot off. He would have rather removed his shirt also, but didn't dare take any more time. Praying he got to her in time, he surged toward the bubbles and reached for Keelan's limp arm.

For the second time today, his heart stopped.

CHAPTER 21

A DEBT WELL PAID

S he was going to die.

It was impossible to resist the instinct to inhale. Water crushed her chest and the last of her air bubbled to the surface. She battled the urge until her lungs burned and she could no longer resist. As water entered her throat, a strong hand circled her wrist and tugged. She instinctively clutched it. The water moved around her as she was pulled back to the shallower depths. Another corded arm clamped around the back of her waist, and she was hauled coughing and sputtering against a hot, hard body.

It took several moments before she could draw a complete breath of air without breaking into another fit of hacking and snorting. When she opened her eyes, she found a pair of flashing sapphire ones locked with her own. Droplets of water still streamed down his thunderous face, his ebony hair glistening with an almost blue light. The muscles in his jaw rippled his shortly trimmed beard. His fingers dug into her upper arms.

Hart's voice was edged with barely contained fury. "Do you have a death wish, or does scaring the life out of me serve as your favorite form of entertainment lately?"

Shock stilled her tongue. He radiated so much heat she wasn't sure if it was because of her lake-cooled skin or the anger pulsing through his. Mortified, she tried to bring her arms up to cover her chest, but Landon Hart merely growled and jerked her firmly against his chest.

She became painfully cognizant of her legs pressed against solid muscular thighs. A familiar blush moved up her neck and all the way past her eyebrows.

After a moment, he released a long breath and gently swept her wet ringlets aside. "Are you all right?"

"Y-yes...I...th...th...think so," she stuttered. "C-Captain H-H-Hart." *Gah!*

A slow smile pulled the corners of his mouth up. The twinkle returned to his eyes. "Please, now that our relationship is more intimate, call me Landon. I *insist*."

They were in thigh deep water. Her discomfiture deepened. There was no tactful way to extract herself from his embrace without causing additional humiliation. In fact, the only way to keep him from leering further at her naked body was to stay exactly where she stood. How long had he been there ogling her?

Keelan opened and shut her mouth in flustered silence. Now, that rash decision to flee the house without an escort seemed like a horribly disastrous one, indeed. As much as she wished she could place the blame elsewhere, this dilemma was entirely her fault. She groaned inwardly.

Why, why, *why*, when in the presence of this man, did she always act boyish, impetuous, and clumsy? Not to mention ridiculously foolish. He must think her an addle-brained child.

Even more vexing was that his opinion even mattered to her.

The only thing worse than returning home with a loosely tied riding habit and mussed hair, would be returning home with a loosely tied riding habit, mussed hair *and* Landon Hart.

That's it.

Her life was over.

Unless, by some miracle, she managed to get to her room

unseen by the entire household, there'd be no avoiding a wedding now.

Hart's expression, while somewhat masked, did not completely hide the mirth still swirling around the corners of his mouth. Steeped in embarrassment, her anger blazed and she shot him an annoyed look.

"Captain Hart, what are you doing here?" She snapped, intentionally ignoring his request she call him by his given name; it was better to stay focused on the anger, rather than the current predicament. It seemed easier and less horrifying.

"When our business concluded, your uncle suggested I take a ride through the plantation, since I had earlier mentioned my curiosity." His fingers started making distracting circles on the small of her back.

"You... you, should have made your presence known much sooner." She glared daggers. At least that wasn't a *real* stutter.

"I am happy to report that the sights," he continued as if she hadn't spoken, "are impressive indeed."

"You—augh!" she sputtered, giving up the argument. "You are the most frustrating person I've ever met."

"And you are the most intriguing person I've ever met." He gave her a mock frown. "I had hoped you would change your mind and wait for me to join you."

"So, you *searched* for me?"

His broad chest rumbled. "It was not difficult, love. I merely followed the trail of departed garments." His eyes sparkled with unbridled humor. "Little was I aware how many had actually... departed."

Her mortification intensified, scorching her cheeks and ears. In fact, it radiated between their bodies in a dangerous wave. "Sir, spying on a lady is indecent." She could hardly breathe out the words.

"I did not intend to spy. It was simply my unexpected good fortune to behold such beauty that my breath nearly bid my body farewell." His eyes drifted closed and he let out a dramatic sigh.

She scowled at his mocking tone. "You truly are a rake!"

He opened one eye to peer at her, then leaned in and brushed her earlobe with his whisper. "And you, my love, are beautiful beyond words." The circles moved from her lower back to her waist.

All she could think about was the swirls his long fingers made on her bare skin. When his storm-blue eyes paused on her lips, her lungs stuttered and she couldn't draw even the smallest breath. A strange tingling sensation shot through her belly.

His touch affected her in a way she was couldn't define. He had to feel her heart ramming against his chest. She needed to put some distance between them, but she was much compromised at the moment. *Obviously.*

Pushing him away would be the appropriate thing to do, but then she'd be utterly exposed once again. Worse, her feet were strangely rooted. How could she possibly win this one?

She expelled a resigned puff of breath. She could only plead her cause and hope for the best. "Were you a gentleman, sir, you would turn away and permit me to remedy my plight."

He gave her a horrified look. "And risk having you fall victim to the raging waters of this lake? I forbid the thought!"

Keelan closed her eyes and groaned, "Must you continue to humiliate me, Captain Hart?"

"*Please*, call me Landon," he repeated in a too-cheery voice.

She groaned louder this time and dropped her head in frustration. She couldn't look into those crystalline eyes one more moment. Her forehead contacted his chest with an unenthusiastic thump.

He chuckled lightly. "Fear not, fair Keelan, for I shall lead you to safety without further injury to your person or your pride, like I did with that poorly mannered shrub a few days ago. You do recall the arrangement we agreed upon?"

Warning bells jingled in her head. "I recall our arrangement quite well." Although her knees were liquefying, she forced herself to look up. She didn't want him to notice how weak she really was, what little control she maintained. The color of his irises deepened to a sultry velvet blue.

His gaze never left her face as he took her fingers firmly in his hand and gently kissed the tips. Her breath froze in her chest, and she struggled to calm the shivers that raced up her spine. With his lips, he forged a path to the center of her palm. The best course of action would be to withdraw her hand. Use it to push against his torso and step away. Maybe even slap some manners into him. Although it was quite possible, that might re-ignite his temper, something she couldn't afford to do out here in the wilderness. Alone.

But it was so tempting that both palms itched.

If she moved now, she might catch him off guard enough with a hard shove to send him backwards into the water. It would give her a few precious seconds to dart behind the boulder near her clothes.

Her mind nudged her to do so, but the sensations Landon Hart was stirring were also commanding her attention. The kiss she owed him hung over the two of them, drawing them together like a silvery moon pulls at the tide.

If she paid her due now, she'd have no reason to cross paths with him ever again. Surely, the dangerous temptations he had awakened in her would go silent without him so near. Surely, she could focus more intently on her future if she put all this behind her. Surely...

It made sense to kiss him now and be done with it. Heaven knows she wouldn't have the strength to ward off his advances again.

She pulled her hand away, but in doing so, her fingers brushed his mouth, drawing a sharp intake of breath from him. Curious, she skimmed her thumb over it and along his jaw, marveling at the roughness of his cheek compared to the pliant warmth of his lips. A sudden desire to plunge her palms into his inky hair had her hand moving past his temple and behind his neck.

She lost the ability to think when she shifted her attention from the shiny black curls to his face. Landon's intense stare smoldered with interest, making her feel like she was melting.

Her rational mind abandoned her. It no longer mattered where she was, or what problems weighed on the day. The last kiss they shared had plagued her every day and night. Were all kisses so heated and heady? She'd been ill prepared for the first one. Now she had an idea what she should expect, and suddenly the overwhelming need to experience it again took over. She pulled his head down.

His lips moved across hers; he ignited that fire in her belly, slashed her resolve, and robbed her of thought. His hand trailed across the small of her back. Her knees grew weaker against the onslaught of the kiss. Should he decide to take even more liberties, she would be quite helpless to argue. Because... she didn't want him to stop. And she couldn't keep herself from wondering what those liberties might entail.

What was this? Was it passion or simple lust? Was there a difference?

Did it matter?

Too soon, his lips abandoned her mouth only to ignite a hot moist path to a flammable spot beneath her ear. His husky whisper slid like silk across a polished marble floor. "Consider your debt very, *very* well paid, my sweet Keelan."

CHAPTER 22

A THUNDER BOLT

L andon took a jagged breath. Keelan fought to refocus, his kiss was as potent and intoxicating as wine. Past his shoulder, Orion stood grazing next to her bonnet and Hart's discarded boots.

Wait. She'd been drowning, and he paused long enough to take off his...

Her jaw unhinged. It was a moment before she could speak. "How long did it take you to remove those boots?" She almost spoke the words evenly, but couldn't keep herself from leveling a furious stare at him.

He glanced back at the shiny, black boots lying in the grass. "I had those specially made by an Italian cobbler. I find the left one a bit snug, but it'll stretch in time." He turned his attention back to her. "Why do you ask?"

The bewildered words he used didn't fool her. He knew exactly what she'd meant. She spoke through clenched teeth, "I was under water *drowning*. Thanks to *you*, yet you took the time to pull off your boots before coming in after me?"

He tilted back a little more, in feigned shock. "Those are my favorite boots! The water would have ruined them." He gave her a

144

wry smirk. "I still saved your life, don't forget that part." He cocked his head and folded his arms around her. "In some parts of the world that would mean you now owe me a life debt and will have to accompany me everywhere as my servant until you are able to save my life in return."

She shook her head, incredulous. "What makes you think when the time came along, I would bother? I imagine it would be much more satisfying to witness your demise."

Landon froze for a second, then threw back his head and laughed. Seeing him so heartily amused made it difficult for her to stay stoic. His laugh rolled genuine and boisterous, with a weight similar to the baritone of his voice, but richer, stronger. It passed along a genial joy and reckless glee like a sudden gust of wind flings bonnets on a blustery spring day.

He tucked another wet ringlet behind her ear, before tracing a finger across her jawbone. His eyes smoldered. "Ah, but sweet Keelan, I'd take the chance anyway because, for me, just having you by my side would be bliss."

Before she could retort, he pulled her against his chest again and kissed her soundly on the mouth before turning and sloshing from the lake.

She did not trust herself to speak and instead stared in disbelief at the man who was walking toward his horse and precious boots. What was it about this infuriating scoundrel that made her stomach tingle and her heart hum in her chest? And why in the world did her body ignore her brain when he was near?

Again, he'd mocked her and used her for his own arrogant entertainment. Or was it she who had used him? She snorted in vexation and splashed toward her clothes, her eyes locked on his retreating form.

The white shirt on his back was almost invisible from the effects of the water, and it stretched tightly across his broad muscular shoulders. Landon's torso was lean and tapered. His breeches clung to his powerful legs. Keelan marveled at the way his muscles rippled with every movement. Smoldering lava still churned in her belly.

Hopefully her clothes were now dry and warm from the sun-baked rock. She scampered behind the boulder to dress. Drawing a shaky breath, she tried to cease her trembling, while her fingers fumbled with her clothes. What had she been *thinking*? She pursed her lips in irritation. How many times must she remind herself of the danger he presented to her virtue and reputation?

Apparently once more.

Even her own body betrayed her.

Again.

And now, she stood perched on a precarious edge. They were alone together, far away from a chaperone. She was dangerously close to putting her recently hatched plan in jeopardy. Here without Slaney or suitable companion, she deserved no better, she supposed.

Unless she could make it back to Twin Pines before Landon Hart and before Uncle Jared arrived home from the mill.

Keelan twisted her hair into a braid, unable to replace her locks in the manner Slaney had so skillfully arranged them earlier this morning. A new idea sparked in her mind. She could hide in the kitchen house until the maid could come and put her in more presentable shape.

She might be able to salvage her future after all.

No doubt, Hart would wed her, bed her and then sail off to other ports, other women. She'd seen this happen time and time again in Chatham, England, the small naval town where she'd grown up.

Was it so wrong to desire love?

Or a husband who desired her company beyond their marriage bed?

Reaching behind her back for the skirt stays, she huffed in exasperation. She was an idiot. What had she been thinking? She had been so very over-heated and sweaty. The cool lake had called to her and lured her in with its sparkling surface and cleansing water. She didn't regret it.

She should have enjoyed it *without* disrobing.

She should have paused long enough to deliberate the difficulty of dressing herself. Her cheeks flushed anew at the growing realization that she must ask for Landon Hart's assistance. She squared her shoulders and clenched her fist around the stays. *Reckless.*

Again.

When she emerged, Hart had already removed the hobbles from Sham's legs and tightened the saddle straps. He led the horse to her.

Sham tossed his noble head at the sight of Landon's stallion tethered nearby. Nostrils flaring, he pranced sideways; Hart spoke low and commanding until the horse quieted to a more docile walk. He secured the reins around a branch and patted Sham's neck before turning to approach her. He was no longer the smiling jester. He'd shifted to a commander.

"Keelan, this is a fine steed but not an appropriate mount for a lady." His voice was even, but she still heard the chastisement. She stiffened as he pressed on, "I understand you are an accomplished equestrian. However, this stallion requires a rider with much more strength."

She lifted her chin. "I am quite capable of keeping my seat. So far, this creature has given me no trouble."

Almost no trouble.

Approaching Sham, she caressed his velvety nose. "He has been the perfect gentleman today." She chanced a sideways look at Landon. "Unlike some males with whom I am acquainted."

He smiled down at her. "'Twill be interesting to see how well you keep your seat while also maintaining mastery of your garments." He raised an ebony eyebrow while leaning over to glance at the back of her skirt. "Or would you like some assistance to that end?"

She took a breath and prepared for more mockery. "I have done the best I can do," she stated, "but I worry my efforts at tightening these might lead to my continued embarrassment." She hesitantly turned her back to him and peered over her shoulder. "Would you mind...?"

Without hesitation, he nimbly grasped the ribbons. In a matter of seconds, they were deftly tied, neither too loose nor too tight. Slaney could do no better. It made her wonder, how many times in the past this same opportunity had presented itself to the rake.

"You seem quite good at this," she quipped.

"Aye," he said. "But I am much more skilled at removing them." He reached up and playfully tugged. "Would you care for a demonstration?"

She whirled away from his reach. "Certainly not!" Seeing his amused visage, she let slip a sheepish grin, relieved for once that he was teasing her because heaven knows how hard it would be for her to refuse one more advance from him. She attempted to regain a more composed countenance. "No doubt, you have much experience to that end."

He grinned as he untied Sham's reins. "I never kiss and tell, fair maiden."

She couldn't help but roll her eyes. She was painfully aware of her tousled appearance, certain she looked nothing like the ladies of the captain's past.

Landon's joviality faded when he shifted his steely gaze up and scanned the darkening sky. "The other reason I followed you, was because the storm that's approaching is likely to turn violent. It appears it'll soon be upon us. If we're to make it back to Twin Pines before it hits, we must make haste now."

She followed his gaze and caught her breath at the sight of the purple and green hues coating the sky above them. She hurriedly wrapped her braid into a twist at the nape of her neck, and began to place the pins by feel alone.

"Would you hand me my hat, please?"

He shook his head as he retrieved her bonnet. "My dear, the gesture is valiant. Still, I'm afraid the ride and the wind will destroy your efforts."

He obviously had no idea how precarious her situation had become. It would have been easier to take the admonition from her father and uncle for leaving without a chaperone than it would be for arriving home with Landon. Doreen might have already gleefully informed Papa that the two had ridden to the mill together. In fact, she'd bet on it.

She exhaled in irritation. "First, I am not your *dear*. Second, were I to return with a proper escort in this disheveled state, my reputation *might* remain intact." She lowered her brows at him. "Returning with you as an escort will certainly tarnish it beyond all hope for repair. My uncle and my father will undoubtedly believe you seduced me with your handsome face and irresistible charm."

She poked him in the chest. "You might take this lightly, but I assure you, I am most serious. I do not want to be shackled in marriage to a lecherous sea captain, an old codger, or a bumbling doctor." She gestured to him. "I must do what I can to preserve my integrity as well as my unsoiled state. Now if you don't mind, please give me my bonnet and my jacket."

He gave her a resigned sigh, willing to retreat. "As you wish." He held her coat as she shrugged into it, then gave her the hat. He cocked his head and studied her for a moment. "Do you truly believe I have a handsome face?"

She choked back a laugh. "I truly believe that *you* believe it."

He grinned, revealing those dimples again. It was hard not to stare at them. They gave him a more boyish appearance, more innocent, which of course, made him more dangerous.

He took a step closer and whispered, "You think I'm handsome and charming. You just said so."

She secured her bonnet on her head. "Just because someone

might say you're handsome, doesn't mean they want to marry you."

Hart stepped closer and stroked his finger across the back of her exposed neck causing her skin to zing with the contact. "You want to marry me?"

She was momentarily speechless. For one thing, it was impossible to talk because the sensation he was creating with a single finger was completely unsettling. Was this the game he played...to charm and seduce? It might amuse him, but he'd no longer find her an easy mark.

As long as he didn't kiss her.

Or come near her.

Ever again.

Or touch her.

Ever again.

Finally, her voice returned. "I didn't say I wanted to marry you. If you recall, I specifically said I *didn't*."

He clutched his heart and staggered backward. "Woman, you wound me with your sharp tongue and harsh words. But to describe our sweet bond as *shackled*, leaves me broken-hearted."

He gave her such a sorrowful look that for a moment, she nearly took pity on him. Keelan turned her face away and chewed her lip stop a smile. He would likely consider her amusement as encouragement. It was best for him not to see it.

"You are a strong, healthy man with a thick shield of arrogance, Landon Hart." She almost succeeded in keeping the laughter from her voice. "I'm sure your heart will recover at a record pace."

His head perked up. "But I'll be forever scarred," he replied, laughter lacing his words. "Besides, you called me Landon. You *do* love me."

She rolled her eyes and searched for a stump or a rock she could use as a mounting block.

"Allow me, love."

She quirked a brow. "With the exception of your aid in saving me from the depths, I am quite certain you have 'helped' me enough today." She perched her fists on her hips. "Exactly what do you plan to do? Throw me across the beast's back like a sack of rice?"

Tossing her a cagey grin, he sank to one knee and laced his fingers together. "My intentions are more chivalrous, I assure you. I mean only to give you a step up."

There appeared to be no other option, so she relented and placed her boot into his waiting palms.

He helped her into the sidesaddle, and boldly guided her foot through the stirrup, ruining her intention to evade his touch from now on. She should thank him for rescuing her. If only he wasn't such a scoundrel, and an arrogant mocker of impulsive young ladies, then the words wouldn't stick in her throat so tenaciously.

But it had to be done.

Even though it was his fault she'd lost her grip on that rock.

"Captain Hart," she said, touching his shoulder. She caught herself too late. Now her hand burned. She curled her fingers into her palm.

"Landon," he corrected, lifting his eyes to her face.

"Landon." She swallowed her pride and hoped her voice wouldn't falter. "Thank you for saving my life. It was foolish of me to go in to begin with. I would have drowned had you not pulled me out."

"It was my *greatest* pleasure, my lady." A spark flared in his eyes, and ignited her cheeks. She should have expected that response. She adjusted the reins. Sham seemed to sense her tension and pranced and fidgeted.

The low, angry rumble of thunder echoed through the pines. The gentle breeze of the afternoon had dropped in temperature and picked up speed. A fat drop of rain splattered on her hand; she'd have to hurry home to beat the storm. The ground was already spotted with large dark blotches where raindrops plopped and tumbled in the soft thick dust. They began to fall with more frequency. A rivulet of water dripped off the back of her hat and down her neck.

"Keelan." Landon's expression was serious now. Both his hand on the bridle and his tone made her pause. "It would ease my mind if you would allow me to lead your mount. I can tether him to my saddle and keep him better controlled if the weather worsens and unsettles him."

She eyed Landon warily. "I think not." She lifted her chin. "I appreciate the offer. However, I am perfectly capable of handling a horse." She reined Sham away from him and gave the stallion a smart heel. She had to make an effort to get back in time. She could act as if she didn't know Landon had been riding about the plantation.

She didn't expect him to attempt to stop her.

He lunged for the reins and succeeded in getting a couple fingers on one of them, jerking it from Keelan's hands. His quick movement startled Sham, who spun away, nearly unseating her in the process. She grabbed at the saddle, an angry admonishment on her tongue. As she tried to jerk her body upright, her heels clipped against Sham's side, which sent him leaping forward.

A scream erupted from her throat before she could stop it. The panicked shriek only spooked the horse more, and he took off at a dead run.

Without warning, a bright flash of lightning and earsplitting crack of thunder ripped through the air around her and shook the ground. There was a loud snap, then the screech of ripping wood. Sham skidded stiff-legged to a stop, squealed, and reared up in fright. Keelan clawed at the horse's mane in a frantic attempt to keep her seat. Landon's warning shout echoed behind her as a large pine to her right toppled.

A bone chilling terror banded around her chest, and she instinctively thumped Sham's flank. The horse jumped forward, dislodging her lower foot from its stirrup, and jolting her off-balance again. Only by twisting her hands tighter into the mane, did she manage to stay on his back. The powerful stallion flew down the lane at breakneck speed, and the next loud thunderclap almost drowned out the drumming of his hooves as well as the tree crashing to forest floor behind them.

CHAPTER 23

A WILD RIDE

Terrified, Keelan clutched a bigger handful of Sham's mane and held on until her knuckles whitened. Her hair again whipped free from her bonnet and slashed across her face and neck, impairing her vision. Seized by panic, a new horror gripped her when she realized she'd dropped the other rein in the fight to maintain her seat.

She now had no way to control the beast or slow him down.

"Stop!" she screamed. "Whoa, Sham!"

The stallion continued at a thundering gallop, with Keelan powerless to halt him. He sensed her fear and reacted in kind. She choked back a terrified sob and again shouted the command to stop, but the rising wind swallowed her voice. The furious storm-chased drops pelted her face in a blinding assault. Her insides churned with icy dread; she clenched Sham's mane as tightly as her trembling fingers would allow.

All she could do was pray.

"Keelan!" Landon's shout was close, and she cast a wild glance over her shoulder. His horse was only a length behind. Orion soon stretched up alongside them.

He leaned to the side, reaching toward her. His arm shot out and clamped around her waist like a steel band, plucking her off Sham's back like a rag doll. He pulled her sideways across his lap; she impulsively wrapped her quivering arms about his neck, buried her face against his shoulder and inhaled the scent of rain and leather and Landon Hart. Tears threatened, and she tried to close her mind to the image of the toppling tree or of her crashing head first to the ground. His muscle-hardened arm tightened, providing comfort and safety.

The swirling wind dipped and danced about them and the hail, like small stones, stung their flesh. He reined his horse to a soft canter, then a light trot, and finally a walk before he turned from the path. She numbly heard his voice vibrating in her ear. "You're safe, Keelan. I have you."

Thank the Lord!

The words passed her lips before she had time to think, "Landon, please don't let go of me!"

"I won't let you go, love. I promise. Not ever."

Her shoulders were quaking uncontrollably, and she fought to take a deeper breath. A crash of thunder shook the earth, and another bold streak of lightning split the heavens. Blinded by the flash, disoriented by fright, she threw her arms up to shield her face. Her entire body trembled with racking, hysterical sobs. The huge pines, which made up most of the forest on either side of them, shielded them from the rain's nearly horizontal attack.

It was as if something stole the surrounding oxygen. She couldn't keep air in her lungs. With a low curse, Landon trapped her wrists in his hand and forced her arms away from her face.

His words came from far away "Keelan! Look at me. You're safe. I have you."

He scowled, slipped his hand behind her neck and pulled her face to his. His mouth collided into hers with the same fierce intensity of the tempest raging around them. A shock coursed through her body as if lightning had struck her. Unconsciously, her fingers curled around the wrist of his hand cupped firmly at her nape. He can't. He can't touch her like this—kiss her like this, or she wouldn't have the strength to guard her heart. A few days or weeks of joy weren't worth the months and years waiting alone for a man who may never come home.

With a shocked gasp, she opened her eyes and jerked away. Before he said another word, she landed a stinging slap against his cheek. She was rewarded with a lopsided leer and a burning palm.

"There you are," he said with unmasked satisfaction.

"How dare you!" What kind of man takes advantage of a woman when she's hysterical?

Ugh.

What a ridiculous question to ask herself. Landon Hart, of course, was a man who'd be so bold. It had taken her a moment to register the kiss, but it was glorious, and the lure of this man could very well be her undoing. Why was she so *weak*?

Now they were about to arrive home on the same mount. She was *doomed*.

A warm finger touched her chin, and she glared up at the source of her own personal storm. The man stirred such a turbulent tide of emotions in her heart, that it pitched and rolled hither and yon like a small dingy in a roiling sea. She had no control over it, and that petrified her.

Landon's eyes clouded with concern and stared intently back at her. His nearness unnerved her, and her senses reeled again from the manly scent of him.

"My apologies love, but it was the only thing I think to do to shatter the state of near hysteria that took you." He grinned. "I am extremely pleased with the results, although somewhat worse for the effort," he said, touching the red outline of her hand on his cheek.

"You'll not get an apology for that," she retorted. "You most certainly deserved it."

His grin widened. "Well worth the price paid."

She pressed her lips together and glanced away. He was so...irritating. She didn't enjoy his absurd admission. Not one tiny bit.

"I blame myself." His mood sobered. "I should have never let you get on that horse. Instead, I should have bloody well thrown you over my saddle and tied you there!"

She gave him a cool smile. "It would have been interesting to see you try."

His eyebrows jumped up; his chest rumbled with a chuckle. "A fascinating physical engagement." He leaned forward. "I would have enjoyed the win immensely."

She managed a feeble smile. Hard, dense rain soaked her clothes, and the wind howled around them. She shivered. Animals had a gift for finding their way home, but she still worried about Sham. They stopped at the cluster of abandoned cabins she'd passed earlier in the day.

What was he doing? She turned her questioning gaze toward him.

He spoke into her ear over the howling wind. "The gale will be upon us before we can return. We need to find shelter *now*."

Alarm exploded in her chest. "Nay! I cannot!" She glanced wildly at the sky. "We must get back. It can't be very far, and Sham is still running loose. We must find him!"

He ignored her tirade and urged Orion forward to a shanty near the edge of the clearing. Wind gusts hissed through the pines with frightening ferocity. The torrent hammered down so hard it hurt her head.

Even as she realized the lunacy of her demands, she pushed against his chest and tried to raise her voice above the roar. "Please, Landon, please take me home!" There was still a chance they could get there before Uncle Jared if he waited out the storm at the mill. If they delayed, her absence would become obvious. They'd be watching for her. Papa would worry.

He grasped her shoulders, shouting over the wild storm. "Keelan, can you see what's happening?" He swept an arm wide. "The wind has picked up several knots, and soon it'll be strong enough to pick up debris as well." He slid his hands down her arms until he could grasp her elbows. "Your safety is more important to me now, than your precious reputation. Surely your family will agree." His voice strengthened into a commanding tone, which allowed for no further argument. "We shall seek refuge now. My decision to protect you is firm in this regard."

She hid her agitation by lashing him with her words. "A comfort, to be sure, Captain."

But who will protect me from *you*?

His eyes darkened to the blue-gray of a chaotic sea. "Your virtue will remain intact while you are under my protection. I give you my word, as a gentleman."

She couldn't hold back a snort. "Gentleman? Do you even understand the definition?" she asked, unable to break his stormy gaze. Captain Landon Hart's mere presence was dangerous. Reason and logic seemed to disappear faster than Ruth's pecan pie when he was around her.

He cut her a wry look. They'd halted beside a structure with one corner of the roof missing, giving her cause to wonder how many creatures their visit would disturb. The front door hung askew by the bottom hinge, and both windows lacked shutters for protection.

She peered through the deluge and raised her voice above the wind. "I don't understand how this feeble structure will protect us."

He dismounted, then lifted her down.

"This one has a cellar." He gestured to the entrance near the side of the cabin. He turned to remove the saddle and pack, speaking over his shoulder. "We'll be safer here." He placed the tack on the ground, then reached up for the blanket.

She opened her mouth to argue, but a wave of dizziness

crashed over her, cutting off her retort. A loud roar filled her ears and her world swirled and dip. Flashes of sensation hovered just out of reach from the fringes of her consciousness. A numbing pulse seeped into her skin, darkening her vision, followed by the jarring impact of the rain-soaked earth.

CHAPTER 24

A STORM SHELTER

Landon's scent, mingled with leather and fresh lake water, awakened her in the semi-darkness. Confused, she searched for a familiar sight before she remembered she was in a cellar below the shanty.

On the dirt floor, a cheery fire crackled merrily, the smoke escaping through a yawning hole in the ceiling above them. Only about half the main floor above remained intact; the rest was gone. Up there, the dark gaping maw of a brick hearth loomed in the shadows, standing quiet and cold at the far end of the first floor room. Farther up, cobwebs coated the rafters, obscuring the shaggy remnants of several abandoned nests tucked in the corner eaves. The musty scent of neglect, mice, and damp dirt surrounded her. Straight ahead were steps built into the side of a wall, leading up to a small hinged door, which appeared to open next to the hearth above. The cellar was oddly larger than the cabin itself.

She couldn't see into the alcove on her right. Probably another storage area.

The structure was deserted, still she had an uneasy sensation she was intruding. There were old burlap bags stuffed with straw and a basket of turnips and potatoes, along with a couple of well-used blankets, as if the occupants had tried to live in the root cellar, rather than up in the old cabin.

She had been resting on a saddle blanket; Landon's coat had been rolled into a makeshift pillow and placed beneath her head. She lifted it to her nose and inhaled. Glancing about, she spied his saddle leaning against the far wall.

Keelan's skin crawled at the sound of the angry wind lunging and clawing at the tiny cabin, causing the frail structure to shudder and groan. A loud thunderclap made her jump, and she glanced up through the hole in the ceiling toward the open windows. The rain fell harder and blew through to the floor. She was immediately grateful for the fire's comforting glow.

The furious slapping of the crippled front door, with its single hinge, couldn't drown out the hailstones clattering on the porch and against the clapboards. She barely heard the clip of boots over the whistling gusts of wind and pelting barrage. The hinged door in the ceiling opened and Landon ducked, stepping down the cellar ladder, then closed the hatch behind him, his pack slung over his shoulder. He deposited everything near the saddle and glanced about, as she had done a few moments earlier.

With every movement of his shoulders, muscles rippled beneath the dripping shirt. The confident set of his jaw and the sinuous fluidity of his stride added to that now familiar air of authority which seemed to surge toward him, envelop him, radiate from him. He was used to leading men, and obviously comfortable with the responsibilities that went hand in hand with such a position.

He began to step closer, but stopped when he saw she'd awakened. "How are you?" He seemed oblivious to the fact he was soaked and water still streamed down his face and neck.

Caught staring, she could only give him a blink and shrug. She brushed her hand across her brow in a vain effort to wipe away the cobwebs from her mind before she mumbled thickly, "A bit muddled."

Landon picked up his pack, and moved to kneel beside her. He loosened the straps and withdrew a cloth-wrapped bundle and a flask.

He unwrapped it, revealing a loaf of crusty bread. Using the cloth, he wiped the water from his face and hands. "When did you last eat?"

Keelan couldn't quite remember. She'd meant to grab one of Ruth's muffins at dawn, prior to training with Daniel, but in her haste, forgot. She missed breakfast. Of course, after Everett's proposal, she'd lost her appetite for lunch and soon after went for a ride.

"Last eve," she said.

"Keelan." He eyed her sternly. "Going without water or food in this climate can be taxing. Add to it the shock you've had, it's no wonder you're faint."

She bristled at his chastisement. She was not some weak maid who swooned at every turn of events. Even if it had become obvious she had less control of her actions and decisions when this striking captain was near, with his cobalt eyes and broad shoulders. It all added to her frustrations. "Not as taxing as fighting off your roguish advances."

Landon's storm blue eyes smoldered with a silent challenge. "That remains to be seen, my sweet Keelan."

He gestured to the flask and bread he had removed from his saddlebags. "There is more than enough here for two." He had a mischievous gleam in his eyes. "However, the rules of the high seas demand you earn your share."

She pushed herself upright and tossed her storm-combed hair behind her. If this arrogant man expected she would "earn" her share, as would a doxy from the docks, then he had a lot to learn about the daughter of Commodore George Grey.

"I will not be manipulated." She narrowed her eyes. "If you

think I might serve you favors in exchange for a crust of bread then your senses have taken flight. I would choose to starve than bend to any more of your prurient whims."

He cocked a quizzical brow. "Aye." He nodded. "I believe you would." With a dramatic flourish, gave her an exaggerated, albeit seated, bow. "I humbly beg your forgiveness, my lady. I only seek to barter for pleasantries. I resolve to halve my share with you in exchange only for warm conversation and your beauteous presence." He placed his hand over his heart. "Put away your barbed tongue for the rest of the day, and I'll gleefully starve myself instead."

She couldn't keep from smiling; still, she gave him a wary look before responding in kind, "Dear sir, your price is too steep, for I can think of no other way a lady can fend off your rakish tendencies, unless you pledge your protection in addition to the treasures you would provide." She pretended to examine her nails. "I shall demand protection from all rogues, including and most especially...you."

He dipped his head and gave her a crooked grin, making the dimple in his cheek deepen. The firelight gleamed off his dark hair, still wet from the rain. "The bargain you demand is a rigid one, my lady, but I pledge to you my fealty. I shall fight for your love and honor until death removes me from your sublime presence."

Gah! He should have taken to the stage.

Keelan feigned a tight-lipped smile, while patting the space beside her makeshift pallet. "Come then, sir, and sit, for my throat is parched and my stomach rumbles louder than the storm outside." She'd never conversed in private so casually with a man before, other than Daniel, but he didn't count. She found it oddly pleasant and relaxing. Had her parents shared a similar relationship, did they talk and tease each other when they were alone?

Somehow, she didn't think so.

Landon moved near her and reached for the flask. He broke

the seal and handed it to her, "Sip this slowly," he warned. "It's water heavily laced with rum."

Heeding his advice, she sipped cautiously. She guessed the water was from his ship's supply, where they mixed rum with it to keep it drinkable while at sea.

He pulled out a round of wax-coated cheese and several odd crispy rolls. He handed one of them to her and smiled at her curiosity. "Marcel, the ship's cook, learned to make these while we were trading in the Orient."

She took a bite. "Delicious," she said gratefully. "Ruth makes something similar, but not as delicate. She calls it a fried pie."

Landon broke off two chunks of bread, and used his knife to cut into the cheese. The fire cast quick, sprite-like shadows, which flickered and danced on the walls. Late afternoon had fallen, but the day had darkened to an eerie blue-green hue of dusk. They shared the small corner of the cellar, seeking comfort in whatever small amount of protection it provided. As they sated their hunger, the gale continued to rage.

He cocked his head and listened. "It's gaining strength. 'Tis good we found shelter when we did."

She eyed him, curious. "How is it you know so much of storms?"

"Over the years, I have sailed around many and through even more. Although we map our routes and time our trips to avoid the worst tempests when we can, one cannot often second-guess the elements."

Keelan picked up the flask and reclined against the rough cellar wall before taking a sip. "You must enjoy the sea very much to spend so many years upon the water."

Landon shrugged. "Everything good that's ever happened to me took place on the water. I've made my fortune crossing oceans and have seen many strange and amazing sights." His eyes turned a molten blue. "However, none can compare to the vision of exquisite beauty I witnessed today."

A flush crept up her neck. *The blackguard.* He enjoyed making her blush. "Should I one day hear tales of you becoming a pirate, or a privateer, scouring the high seas for weak merchant ships to plunder, I would have no trouble believing them." She took another careful sip and studied him warily. Captain Landon Hart certainly was *not* a gentleman and that particular character defect was sure to cause trouble for her.

It already had.

"Slaney says men of the sea have women in every port and isle. How many maidens have you tarnished in your conquests?"

Landon paused, his fried roll partway to his mouth, then threw back his head and laughed. The genuine sound was contagious. Amusement lingered in the corners of his eyes for a moment, then he sobered and leaned toward her.

Her smile faded as she pressed her back against the wall in a vain attempt to keep a fair distance between them. Landon's eyes glittered dangerously and she squirmed, now slightly unsure of her choice of topics.

When he spoke, his voice was low and smoky, making the air in the room thin, and she caught her breath. "If I became a pirate, my love, you would be in dire need of a champion. I'd deem you a most valuable conquest indeed, and wouldn't wait long before claiming you as my own."

Keelan swallowed. This maddening talent he had, turning her words to his advantage, both vexed and heated her, spurring the urge to deflate his ego to a more manageable level, and her trepidation at the possible consequences of doing so.

She plunged stubbornly on. "You must have no desire to take a wife or start a family, or surely you would have done so. How long do you stay in a harbor? A few weeks? That's not nearly enough time to court a prospective bride. I can only conclude, you have no wish for a family of your own. Do you enjoy the freedom? I know I would."

Landon reclined against the adjacent wall, rested a hand over his bent knee, and finished chewing his fried roll before answering. "Aye. 'Tis true in part. I don't normally stay for long when I run the trade routes." His gaze locked with hers. "While I would treasure having a family, marriage does not seem to suit me." His gravelly voice dropped.

How would he know unless he tried it? It dawned on her. "You've been married before," she observed. Curiously, he must have tried to keep a life on land while also maintaining one on the water. But like any sailor the temptations are too many. The ability to stray with no repercussions had to be hard to resist. No union can weather the battering of that kind of storm unless neither spouse cared.

"Aye," he whispered to the flames. "I was married, once."

"And?" she prompted. For some twisted reason, she wanted him to prove her right and say it was impossible to remain faithful, that the sea would be his only love.

"She died in childbirth," he stated numbly. "While I was away."

His words jarred her as if she'd been struck. This wasn't what she expected to hear. A dark cloud of guilt settled on her shoulders for her faulty assumptions. "I'm sorry for your loss, and for my insensitive questions."

He shrugged then reached over and tossed a broken clapboard on the fire. "But, you are correct," he mused. "Courting a worthy bride cannot be accomplished in the span of time I'm in port." Leaning forward again, he traced a finger along her jaw, tilting her face toward his before lowering his voice to a husky whisper. "I must admit, my lovely Keelan, your beauty, spirit, wit, and courage have all given me pause to consider *making* the time."

Her breath froze her lungs. Keelan tore her eyes from his and busied herself, cutting another small slice of cheese, annoyed she was once again flustered by his frankness, so much so, her hands were shaking. She wished she could attribute it to the lack of food and the recent terror she experienced. She must look as wobbly as a new foal. Even the dagger became an awkward tool, and she fumbled with it.

Landon's warm fingers closed around hers and gently removed the rebellious utensil. He cut a chunk of the cheese and impaled it upon the tip of his blade. He passed it to her, and she plucked it from the knife and sent him a small, embarrassed nod of thanks.

His damp, black curls fell forward around his face, giving him a roguish countenance, and she wanted to reach over and brush them away. She occupied her fingers by wrapping them in her skirt. What was it about this man that drew her to him? Her body foolishly defied her common sense at every turn.

It was so frustrating.

He'd been wed before; he should know that it requires more than spirit and wit. "Beauty doesn't make a marriage. Nor do riches or passion. I will marry only for love or not marry at all." *Not at all* was preferable given her current options. She'd not live in another house made lonely by a husband's gaping absence. And she wouldn't marry a man she didn't love. As soon as she safely could, she'd break her engagement with Dr. Garrison, and pray he'd forgive her.

She passed the watered-down rum back to Landon. "I witnessed what my father's leaving did to my mother. " She rested her head back against the wall and stared at the web-thatched ceiling far above them. "I'd prefer to stay unmarried and open a shop in Charleston where I could sell all kinds of exotic fabrics, spices, and goods from across the ocean. I could never be lonely doing that."

She flicked the back of her hand at him, as if swatting a swarm of gnats. "And no matter how handsome or silk-tongued he is, I would never wed a man who comes home for a few weeks time, only to get me fat-bellied with child, then leave for months. And months."

He remained silent.

Oh, dear. She was an idiot.

That was a heartless thing to say after he just admitted that his wife died in childbirth. She should have bit her tongue. Now, she felt like a cruel harpy. "I'm sorry, I didn't mean... It wasn't my intention to—"

A gentle finger on her chin cut her off and guided her gaze back up to his. A liquid flame sparked in his eyes. The humor had left, and in its place was a smoldering blue fire glittering with a mesmerizing luminosity. The intensity of his stare made her ears ring. He leaned forward until his face was inches from hers.

"Any man who would leave you alone for even an hour would be a fool," he said softly.

Landon lowered his lips and her heart slammed violently against the sides of her ribs, sending tremors straight through her chest. They stopped below her belly and exploded, creating a dense heat. Her mind screamed for her to retreat, but she wanted the touch of his lips against hers again, and the power of his strong arms pressing her against his body.

She no longer cared what she should or shouldn't do.

CHAPTER 25

A RARE JEWEL

L andon inhaled the woman who had stirred his interest so strongly and his passions so wildly and pulled her closer still. She was like a sprite flitting and dancing beneath the wide, waxy leaves of a magnolia tree; sometimes still and pensive, others quick and carefree. He thought he'd discovered the real Keelan earlier at the lake, but now he wasn't as sure. Was she the boyish imp dueling so bravely? Was she the stunning, yet haughty maiden preparing to dash his heart into the flames? Or the beautiful fire-haired water nymph who drew him to her like a fish on a string? The mystery only stoked his curiosity, making him even more determined to solve it. For reasons he couldn't fathom, he was drawn to her. It went beyond human desire, too. He wanted to make her laugh, shield her, and keep her safe, fulfill her dreams.

In the twilight of the storm-darkened afternoon, her eyes glowed a jeweled green. It was like looking into the untamed gaze of a dragon, shimmering with fire and energy, ready to erupt into heat and flame. His need to kiss her was fueled on by an unexplained urgency to capture without conquering, to yield without surrendering, and to protect without imprisoning.

She hadn't hidden her distrust of him. The barrier she fought so hard to build slipped only in the height of an impassioned kiss or during a sparring match of words and wit.

Yet it slipped.

For a few brief moments, she allowed him to view something more than aloofness in the depths of those emerald eyes. A competitive spirit. Humor. Longing. A thirst for motion. Ambition. She was not afraid to take risks. He liked that.

But her assessment of him was accurate.

He would never abandon his business or his crew and leave the sea for a married life. Adventure and the thrill of experiencing new things was like air. He needed it. It was as much a part of him as his skin.

Could a young lady like her possibly care for a man who offered love, but not marriage; loyalty, but not lands; riches, but not lineage? She'd admitted she cared nothing about titles and wealth, but could love alone truly satisfy her?

Could love alone, really win her heart?

Could a lifetime of devotion, loyalty, and protection be enough to claim her? His heart jumped at a new thought. If he asked, would she *join* him, share a life with him on the water? Her eyes flared with a passionate light when she spoke about her shop. Would she give up her dream for him? It was selfish to even consider asking such a sacrifice from her. He couldn't bare to be the brunt of her resentment later.

He'd known her a few days, yet it seemed they'd known each other for years. She wanted him even as she tried to refuse him. Her drive for independence was as strong as her spirit. He could never tame that part of her, nor would he ever want to.

She pulled away to stare at him. He stroked the soft skin of her cheek and neck. The little noise she made deep in her throat vibrated lightly against his fingers, and he sucked in his breath. Self-control was almost impossible with her so close that he could see the burning flecks of gold in her irises. She was a siren, and he was helpless.

He stared at the beauty who gazed at him with raw, wild passion. She did not know the affect she had on him, the power she wielded. Was he strong enough to keep himself in check? Common sense urged restraint. Here was a rare jewel, one he must earn. To take her this moment would only provide fuel for her hatred later.

Normally, there wouldn't be a later, and now he surprised himself by looking forward to it. Hungered for it like a starving man hungers for bread.

Keelan's lips parted, and she took a ragged breath. His need for her intensified, and with a low curse, he pulled her against his chest and eased her back down onto the saddle blanket. The mere thought of kissing her tore at his control. He lowered his head and pressed his lips against the sweet skin of her neck.

He was weak.

KEELAN HUNGERED in a way she couldn't describe. The taste of his lips on her mouth, the hard, warm press of his body, the air she could barely draw into her lungs left her *intoxicated*. She craved the sensations his kisses created, like she'd craved air below the surface of the lake.

He moved to that impossibly tender place behind her ear, and she lost all sense of time and space. She wasn't sure of anything except that she didn't want this to end. A strange thrill fluttered just beneath her skin, tingling and vibrating. She put her hand under his jaw, brought his lips to hers, and kissed his lower lip. He drew in a harsh breath and slid his palm around the back of her neck, cradled her head and crushed her to him.

His mouth ravaged her, stealing her breath, leaving her swirling somewhere high above the storm. How could anyone tire of kisses like *this*? Kissing him was like breathing; it was a requirement.

She should want to move away. But she didn't.

She wanted more. Needed more, but she could not allow herself to take it.

KEELAN'S HAND closed around Landon's forearm, stilling him. He would not push her beyond her desire. For a reason eluding his logical mind at the moment, he needed her to crave his touch, even demand it. It baffled him. He raised his head and searched her face for the command he needed. Her breath came in light pants.

"You have branded me heart, Keelan, lass," he whispered hoarsely. He kissed the place that pulsed wildly on her neck and she whimpered.

"Touching your skin is like touching the sun-warmed marble."

Because she had intrigued him, he'd wanted to lure her to his bed and seduce her. Fool that he was, he'd thought he could enjoy a tussle or two and be on his way. Just the thought now sickened him and writhed sour and twisting in his gut.

She opened her eyes, and he lost himself in the darkened pools of green. They were filled with wonder and bewilderment. The pull was impossible to resist. He could barely find his voice. "What is it that makes me want to breathe you in as if you are the last breath of air on earth?"

"Sometimes," she breathed, her eyes still locked with his, "the same thought flows through my mind."

His heart jolted and his mouth went dry. For once, he had no words. She reached up and pulled his head down and kissed him, and he fell into a pool of fire and emeralds.

"You were made to be worshipped, Keelan," he rasped. "I want to show you how a man should pay homage to a goddess."

CHAPTER 26

A WEAK MOMENT

S anity had abandoned Keelan's mind. Even as warning bells began to bang harshly in her head, her body continued to fight them. She wanted to experience more of this; she wanted Landon to be the one to teach her how to make love. And she was only a caress away from begging him to do so.

What next, then? Her mind asked sluggishly. *A wedding? Followed by a farewell? Would he still make you happy, then? Or perhaps, no wedding for you and no commitment from him. Remember his game; you may be nothing more than a pawn, insignificant and expendable.*

Did she care?

Where was her *head*?

Her weakness around this man was appalling

She finally caught her breath enough to speak. "Landon, please stop. We can't…"

He brought his lips to hers and kissed her. She should've moved away before she lost herself again, but this kiss was different. Gentle, lightly probing…tender. It was *tender*. It mesmerized her like a cobra to a lute. It took a long moment, but she managed to brace her palms on Landon's chest and shove. A little. It wasn't particularly hard, but it worked and he released her.

"I can't let this happen," she gasped. "No matter—"

"No matter how you feel about me?" His words were soft and quiet, but they hit her like a stinging slap.

"I...I don't know how I feel about you." She lied as she scooted away from him. Her chest heaved as if she had run for miles. Heat still smoldered in the center of her body. His touch had done things to her that she never imagined were possible. She couldn't even slow her breathing and compose herself.

She had acted like an addle-brained fool. Was a moment of bliss, the rapture of a caress worth the cost of her future happiness? Who was she to him, anyway? All he wanted was to seduce her. He had accomplished his goal, then.

Shame and anger seeped through her.

She choked, still barely able to form the words. "You lied."

He quirked a brow. "I promised your virtue would remain intact. It did."

"You promised to protect me from—" Embarrassed by what she had permitted him to do to her pulled hot tears from her eyes. "You took advantage."

He peered at her closely. "Are you saying I am solely responsible for what happened between us?"

"Yes. No." Keelan sat up and inched further toward the wall behind her. Thinking back to the way he gave her such intense pleasure made her heart limpid and vivacious at the same time. "No, not entirely. But,I let you manipulate me, and that was a mistake. I know to never trust your kind. I knew that, and I still —" Anger at her own stupidity had her hissing through her teeth.

"My kind?" Landon's eyes narrowed. "What is my *kind*, exactly?"

Her embarrassment had reached its peak. A harsh laugh clawed from her throat; she whispered hoarsely, "You know what type of man you are, one who seduces women for sport. It's a *game* for you. I'm well-aware I'm nothing more than your current fancy, a way to bide the time while you're in Charleston." She dropped her chin and flattened her lips. "And I'm embarrassed to admit that I'm soft-headed. And gullible and apparently easy to seduce."

Somewhere in the back of her mind, she wanted him to deny it, convince her how wrong she was, tell her that she meant more to him than anyone he'd ever met. That he loved her as much as she—

But instead, his stormy eyes turned flinty and his expression chilled.

Hope twisted into a black shard and sliced her heart open; the sharp searing pain stole her breath.

She didn't want to be right. But apparently she was.

She willed the tears burning the corners of her eyes away, then tucked a loose strand of hair behind her ear. "That's not a role I want to play." She turned her head and spoke before he could cast his spell on her again.

He heaved a sigh. "You're not a part of a game of seduction, Keelan. I care about you—"

"I wish I believed you." She gave a dry laugh that burned the back of her throat. "But I don't. Your sweet charm and easy smile is very seductive, but it's not real, it's an act. A lie. Find another to warm your bed. I'll not sacrifice my virtue for your simple, primal pleasures. I want you to stay away from me." She choked out a whisper. "Please, Landon, I beg you."

Yet, she was aware that even as she said the words, the image of him kissing another woman twisted her stomach. As hard as she had tried to avoid it, she allowed her heart to slip and tilt her center of logic.

Soon, he would sail away from the port of Charleston, and she would be left bearing a yoke of misery because she wasn't strong enough.

He'd already created a raw bleeding wound.

Blast that man.

His voice dropped. "I see."

The chill in his tone made her wince. She lifted her nose and ignored the bite of his words. She combed through her storm-blown hair with trembling fingers, doing her best to banish the thoughts and images of the exuberant sensations he stirred.

"Boy, girl, temptress, lady, now shrew, the many faces of Keelan Grey." The quiet words he spoke affected her more than if he had shouted them. "Which will you show next, I wonder?"

He did not know how each word sliced off another chunk of her heart.

"Our lives follow different paths," she whispered. "You're a man of the sea. I could never love you," she lied. "I'm a woman who enjoys the busy atmosphere of the city. I want to run a shop and have a family someday." She wanted more than that, now, thanks to him, something she'd never attain.

His voice was low and hoarse, "Then 'tis a dangerous course you tread now, my sweet." He leaned back against the wall and closed his eyes, dismissing her from his sight.

She turned her back to him and wiped away the hot tears before they traveled too far down her cheeks. Disappointment, hurt, and humiliation smothered her like thick smoke.

They sat in silence as the wind wailed forlornly; branches and debris hit the outer walls. Gusts clawed and slashed at the shingles around the damaged corner of the roof. The pelting rain found its way further into the small structure, causing the fire to sputter and hiss angrily at the intrusion. Landon jumped up and quickly doused the flames, which extinguished much of the light.

"Why did you put it out?" she cried, thinking there would be no way to dry their rain-soaked clothes.

Landon answered from a few feet away. "The hole in the floorboards above served as our chimney, but if it becomes covered with debris, the cellar will fill with smoke," She could almost make out his silhouette in the diminishing light.

Seeking something solid for support, she groped for the wall behind her and scampered backward until her spine pressed against it. The storm was a giant, angry beast and when it ripped away another portion of the cabin, she screamed. The force yanked away a large section above them and tossed it straight up into the sky. She let out a strangled cry and ducked her head as splintering wood shrieked into the howling wind.

Landon's hard arms gathered her close, his deep voice firm in her ear, "I have you, Keelan. Don't be afraid." He murmured something else, but a loud screech drowned out his words. He pushed her back to the ground against the wall and covered her body with his, as shards of planking and rubble rained down on them. She squeezed her eyes closed, wrapped her arms around him, and clung with every ounce of strength she had. She shouldn't be so relieved to be this close, but it would be useless to pretend otherwise. Truth was, she'd rather be the recipient of his anger instead of that cold indifference she felt moments ago.

More of the shanty collapsed above them, plunging them into complete darkness, and muffling the sound of the storm outside. He held her tightly, and she prayed the structure wouldn't completely fall into the cellar. They stayed that way for a long time, while the wind and rain lashed the land. His hard chest, hips and thighs blanketed her, creating searing warmth where they touched. She nuzzled her face into the pulse on the side of his neck and when she opened her eyes, her lashes flickered against his skin. He started and then chuckled.

"I remember my mother doing that to me when I was a young lad," he said, a smile in his voice.

"Doing what?" she asked, confused. It was too hard to ignore the lovely pressure of his body long enough to figure out what he meant.

"This." Landon blinked against her cheek, drawing a surprised giggle from her. "She called them 'fairy kisses.'" He dipped his head and did it again.

"I like fairy kisses." She was unable to contain her laughter at the ticklish sensation his lashes created. "Have you told her how you cherish that memory?"

"My parents died of a fever during the voyage from Ireland to Boston when I was young."

"Oh," she said, saddened. "How awful for you. What did you do? Where did you live?"

He shifted his weight to the side. "Conal's uncle took me in and taught me about sailing ships and bartering for goods. Eventually, Uncle Fynn rented a small space in his hold to me, and I would purchase cargo and sell it at a profit. When I saved enough money, I bought my own brigantine, the *Desire*. Conal took over the *Seeker*. After a few years, Fynn turned his trading company over to four of us: his sons, Ronan and Brendan, his nephew Conal, and me. Brendan was Fynn's first mate on the *Reward*."

"What's the name of Ronan's ship?"

"Ronan is only fourteen. The fleet was running a new trade route together a few weeks ago when we were attacked. We came here to try to complete Fynn's original plan while our ships were repaired. Brendan Ahern and the *Reward* are awaiting us in Harbour Town"

Keelan already suspected Fynn's reasons. She took a resigned breath, wishing she didn't have to admit to him something that might have horribly affected his adopted family.

"I might be able to clarify why Uncle Fynn wanted to speak with my father." She was now grateful for the darkened cellar; he wouldn't be able to see the embarrassment in her eyes, although it was uncertain if she could keep it from her voice.

"My father inadvertently gave orders to sink a vessel off the coast of Ireland about two years ago. He assumed is was a French privateer being duplicitous by flying American colors. Unfortunately, it *was* an American passenger ship. Almost everyone drowned or was killed. There was a large public outcry. He was court-martialed, and if it hadn't been for the influence of one of his old war comrades, he would have even been hanged."

Her mother had to close and board up the shop after stones

had been thrown through the front windows on two different occasions. Less than a week later, she was dead.

"We suspect it's the reason our family was targeted by an assassin. Someone seeks revenge against my father. My mother was murdered, then my aunt and cousin. Papa's friend managed to help us escape to Charleston, where we hoped we'd be safe."

"So you're wondering if Fynn Ahern had a family member aboard," Landon stated.

"Yes."

"No," he mused. "I don't think that was the reason. Fynn was like a father to me, so I know Conal's entire family. They had no such a tragedy. I doubt Fynn journeyed here for retribution," he added, as if reading her mind.

She made a mental note to speak with her father about it at the first opportunity.

The wailing wind eased, and the fierce din of angry hail changed to the gentler slap of a spring rain. How long had they been talking?

"It seems the worst has passed," he said, echoing her thoughts. "Let's see if I can push the hatch open."

As soon as he lifted his weight from her, the cool air blew away his warmth, leaving her chilled and exposed. A moment later, she heard the sound of his shoulder pushing against the door, then a grunt. No creaking hinges followed. He tried again and was delivered the same result.

"It won't move even a little. If I had to wager on the cause, I'd say the chimney wall above has collapsed on it," he said.

They were trapped in an abandoned, now demolished, shanty miles from the mill and the main house. The chances of anyone finding them soon were tiny. And there was nothing they could do about it.

"Maybe if I help you, we can open the door together." She did a horrible job of hiding the tremor in her voice, as she scrambled to her feet. Keelan reached out and when her hand found the wall, she began to grope her way along the rough, damp surface toward Landon's voice.

"There's not enough room for both of us to stand on the step," he answered. "But, I fear our efforts would be in vain. I noticed no give at all."

The thick air invaded Keelan's chest, and her breaths shortened in response. The walls loomed around them in the murky blackness. Something brushed against her hand and she jumped, unable to restrain a surprised squeak.

Landon's long, firm fingers twined with hers and he gave a squeeze. "That was just me, trying to find you."

She allowed him to pull her into the comforting circle of his arms. "What now?"

"An opening exists above the remnants of our fire, but the floor here drops sharply and I can't reach high enough to move the debris enough to fit through." Landon's words were carefully even.

"Then we're trapped here," her voice quavered and she swallowed. She really should have just stayed in the house this morning rather than take her problems on a ride through the countryside.

"There is one thing we could try," he mused. "But it won't be easy for either of us." Was that a smile she heard in the dark? Was he *smiling*? She could think of nothing that was even the tiniest bit humorous.

"What is it?"

"If I lift you, and whatever covering the opening is moveable, you might be able to shift it enough to squeeze out."

He waited patiently while she mulled over his plan. Surely, she could think of something that would work better. But nothing came to mind.

Think of something. Anything.

She let out a beleaguered breath. There was no alternative to even consider.

"Tell me what to do," she said resignedly. She had a feeling the captain would be more comfortable with the situation than she. The only satisfaction for her was that she would be spared seeing his rakish leer.

Suddenly, the darkness seemed less intimidating.

CHAPTER 27

A FREEDOM RUNNER

"**R**eady?"
No.

"I'm ready." She tried to sound nonchalant, but her voice came out lumpy with trepidation.

Landon had explained how he would wrap his arms around her legs and lift her up. He was strong enough to do so effortlessly, but she still wasn't comfortable with being hoisted off the ground in total darkness.

Holding her hand, he picked his way through the stifling darkness, stopping when his boot crunched on the charred wood remnants of their fire. She heard him move behind her, the heat from his large body pulsed against her back, and the tiny hairs on her arms and the back of her neck twitched.

Perhaps this wasn't the best idea after all.

She trembled slightly, but still managed to stay mute as his hands moved down her ribs, over her hips. Keelan wasn't about to give him the satisfaction of knowing how his touch affected her, or a reason to mock her for chastising him for it. She'd had enough for one day.

His hands continued down the outside of her upper legs with

agonizing slowness. She tensed in response, about to lose the fight to remain silent. Before she could open her mouth to snap at him, he hugged her knees and lifted her off the ground.

"Oh!" She gasped and flung her arms wide. There was nothing to cling to. Good Lord, she now sat on his shoulder. He had one arm over her thighs and the other on the small of her back, dangerously close to her bottom. She reached down and grabbed the fabric of his shirt.

"Stay still," he grunted.

"Get your hand away from my backside!" she hissed. He was intentionally trying to irritate her.

"Keelan—"

"Now!"

He released a frustrated sound. "As you wish." He slid his hand up her back and around her ribcage to rest right beneath her right breast, nearly covering her entire side.

"Landon Hart!"

"If I don't hold you, love, you'll fall," he said with a hint of exasperation in his tone.

Keelan rolled her eyes. He could find a way to keep her secure without all this groping. "This is your way of protecting my well-being? Surely it can be done with your hand somewhere less improper."

He glided his hand around her ribs so slowly it felt like a caress, heating her skin and making her want to close her eyes and savor it. Not that she enjoyed it. Well, she shouldn't have enjoyed it, considering the predicament they were in at the moment.

He stopped between her shoulder blades. She wobbled without the protective band of his arm, a startled yip escaped her throat. His hand jumped back to the front of her ribcage, and it was a moment before she realized she was gripping his forearm with both hands. It would be better if he slid his giant hand an inch lower, but she didn't dare ask. Who knows where it would end up?

"Don't do that again!" Her breath came out in short pants. "Stay this way, it's safer."

He chuckled. "Yes, my love."

"Stop that." Irritating man.

"Stop what?"

"Calling me your 'love.'" It was entirely too unsettling, too intimate, and too wonderful.

And too false.

"But sweet Keelan, you—"

An unintelligible murmur of voices filtered through the rubble above. Keelan's heart leapt. Someone was out there! They would soon be discovered and rescued. Thank goodness!

Landon gently lowered her to the ground and slipped his hand over her mouth before whispering, "Let's listen before we alert them to our presence, in case they are not well-intentioned."

Of course, how naïve of her. She did her best to swallow her fear, but it was impossible with a dry mouth. They might be vagabonds or worse. She'd been ready to shout out, which could have put them in danger.

She nodded and he removed his hand. Footsteps sounded on the planks above, but the voices remained muted and she couldn't make out any words.

"What should we do?" She wanted to yell for help, but what if the strangers were indeed highwaymen taking advantage of the chaos following the storm?

He slid his hand down her arm in the darkness and before she could question his motives, the handle of his dagger pressed into her palm.

"Keep the knife handy in case things go awry."

Before he could proceed with his plan, a dim glow appeared from within the small alcove. It took only a second for her to conclude that it was an entrance to a small tunnel, rather than a storage area, and the people who were outside a moment ago were now on their way *in*.

They were trapped.

Landon moved swiftly, dragging her with him. He pressed her against the wall adjacent to the tunnel's mouth and touched his finger to her lips to remind her to be silent. In the slow dawning of light, he withdrew a pistol from one of the saddlebags. She barely breathed.

The glow grew brighter and a brown arm holding a lantern appeared. A young man, perhaps in his early teens crawled from the opening. As he straightened, he locked gazes with her, and his eyes widened. Landon crept up behind him, put a hand over his mouth and pressed the pistol into his side. He pulled the young slave away from the lantern and into the shadows.

A woman emerged next. She stood and brushed her skirts, then turned to help a man crawling behind her. As he straightened, she could see he was cradling his arm, and blood had seeped through the sleeve of his shirt. The man froze in place, but he seemed to coil like a viper, every muscle active, eyes fixed on Landon and the boy. The woman reacted to the tension of the man next to her. She whirled and stifled a scream with her hands, as her gaze fell upon Landon's pistol and the young man he held.

The last person to emerge made Keelan gasp.

It was little Joseph's father.

"Simon!" she said with surprise and relief.

He jolted as if struck. His head whipped up, and he spun to face her. A multitude of emotions fluttered across his face. Shock, relief, fear.

"Miss Keelan! Praise the Lord you all right! Ruth an' yo family has worried themselves sick."

The enlarged root cellar made more sense, now. The baskets of vegetables, the small sacks of rice, the tattered blankets and straw pallets, were enough provisions for a few people who might need a place to rest without drawing any attention.

"What are you doing here, Simon?" she asked quietly, already knowing the answer. She had heard of a secret society who helped slaves escape to the north. What were they called? Freedom Runners?

The house slave shifted his weight from foot to foot for a moment. Landon had released the boy, but still had his weapon pointed at the group. He changed position to stand next to her.

With trembling fingers, the woman reached over, grasped the boy's arm, and hugged it to her stomach. Finally, with watery eyes, Simon appealed to her. "Miss Keelan, these folks here...they jus' need a short stopover on their way...along." He gestured to the other man's bleeding arm.

"Along where?" She really didn't need the answer.

She already knew.

CHAPTER 28

A RIDE HOME

Runaways.

Simon stared at his toes. The woman began to weep softly; the boy stood stiff as a statue. The wounded man put his uninjured arm around the woman's waist. "Hush, now, Nettie," he murmured.

Landon whispered in her ear, "I think it's best for us if we don't know their destination." He holstered the gun. "'Tis obvious they're runaways. Unless you wish to force them back with us, the less we know, the better."

She wondered what Simon's part was in all this. Unlike her father and uncle, she hadn't been able to adjust comfortably into the Lowcountry society of plantation owners and their families. If she were a slave, she'd run away too. She might still, depending on what transpired when she returned home.

She jerked her chin toward the other man's wound. "Let me see your arm."

He straightened, and gave a sideways glance to Simon, who nodded. He peeled back his bloodied sleeve to show a deep, jagged slash. She glanced at Landon. "I'll need your rum-laced water, unless you have straight whiskey?"

"I do have a small flask of whiskey," he replied. He rummaged around in his saddlebags and pulled it out.

She addressed Simon. "Please see if you can find some garlic in those bags in the corner."

While he searched for garlic, she took the dagger and slit strips from her shift. Remembering Slaney's words in the kitchen house, she doused the wound with Landon's whiskey. The man had a stronger countenance than she, and showed no sign of pain, except a slight hissing intake of breath. Simon handed her a needle and thread, and she glanced at him in surprise.

"Found it near the garlic," he said not meeting her gaze.

Stopover, indeed. She wondered what other supplies were hidden in the cellar.

Keelan stitched the wound. When she finished, she perused it smugly. Her needlepoint might be horrendous, but she could stitch a wound quite effectively. She poured a bit more whiskey over it, then crushed the garlic, using the blade's handle. She pressed it over the cut then wrapped everything securely. She gave the left over strips to his wife, along with the rest of the clove.

"Use these later to change the dressing."

"Yes'm." Nettie took the items and placed them in her apron pocket. Her eyes were still wary.

Keelan calmly studied Simon. "Will you be going with them?"

He gave her a surprised look. "Why no, Miss! I wouldn't leave my family. We together. I ain't runnin' Miss Keelan."

Family. She recalled Ruth and Joseph, and how they had clung to each other in the kitchen yard. She came to a conclusion. Hopefully Landon would go along with it. Turning to him, she handed him the blade. "It has been an exhausting day, and I'd like to go home." She spoke to the runaways before she exited. "We'll make no mention that we saw you. God speed on your journey."

Landon's face softened. "Go on ahead, I'll gather my gear and meet you outside."

The tunnel itself was cleverly hidden within a cluster of shrubs and rocks, several paces from the old shack. She climbed out and perused her surroundings. In the aftermath an eerie, golden, pink veil had settled about the countryside. The evening sun began to peek from behind the dark purple clouds now moving northwest.

She stared at the remnants of the small shanty that had been snuggled into the grove. A massive tree had flattened it. Her throat constricted at the devastation surrounding them. A path of trees, snapped midway up the trunk, trailed away from the cabin as if a giant had swung a great scythe. The ground was littered with shaggy tresses of Spanish moss, dark prickly pine cones the size of her boot, and a carpet of twigs and green leaves. She couldn't restrain a shudder. They were lucky to have escaped injury. Thoughts of her family had her eager to head home, concerned for their well-being.

Landon emerged, then dragged an old plank across the entrance to hide it.

"I'm glad your knowledge of storms is sound, Milord Pirate," she murmured.

"Been through enough to see them coming, most times," he replied, taking in the demolished structure behind them.

It was as if there was an unspoken agreement between the two of them to avoid discussing Simon and the runaways, almost as if ignoring them made them invisible and kept them safe. It would be nice to forget the harsh words they exchanged too. Although it might be better for her to stay distant.

Worry churned in her stomach and she prayed that the horses made it through unscathed. "Where did you hobble Orion?" That horse now held a special place in her heart.

"I didn't," he responded. "In conditions like these, it's best to allow the animal's instincts to see it safely through. I trust Orion found adequate shelter." Glancing at her he added, "Sham would have, too." He gave a loud piercing whistle and waited.

She heard the pounding hoof beats before she caught sight of the stallion. He rounded the toppled shanty and skidded to a muddy halt before snorting loudly in greeting. Landon spoke to his horse in soft tones, while he moved his hand over the mud-streaked shoulders and quivering flanks. Aside from several twigs tangled in his mane and tail and a few streaks of red clay, the steed had weathered the elements well enough.

Satisfied he was sound, Landon quickly saddled him and turned toward her. "At a leisurely pace, it shouldn't take long to make it back. Come, I'll help you mount."

She stepped into his waiting hand, and he hoisted her easily. It'd been many years since she'd had ridden astride a horse. Her father insisted she learn how to control a well-trained mount with her knees and heels before she attempted to ride sidesad-dle. Even so, it still seemed strange and unfamiliar as she wiggled in her seat. Her shortened shift hindered her ability to keep her legs open enough to comfortably straddle Orion's back, so she pulled it up and allowed it to bunch above her waist beneath her skirt.

Landon secured his bags, and swung a leg up behind her. Keelan's back went rigid at the shock of his hardened thighs against the backs of her own. His arm looped with bold famil-iarity around her middle. Even more shocking was the scalding heat of him against her backside. She squirmed forward as far as she could.

His chest rumbled behind her. "Methinks the ride back should be a pleasant one."

She made a point of removing his arm and placing it on his own leg. "Keep your hands to your own person, Captain. I'll not tolerate your oafish groping. Despite your roguish conduct today, I will continue my efforts to preserve my reputation and my virtue. Being seen in your presence will do enough damage to my good name as it is."

He gave a short laugh. "My touch did not seem to tarnish your reputation during the violence of the gale. Indeed," he continued in a thoughtful, yet mocking tone, "the high and haughty Miss

Keelan seemed to desire the warmth and protection of my arms, making me wonder what other services I might provide."

There it was. He probably didn't mean to reveal that information, but he'd just admitted to her that the kiss they'd shared was driven by lust. *Services, humph.* He spoke as if he was a stud and she a brood mare. Now that she understood both his place and hers in their relationship, there was no need for her to say more. It didn't matter, and it would change nothing, not the way he felt about her nor the different paths their lives would soon take. There could be no satisfaction in bringing it all to light. If anything, it would only cause pain.

Well, *more* pain.

His warm breath against her nape flashed across the skin on her neck. She shivered involuntarily and, annoyed with her body's response to his close proximity, she brought her hands up to her hair.

"Thanks to a spring rain, my appearance has been much damaged." She groaned. "What will my family think?"

She felt him shrug as he nudged Orion into motion. "This was not a mere rain shower, Keelan. If they care about your safety, they will welcome you home, relieved you were able to weather such a fierce tempest. I'm afraid many may not have shared our good fortune."

She pondered his statement as they plodded through the clearing. The other abandoned shanties hadn't survived the ravages of the winds either. Shingles, clapboards, and splintered planks littered the earth.

A thought hit her, making the back of her neck tingle. How did Landon know the cabin in which they sheltered had a cellar?

While she pondered the possible reasons, the horse picked his way nimbly through the debris. Landon steered them toward home. He shifted slightly, and Orion leapt into a slow easy canter.

She almost squealed at the unexpected change in gait and grabbed the mane with both hands. Landon's arm snaked around her and settled her firmly back into the seat. This time she did not remove it, choosing safety in exchange for pride.

The rest of the journey back was uneventful, and she couldn't help but enjoy the easy conversation she had with Landon. He was a talented storyteller, keeping her holding her breath in suspense or holding her side from laughter.

"It is no wonder you love sailing the ocean. If I were a man, I think I would choose the same profession. It would be fascinating to see such exotic sights and live such extraordinary experiences."

"Just say the word, my lady and I will be your most devoted escort."

She sighed and became quiet as her thoughts churned. He spoke the words lightly, but their weight was palpable. Circumstances with her father and her own troubles made such a life appear no more than a childish dream. Remaining practical and following her plan of opening her shop should stay in the forefront of her mind.

Everything else should stay distant.

Exposing her tender desires to a charmer like Landon would only add more torment to an already broken-heart. She had to steel her emotions from the potent lure of the man, and somehow maintain a cool and aloof demeanor. Keeping a snowflake from melting on a hot July day in South Carolina would be easier.

Both marveled at the destruction. The storm had cut a swath of devastation through the forest along the southern side of the trail. Entire trees had been uprooted. Some looked like broken broomsticks; their trunks twisted and snapped several feet from the ground.

"It headed northwest," Landon quietly observed.

She chewed her lower lip.

Toward Twin Pines.

CHAPTER 29

KEELAN'S CHOICE

The stable roof was in shambles.

From what she could see, it lay in pieces scattered about the barnyard and as far as Aunt Sarah's garden. Men, women, and children dotted the landscape, picking up the debris. Somehow, the main house had escaped damage. Keelan expelled a thankful sigh.

Thomas worked hitching horses to Uncle Jared's carriage. Nearby, additional mounts were saddled and tethered to the fence.

They rode into the yard. Upon recognizing them, the young groom let out a whoop and ran off into the house.

Landon dismounted. "It appears we have caused a bit of a tizzy."

She blew a curl from her face. "A search party has been assembled." She glanced worriedly toward the house wondering if it was for them or the runaways. "I worry Simon won't make it back before his absence is noticed."

Landon wrapped the reins around a fence post. "He is a very resourceful man," he answered, his expression shuttered.

She shot him a narrowed glance. "How would you know that? You have only seen him twice."

Landon shrugged. "He left a strong impression." He reached up and circled her waist with his hands, then pulled her from the saddle.

"And how did you know about the cellar in that—"

There was a fierce tug on her train accompanied by a violent rip making both freeze. She was suspended, held in part by his extended arms, as well as the trapped skirt, snagged on the saddle horn. With a wary swallow, she peered over her shoulder then gasped. The back of her skirt had separated from the seam, exposing her twisted shift. The result unveiled a pair of ivory-white legs and from the draft, most of her backside as well.

Landon followed her gaze and his eyes widened. She wanted to smack his hard and horribly unyielding shoulder, but she settled for glaring at him. He leered back, crystal blue eyes brimming with humor.

"Put. Me. Down."

His grin expanded. "As you wish."

He began to lower her to the ground, but paused again at the sound of another rending.

"Wait!" she shrieked, immediately regretting her command.

The corners of his mouth twitched. "What will it be, my love? Shall I put you down or not? I enjoy having you in my arms but would desire a more private spot."

"This is no time for jest!" she hissed. "Nor the time to play the rutting stag. My hem is caught, and you know it."

He tilted his head and leisurely scrutinized her exposed limbs. This time, she thumped his chest with her fists.

"Landon Hart!"

"Would you like some help to that end, my love?" he asked solemnly.

His calm, confident demeanor, combined with his ornery teasing, made it hard for her to focus on the issue at hand. She expelled an exasperated breath and hoped she sounded intimidating when she spoke through clenched teeth. "If you are quite through being a scoundrel then, *yes*!"

Landon easily lifted her higher and to her shock, put her over his shoulder like a sack of sugar. His left hand rested boldly on the small of her back, if you could call it that, since its position was either at the lowest part of her back or the highest part of her bottom. Stepping forward, he reached up and disengaged the train. That feat accomplished, he lowered her from his shoulder and released her, allowing her to slide against his body with a speed similar to cold molasses.

He was a rake to the *core*.

She shoved against his chest, which was like shoving an ox. With what she hoped was a chilling glare, she struggled to wriggle the stubbornly tangled shift free.

"Look what you've done!" She swiveled and reached for the torn waistline. She grasped a handful of fabric and tried her best to preserve her modesty. How humiliating. At least no one was near enough to witness her mortification. She decided to ignore the hot flush burning her cheeks. Let the cad think it was anger instead of acute embarrassment, which welled inside her like an overfilled pitcher.

The entire day had been one compromising event after another, and Landon Hart had witnessed or participated in every single one. Embarrassment and shame turned to anger. His proximity made him an easy target. Scowling, she raised her chin to meet his carefully subdued gaze, and poked a slender finger hard on his chest. She stalked him when he stepped back, narrowing the space between them.

"Since I have been in your presence, I have been insulted, ogled, mauled and now, practically had the clothes ripped from my body."

Landon managed to look appalled. "My sweet Miss Grey, I never insulted you."

At no time in her life had she repeatedly felt so discomfited, desirable, passionate, and scandalized as she had since meeting Landon Hart. Why must she ever seem the ninny in his eyes? She painted herself into a very unladylike portrait; and repeated it every time they saw each other. It annoyed her even more that Landon had gleefully witnessed every dreadful moment. She'd even allowed him to seduce her.

And enjoyed it.

Ugh. She was so weak. To be placed in a category with all the other ladies he'd charmed, had her stomach tossing acid up her throat. Even now, she ached for another of his kisses.

She longed for it all to mean more.

The horrible understanding that she'd acted like a lovesick girl, rather than a young lady of grace and integrity grated her pride. Worse, was the way her body reacted when he was near, beyond the annoyance and anger. Part of her wanted to be close enough to breathe him in, thrilling in the way his presence energized her.

Another part of her was frantically clanking gongs and tin kettles in her head in warning.

She wasn't a daft, pampered child of the aristocracy. She'd grown up as a commodore's daughter. Her mother had made sure she understood the ways of men. She'd be wise to avoid letting her reckless emotions override those lessons. If only she could trust her own self-restraint.

Seemingly undaunted by her reprimand, the sea captain was rudely avoiding eye contact as she spoke. His attention was directed over her shoulder.

"Keelan, my sweet—"

"Do *not* attempt to ply me with tender words in hopes of dampening my vexation." Unwilling to yield him the opportunity to toss about any more of his apparently bottomless supply of mockery and charm, she continued, "I am not your *sweet*. I am not your *love*. You act like a charming gentleman one moment and a pirate thief stealing kisses from me the next." She wished she could find the words to slice his overconfident ego and dispel that infuriating grin. She gestured to her person. "Look at me! You have literally ripped the clothes from my body."

His eyebrows lowered in warning. He spoke softly. "Keelan, love, 'tis best to continue this conversation another time."

Her jaw unhinged. Did he think he could simply tell her to be quiet and postpone the admonishment until such a time it was convenient for *him*?

She flung an arm in the air in exasperation. "Do you really think I give a hoot about whether or not you want to hear about what a scandalous debaucher of women you are?" He might be lord, master, and captain of his ship but this was not his domain, and she would not let him bully her into silence. She would speak her mind!

"And you should know, Sir Pirate, if you think your groping and pawing will have me soon falling, willing and lusty, into your bed like a common street trollop then you, sir—" She jabbed his chest again. "Are an arrogant *ass*!"

There. He deserved every last word of that chastisement.

She dropped her hand and tried to better gather her tattered skirt. "Oh, for pity's sake, let's speak no more of it. I'm afraid it's been a trying afternoon, and my patience has been worn too thin." She brushed her hand over her renegade curls. "We should be thankful the worst thing that happened was that I lost my—"

A startled gasp hit Keelan like a cold blast of water.

"...favorite bonnet." She finished weakly.

Landon's face blanked as he fought to remain painfully composed. Who was behind her? Slowly turning, she saw Thomas standing with a small contingent of family and servants. To her horror, Mr. Pratt, Doreen, Aunt Sarah, and Uncle Jared stood on the porch at the forefront, their eyes wide and unblinking. Her father sat on a wheeled chair. Thomas and Ruth did their best to find other sights to peruse, like toes, trees, the sky. Behind them,

Everett stuttered out the front door, making matters truly abysmal.

Her aunt managed to find her voice first. "Keelan, dear child," she choked. "When that beast of a horse returned without you, we feared the worst!" She scurried forward and lightly hugged her. "I am so relieved you are home safe. You appear to be..."

Doreen dug her fists into her hips. "Running around the countryside like some loose floozy!" she sneered, her perusal raking Keelan from nose to toes. "Look at her. Riding hither and yon without a decent escort! It's shameful." Doreen turned toward her father. "Our name will be the laughing stock of the Charleston area, if it's not already, thanks to her!"

Keelan stiffened at her cousin's harsh outburst.

Uncle Jared scowled at his daughter, quickly grabbed her arm, and pulled her behind him. "This is none of your concern, Doreen."

Landon addressed her cousin; placing a hand over his heart, he bowed slightly. "I assure you, Miss Doreen, Miss Keelan was on her best behavior. My reputation as a gentleman has remained intact and not been tarnished in the least by today's events."

Keelan's jaw dropped as the meaning of Landon's words sank in. Her aunt made a strangled choking sound; her eyes flickered nervously between her husband and the other onlookers. Her uncle actually appeared to be fighting back a smile. He coughed into his hand, then scratched his neck and glanced at her father.

But it was Mr. Pratt who acted first, his face a mottled red. His glower shifted between her and Landon. "I came here before continuing on my search for three runaways, to make sure my intended hadn't been harmed by the storm." He turned to her father and uncle. "However, in light of the current situation, consider my previous offer of marriage rescinded!"

Hallelujah! Keelan wanted to dance with glee, but her father's thunderous expression immediately smothered the inclination. Instead, she sent up a silent prayer that Simon helped the family get away safely. They were already at a disadvantage. It's harder to run with three.

Pratt shouldered past the two men and strode down the steps without another glance in Keelan's direction. After snatching his horse's reins from the hitching post, he mounted and dug his heels into the gelding's side. At his shout, two other figures near the stables galloped to join him in his flight down the lane toward the mill.

The family stood in horrified silence, except for Keelan, of course, she wanted to laugh with relief, but didn't dare try to appear anything but grim. Doreen clapped a hand over her mouth. Although, by the gleam in her eyes, she had to assume her cousin enjoyed the entertainment immensely.

Her father was stone-faced. "What have you to say for your actions, Captain Hart?"

She went from sudden elation to instant terror. Her chest turned to hard, jagged stone, weighing her down and making it difficult to draw an even breath. What had she done? How much had they heard?

Landon answered smoothly, unruffled, "I acted with your daughter's best interests in mind."

Liar.

Of course, Landon didn't have the courage to look at her as he continued. "After speaking with Mr. Grey, I took his advice and toured the plantation. I came upon Miss Grey and offered to escort her back to the house. We were unable to make it back in time, so we sought shelter and waited for the hurricane to pass. Unfortunately, the lightening frightened off her mount. I did my best to return her to you, unharmed in every way."

Should she correct him? Should she tell her father Hart had saved her from a runaway horse in addition to the fury of a horrendous storm? Would Papa think it was a ploy to show Landon in a more positive light than what he deserved? Sadly, the damage had already been done, thanks to her regrettable tirade. As hard was it was for her to do so, she slammed her mouth shut.

"According to my daughter, your conduct was unbecoming," her father growled, leaning heavily on the arms of the wheeled chair. "I assure you, knowing Pratt, the sun will barely rise on the morrow, 'ere the rest of the county will be buzzing with the news you have *ruined* her!" His last words ended in a near roar, causing both Keelan and Aunt Sarah to cringe.

Landon didn't flinch. In fact, his face showed no emotion at all. "I have no desire to see your daughter's reputation ruined beyond repair, Commodore. As amends, I respectfully request her hand in marriage, sir, if that will remedy the situation."

"It would certainly help," Jared interjected. "And sooner rather than later."

"Wait!" Everett fell forward, tripping over Ruth's foot as he squeezed between her and Joseph. "I...I also offer my hand in marriage. I have spoken to both the commodore and Miss Grey, concerning such. Keelan and I are in love and are, in fact, already betrothed."

She could only stare at the doctor in shock. What had he just said?

In love?

In...*love?*

She opened her mouth to object, but all that would come out was an odd squeaking noise.

That beautiful plan, the one that started out as a delaying tactic had turned on her like a rabid dog. To make matters even more deplorable, she'd inadvertently moved up the wedding date.

Everything was now completely out of her control, and she didn't do well when she had no control. Papa slammed down his eyebrows, then glared at his brother, who remained stoic. Her mind worked furiously, tossing away one idea after another, but she could find no quick way out, other than fake a complete faint, but that would mean letting go of her skirt.

Drat.

Her father crossed his arms. "My daughter will decide now which of the two she will wed."

Decide *now?*

Marry Landon Hart or Everett Garrison? Choose either a rogue like Landon who flirted with the strings of her heart better than the best trained violinist, or a benevolent, but meek man like Everett, who while kind, stirred no passion in her soul at all.

Good Lord, she lived a nightmare!

She finally found her tongue. "Papa, can we not take some time to discuss—"

Her father swiftly raised a pale, trembling hand and stopped her. "I need no time. My decision stands. You will marry immediately. The only question you must answer is, which man will you take as a husband?"

She could only gape at her father. Her heart screamed Landon's name, but her voice would not. Her body hungered for him, but her heart feared he'd feed it lust rather than love. Then a wicked image crept into her mind of her standing on the pier with a swollen belly, and the women of Charleston talking behind their fans about her husband, who left his naïve little wife behind while bedding every arduous beauty between here and China.

Everett had a growing practice in Charleston. It was likely he would return to it when he was no longer needed at Twin Pines. Already, he'd made several trips back and forth each month. The fastest way to see her dream of owning her own boutique fulfilled, would be to choose Everett. Better to chain herself to the one she didn't love, than the one who would shatter her heart and leave her bitter and lonely.

It would be safer, less painful in the end.

Her shoulders sagged, as if Orion had just climbed on her back. She stared at her father and swallowed. "Fine then. I'll take…" She closed her eyes. "Dr. Garrison."

Doreen inhaled sharply before she whirled, wrenched open the door, and ran into the house.

Next to her, Landon released the slightest expulsion of breath. A sigh of relief. Her stomach took a sickening plunge.

So, she'd made the right choice after all. The right choice, not the most desired one. Not her heart's choice.

Now that the decision was made, she hated herself for allowing Landon to shred her stupid heart. How dare her father force her choose now, in front of everyone? She couldn't stand there a moment longer. When she started for the porch, Landon touched her elbow.

"Keelan—"

The world turned red. She reacted instinctively with a fury fed by regret, heartbreak and humiliation. In one smooth motion, she jerked her elbow away and with her other hand, landed a slap on his cheek that could be heard all the way to Jamaica. Whirling back toward the house, she gathered her ruined skirt and stomped up the stairs, people parting a path for her like the red sea.

Blast that man!

And blast her silly, foolish, *foolish* heart.

CHAPTER 30

A NEW PROPOSAL

Landon adjusted Orion's reins and prepared to mount. He'd probably dodged a bullet, both literally and figuratively. Grey would have been perfectly in his rights to demand he marry Keelan today, and at gunpoint. He lifted his sleeve and wiped the small beads of sweat from his hairline. If he ever married, it would be too soon. His line of work didn't accommodate wives very well. And he enjoyed his freedom. He couldn't help looking back toward the upper windows of the house. So why did he feel as if something thorny scraped the inside of his chest?

"Hart."

He turned toward Commodore Grey, who was alone with his brother on the porch. The commodore's pallor was more pronounced, now that his anger had diminished. The veins on his stark hands glared like blue ink on white parchment.

"Yes, Commodore?"

Sighing heavily, the old man cleared his throat. "Thank you for taking my daughter under your protection and seeing her home. We've been sick with worry over her welfare."

He gave the commodore a slight nod, thinking back to his earlier blunder that made Sham bolt away with Keelan on his back. "I'm glad I was able to help, sir. However, I have a distinct feeling that even if I hadn't been, your daughter would have managed well enough on her own. She appears to be most resilient."

Commodore Grey gave him a wry smile. "Indeed."

"Godspeed in finding the missing boy and your stolen property," Jared said.

Landon nodded his thanks. "I appreciate the information you shared. Our search will continue until we find both." With that, he swung a leg over Orion's back. "Good day, gentlemen."

As he rode back to Charleston, it was easy to explain away the dull ache in his gut to hunger. That fiery-haired forest imp of a young woman was better off wed to a bland man like Garrison. The doctor might be able to rein her in and settle down that wild spirit of hers. Keep her safe before she set the country on fire.

The chit was bright, but reckless.

She took risks without considering the impending consequences.

She was fearless. Strong-willed.

What would it be like to have her with him? Would her fire consume him like embers to paper, or would they both plunge headlong over the edge of the universe in a torrent of passion and flames?

He shook his head. It did no good to ruminate over it; she and Garrison were *in love*.

He was better off sailing solo with the wind at his back and the world solid and faithful at his feet.

KEELAN LEANED over her father's shoulder as he sat at the desk in the study, perusing the figures she'd prepared. She'd spent the entire day yesterday studying the ledgers and writing down her proposal for Twin Pines based on her engagement to Dr. Garrison.

It had been a daunting task. Not so much because of the complexity of the financial aspects, but because her mind kept drifting to the memory of Landon's mouth curving up at the corners in that sensual, knowing smile.

She had made the right choice. Right?

Yes, of course she had.

Yet, the base instincts driving the woman in her to deeply desire Landon Hart were crying foul. And would not cease.

Her father glanced up at Uncle Jared who was sitting in a chair. "What do you think, Jared?"

"I think leasing Twin Pines to Pratt is a sound idea. The fact that after five years, he'll have an option to buy the plantation will appeal to him." He ticked off his observations on his fingers. "It'll allow him to generate revenue for the purchase. It will provide Keelan and Garrison time to establish the business, and expand his practice. Pratt's regular lease payments will give you enough monthly income to live in Charleston, as well as enable you to garner a line of credit to provide them the funding to open and stock the store."

George Grey sat back in his chair. Keelan placed her hand on his shoulder. "Papa, you know there isn't anything like this in town. Not the way I envision. I know my boutique will be a success." Bolts of colorful fabric, lining the walls near the ceiling, would draw a patron's gaze from across the street. Shelves of jars filled with exotic spices and teas would stir an aroma just as enticing. Beautiful pottery and china would glitter brightly in the front window on a bed of luxurious, deeply hued silk.

He reached up and patted her hand then squeezed. "I believe you. If anyone can, you can, my dear."

Uncle Jared had unexpectedly become her grudging ally. "Between Keelan's knowledge of your late wife's boutique and my connections on the waterfront, we should have no trouble getting things underway in town. Our entire family would be able to reside and conduct business there. I'll always be close by to help Keelan, should she need it, George."

Jared paced the study. "Garrison can focus on his practice as well. I concur with Keelan's reasoning. Pratt has been coveting Twin Pines since you arrived. I think he'll agree to a lease, contingent upon an outright purchase within a limited time frame." He rocked back on his heels. "When I met with Captains Hart and O'Brien regarding the rental of one of my warehouses, I had an opportunity to review their inventory list, which I have to say, was quite impressive. They trade rare items which would have the people of the Lowcountry salivating."

Her father stiffened. "There are many reliable merchant companies to choose from. I'm sure we can find someone similar."

Jared sighed. "You must admit the Hart and Ahern have very keen business sense. Their company is sound, even after losing part of their cargo. Although I doubt they could recuperate from another loss. They only have to sail along the coast and deliver goods to their buyers. If their journey was to the Caribbean or South America, there'd be a greater risk."

Although she was leery of Captain Landon Hart when it came to his personal intentions, he would indeed be the perfect supplier of out-of-the-ordinary items she'd want to sell. She wasn't sure she'd be able to tolerate any kind of business arrangement with him. Seeing him each time would be like pulling a scab off a partially healed wound over and over. And over.

"Papa's correct. I'm sure we can find another shipping merchant to work with," she said, hoping she sounded as certain as her words. If father would allow her to enjoy a long engagement to the doctor, rather than insist on a hasty wedding, she'd have the opportunity to show she could accomplish both *without* a husband.

Without a husband to disrupt things. And kiss with his teeth.

She'd already succeeded in moving the wedding date to five months hence. If she delayed enough, surely Dr. Garrison would lose interest and break their engagement.

She could at least hope. She harbored no yearning to marry, especially now. How could she tolerate an intimate relationship with someone who could never arouse passion in the way Landon Hart could with a single kiss? Anything less was bound to be a tremendous disappointment. She'd rather remain a spinster.

"It's settled then," her father replied. "I'll pen a letter to Pratt to include with the proposal."

Keelan faced the window and allowed herself a victorious smile.

She should feel relieved, but there was a nagging sensation deep in her belly. Something still wasn't quite right, like a table with one short leg that wasn't noticeable until you leaned an elbow on that one spot that made it tilt.

CHAPTER 31

A SECRET OUT

"Quit yer fidgeting lass, or I'll never get this right!" Slaney, huffed. "Ye be squirmin' like a wee minnow in a child's fist." For the second time, the maid tried to pin a wayward strand of Keelan's hair.

The night of Doreen's ball arrived all too soon.

Keelan sighed apologetically. "I'm sorry. It's just that—"

"You canna wait to be in the arms of yer betrothed?" She couldn't miss the sarcasm in her maid's voice.

Keelan snorted. "Had poor Pastor Braun and his chapel not been blown away by the storm, I'd be a married woman by now. At least it's an announcement and not a wedding ceremony that will take place later this evening." She picked up a mirror and studied the maid's handiwork. "Lovely work, Slaney."

Still, she had an intense desire to don her waif's clothes, stuff her hidden bag of coins into a pillowcase, and slip out the back a final time.

Run.

The chamber door opened, startling both women.

Slaney made a small, strange noise.

Perplexed at the sound and assaulted by the overpowering

aroma of rose water, she shared Slaney's reaction. One glance at Doreen's attire, and she understood the maid's response.

Doreen's evening gown was a magnificent, pale yellow silk creation. Obviously a talented seamstress tried hard to take the latest style and mold it to Doreen's skinny body. On a more endowed woman, the dress would have been stunning. On Doreen's scant frame, it was obscene.

It barely covered what little Doreen had in the way of breasts by showing a daring plunge in the neckline. Uncle Jared would be horrified. How did her cousin persuade Aunt Sarah to buy it?

Doreen pushed her skirts to the side, as she walked past the bed and scowled, shaking her strawberry blond locks in disapproval. "You've ruined my soirée."

Keelan smiled humorlessly at her sulking cousin, although she was careful to add a cheerful lilt in her voice. "Good evening, Doreen. That is a beautiful gown. Has your father seen it yet?"

The young woman sniffed as she gestured to the garment. "I had it made by the best dressmaker in Charleston. She assured me it's all the rage in Paris." She patted a carefully placed curl on her shoulder and lifted her chin higher, while her gaze scraped up and down Keelan. She added snidely, "Papa would want me to have only the best."

That raised a brow. So Uncle Jared *hadn't* seen it.

Her cousin continued. "Since you arrived, all the eligible beaus have come to call and after a few minutes with you, they bolt out and never return! They always want *you*. Please tell Miss Keelan I have come to call," she mimicked. Doreen's face imploded with disdain, "Yet, you toy with them as would .a common strumpet!"

Keelan's temper flared at the lewd words. She hadn't intended to reveal her reasoning, but it escaped before she could stop it. "I was not toying with them, Doreen. I was rejecting them in an attempt to turn their attention to you."

For a moment, the girl was speechless. Her composure shifted and transformed her expression from jealous spite to deep humiliation. Her face paled, and her hand shook a little when she reached up to brush a curl hair from her eyes.

"Well, it didn't work, did it?" Doreen responded in a choked voice. Her lower lip trembled. A dark flush started to creep over her cheeks. "You have managed to draw all the attention to yourself, instead. Again. My party, *my* night, and Father insists on making your betrothal announcement to the whole of Charleston." Doreen's voice cracked, and she whirled away and stood facing the window.

A long moment passed before Doreen composed herself enough to turn back to face them. Her eyes glistened. "You're now engaged to marry the one man about whom I care the most." She swallowed a jagged sob. "Why didn't you simply choose the captain and go away with him? Why Everett? You don't love him. I know you don't!"

No. Keelan froze in stunned silence. Doreen was in love with Dr. Garrison? She took a hesitant step forward. Oh dear. Why hadn't she noticed?

"Doreen, had I known I would have—"

"What, Keelan?" Tears started to spill down her face. "You would have what? Turned his attention toward me like you claim you did with the others, as just another one of your cast-offs?"

"Yes," she said, then regretted the response. She hadn't meant to sound as if she agreed with Doreen's assessment, that she would leave Everett as one might do with an unwanted possession. "No, I mean—"

"I know what you mean." Doreen cut her off, her breathing harsh and jerky. "You are so selfish! Do you do this for amusement? Do you enjoy playing with a man's affections like a child with a doll? Can't you see he was trying to save your stupid, worthless, reputation?" Doreen stuttered the words between sobs. "What's it like, Keelan? What's it like to be so beautiful that every man who lays eyes on you falls in love with you? What's it like to play your game of seduction and then when they are smitten and vulnerable, shove them aside?"

Keelan was shocked into silence. The raw, heavy weight of Doreen's words slammed into the accusations she'd thrown at Landon back in the cabin. Fingers of regret raked across her heart. Her intention was not to steal the man Doreen loved. Given a choice of two evils, she just chose the lesser. How did she miss Doreen's affection for Everett? Had she been so wrapped up in pursuing her own schemes she hadn't caught the most conspicuous tells?

To give her something to do other than watch her cousin weep and feel wretched about it, Keelan went to the tallboy and pulled open drawers until she found a handkerchief. She silently pressed it into Doreen's palm. The best thing for the girl to do now, was to cry it out.

"Don't try to be kind," Doreen said at last, snatching the handkerchief and dabbing the tears. "You don't deserve Everett. He is kind and chivalrous and generous. He's not only been seeing to your father, but also the children on this plantation. I've been helping him. He's been teaching me how to mix up medicine and treat injuries. He's even taught me how to administer your father's. I was hoping..." She choked back another sob.

A horrible guilt seeped into Keelan's chest. Her intentions had never been to toy with anyone's heart. She'd done just that with Dr. Garrison, hadn't she? She'd taken advantage of his besotted devotion for her and used it to bolster her cause.

She was no different from Landon. The irony hit her like a hard punch to the chest.

Now more than ever, she wanted to devise a way to avoid this marriage. But the wheels were already in motion, and the chances of stopping them were very slim.

Run away, whispered a voice in her head. *Just go.*

Her cousin sniffled about the room, picking up objects and absently putting them down again.

Keelan felt like an idiot. "Doreen, I'm sorry. This isn't something I want either. Maybe things will change for the better for both of us."

"Better? How can anything become better?" Doreen clenched her fists at her sides and stomped her foot. "This should be my engagement celebration, Everett's and mine! But you stole him from me, and the worst part is that I know you don't even love him!" She flung the mirror on the bed. Doreen glared at her. "I hate you."

Keelan felt horrible about the deception, but this needed to end before Doreen lost her composure entirely. "Doreen, you should go."

Snarling, Doreen grabbed a water goblet off the nightstand and flew toward her. "Don't ever speak to me again, you greedy, spoiled brat!"

Doreen drew back her hand and swung the glass. In two quick movements, Keelan instinctively blocked with her left forearm and snatched it away with her right hand. The momentum of the charge carried Doreen forward. Being disarmed threw her off balance and she crashed to the floor. Keelan stared down at the fluffy pile of silk and petticoats.

Doreen wailed and floundered around like a drunken trout. "My arm! This will bruise for sure, I just know it!"

"Slaney, please help Doreen up so she can leave."

The maid warily moved behind the girl, slid her elbows under Doreen's armpits, and heaved. After stepping on the stiffly starched petticoats several times, Doreen stumbled to her feet and jerked her arms away. Her curls looked like they'd been combed with a kitchen whisk.

She tromped from the room, yelling for her maid at the top of her lungs.

For a moment, both Keelan and Slaney stood frozen. Waving away the still pungent scent of rose water, the maid moved to close the door. Slaney brushed her hands on her apron then reached for Keelan's gown. "Come now, lass, let's get ye dressed. Guests are beginning to arrive." Leaving the obvious unsaid.

Keelan doubted she'd be able to act the part of a happy fiancée in Dr. Garrison's presence this evening. However, her father's health seemed to improve slightly in the past few days, and he planned on attending for a short while, so she'd do her best. Perhaps she could find the doctor and have a brief word with him before the festivities start. She owed him the truth, that she didn't love him. If he cared about Doreen, he'd jump at the opportunity to break the engagement. She couldn't marry him out of convenience. Papa and Uncle Jared already sent her proposal to Pratt. There was no need for this charade to continue.

Slaney's sympathetic voice broke the quiet of the room, "Perhaps ye could feign a headache and retire early."

"I won't give Doreen the satisfaction of thinking she's bullied me away." Yes, her pride was overriding every thread of sense, but she was too upset and angry with herself to care. She stepped into the shimmering ocean-blue ball gown. Slaney pulled it up over her shoulders and began working the fastenings. Keelan tried to swallow the lump expanding in her throat.

When she finished, Slaney gave her a warm, soft hug and spun her toward the door. "At least the other gents will be leavin' ye be this evenin', since yer betrothed now."

She rolled her eyes. Wonderful. "That's a *colossal* comfort."

CHAPTER 32

A BALL BEGINS

L aughter and music rose from the ballroom below as Keelan left her room. They had opened every window in the house to enjoy the cooling effects of the light winds. The aroma of roasted meats from the fire pit mingled with the heavy scent of magnolia blossoms. Her aunt's voice carried up the stairs as she greeted guests.

Normally, the opportunity to attend such a gala made her giddy. However, the somber blanket of reality smothered any excitement or anticipation. Images of shackles and grey mist bombarded her mind.

Melancholy seeped deep into her bones.

The only bright spot of optimism came with the comfort that she didn't have to worry about Pratt. Even thinking his name made a cold, murky hand clamp her stomach.

Twin Pines had a glorious two-story foyer. The staircase split partway down, much like a wishbone, to hug the side walls. Upon entry, visitors were ushered straight ahead, through the tall archway under the grand stair. She began her descent with deliberate steps. The last thing she wanted was to roll to the bottom in a tumbled heap.

The hard edge in her uncle's voice stuttered her next step. "Captain Hart, welcome."

Her stomach plummeted to her feet at the thought of seeing the mocking countenance of Landon Hart again.

Not him!

Not here!

She sensed his perusal even before she lifted her head. She fought to maintain her attention on her slippers, otherwise that amused, mocking smirk would destroy her concentration. Would he ever treat her as a lady, or would he always see that a boyish chit beneath? Not that it mattered anymore.

There was no way to delay it any longer, so she allowed herself to look at him. Even as tension tightened her lungs, a slow, swirling sensation pooled in her belly. Landon's shiny, ebony locks were secured in a queue. A matching light gray waistcoat complimented the dark charcoal breeches. The black silk shirt accented the sun-darkened skin of his face and neck. His eyes glowed with a blue sheen.

That was definitely not a mocking expression. Instead, he regarded her with a warm glow of admiration. Or lust. Probably lust. His perusal sent a wave of pure heat from the hem of her gown to her hair, causing a shiver to whip across her shoulders. A furious blush crept over her cheeks, as the captain's sapphire stare lingered overlong near the neckline. It took almost all her strength to keep from crossing her arms over her chest and fleeing back up to the safety of her chamber. Instead, she slapped what she hoped was a cool, serene smile on her face and continued down, despite the Albatross flapping hysterically in her stomach.

Breathe. Swallow. Swallow and breathe. No, blast it, not at the same time. Her mouth had gone dry. She clutched the banister more firmly and gave herself a mental tongue-lashing.

Concentrate on the steps, you ninny.

Now was not the time to lose her footing. Before she could

take another step, Landon ascended two at a time and offered her his arm.

"Allow me to escort you, Miss Grey." He gripped her elbow. A warmth zipped through her arm and all the way to her toes. Ignore the touch of his fingers. *Ignore* them. Focus on the steps. Good Lord, if she tripped now the humiliation would vaporize her like boiling water in a teapot.

"Quite honestly, I don't know how you ladies cope with steps and full skirts. Were a man in your shoes, he'd already be a crumpled pile of arms and legs down in the entryway."

Her laugh came out more as a weak warble, betraying the state of her nerves. "It appears they are wise enough to avoid wearing them in the first place," she muttered. "We women bring this all on ourselves."

He dipped his head and chuckled. "And we men are most grateful."

Really, what kind of mindless banter was this? Was he actually trying to calm her with this banal conversation? Perhaps this was an attempt to lure her into a false sense of security. She resolved to stay away from the man, as soon as she descended the stairs safely, for her own sake.

When they reached the foyer, she disengaged her hand from his arm to greet her aunt and uncle by the door, her palm still radiating heat. "What a beautiful night for your daughter's ball."

Her aunt kissed her cheek. "Isn't it simply perfect? We are so fortunate to have this refreshing breeze." Aunt Sarah's eyes twitched from Landon to her husband and back.

Apparently, more droll observations were needed to keep Uncle Jared from making a scene.

Her uncle's perusal traveled approvingly up and down. "Might I say you look stunning, my dear?" His face softened. "I just came from your father's chamber. I'm afraid he's feeling too poorly to join us. He would have been proud to be the one announcing your forthcoming nuptials."

Landon stiffened. She still smiled woodenly at her uncle. If she met Landon's gaze, he'd read it in her eyes.

A lie. It's all a lie.

Her face must have betrayed her heartache as well as her despair. Aunt Sarah gave her a light hug. "I'm so sorry, dear."

Keelan's heart fell hard enough to pull her shoulders down with it. Papa had improved dramatically over the past few days. He even took a walk with her yesterday to inspect the stable repairs. She decided to excuse herself as soon as possible and go sit with him the remainder of the evening.

After pulling Garrison aside to break their engagement.

Landon turned, pulled her hand toward him, and pressed his lips to her fingertips. "I wish you a happy, loving marriage, Miss Grey. Although I am sure several, young men will go home this evening much saddened by such news."

A happy, loving marriage. Everything she wanted. Nothing she'd experience. She focused her attention on the vase of flowers on a nearby table. Don't look at him. Don't look. As badly as she wanted to tell him everything, she didn't dare.

Hart turned his attention to her uncle. "If you'll recall, one of our galley boys went missing during the theft of our cargo. When you and I talked at the mill, you gave me several names of a few who might know about the local men I hired. So far, none provided helpful information. I hope you can introduce me to others tonight, who may have the information I require. I'm most concerned for the boy's welfare."

Uncle Jared clasped his hands behind his back and pursed his lips. "Ah yes. The storm hindered those efforts more than a little, I'm sure. As soon as all our guests arrive, and the ball is underway, we shall meet in my study."

"Thank you, sir." Landon inclined his head.

Simon stepped forward and smiled. He held a tray of unfilled wine glasses. Joseph stood at his father's side, carefully holding a half-filled carafe.

Simon removed a stem, a kind crinkle in his eyes. "Would you care for a glass of wine, Miss Grey?"

She smiled. "Yes, please, I would. Captain Hart?"

Landon's response was curt. "No, thank you."

She flinched at the coolness coating his demeanor. She deserved it.

Guilt enveloped her. She didn't think she could ever hurt his feelings in any way. He played his game with her. And now it was over. Although she hadn't planned on using Landon to ignite her scheme to prevent matrimony to Pratt, everything fell perfectly into place.

Everything but the truth.

CHAPTER 33

A SIP OF WINE

A feminine cough broke the temporary silence. Everyone's attention turned to the top of the staircase.

Doreen posed on the landing, smiling sweetly at Hart.

Keelan raised her glass and took a sip. Doreen's hair had been repaired, her face no longer reddened by tears and anger. She tried to act nonchalant, but the flirtatious gaze Doreen had fixed on Landon fired Keelan's irritation.

She was annoyed even more by the fact that it bothered her.

Immensely.

Then she heard her aunt's small gasp behind her. Apparently, Aunt Sarah hadn't seen the dress either, and cast a horrified stare over the rim of her glass at her husband. A wide-eyed look of panic seemed to have paralyzed Uncle Jared's normally stoic face. His jaw clenched and began a convulsive quivering. When he found his voice, the words fell out like a cup of nails on a tin plate.

"WHAT IN GOD'S NAME?"

Aunt Sarah's elbow shot out from her side and she gave her husband a merciless poke, which sent him into a fit of coughing.

"Captain Hart, you remember my daughter, Doreen," she said thinly, waving a weak hand at the stairs.

Uncle Jared stood like a wooden pillar; his stare was barely visible under his thick, slashing eyebrows.

Since no other gentleman were nearby, and her uncle struggled to breathe, Hart once again ascended the steps and graciously offered his arm. He'd better love the fragrance of rose water, otherwise a pungent trip up and down the staircase awaited the lethally handsome Captain Hart.

As he neared Doreen, he stifled a low cough. Keelan grinned into her glass. Rose water wasn't a favorite, then.

"It is a joy to see you again, Miss Grey." Hart said cordially. "You look lovely this evening."

Doreen gazed dreamily at Landon. "Thank you," she drawled, as she batted her lashes demurely. "It's refreshing to converse with a man with an astute sense of style." She slipped her arm through Landon's and pulled it tightly against her ribs, which smashed a breast up enough to almost fall out. "My! Such strong arms. I truly appreciate your kind escort."

A larger gulp of wine was needed to keep from snorting in disgust at her cousin's shameless and downright blatant attempt at flirtation. The pair descended, and this time Landon accepted refreshment from Simon and Joseph. Doreen continued to cling to his arm while she tried to steer him in the direction of the music.

"Captain Hart, you must come and listen to the musicians my father brought in from Charleston. They play a divine waltz."

Landon smiled politely. "My apologies, Miss Grey, but I have urgent business with your father. I'm sure your dance card must already be quite full."

Aunt Sarah hopped forward and draped her fichu around Doreen's shoulders. "Here, dear," she said, "it's a little drafty this evening." She swiftly tied the garment.

"Mother, I do not need—"

Uncle Jared's voice growled from behind his wife's shoulder, "Daughter, you'll do well to obey your mother!"

"But Papa..." Doreen whined.

At her sire's warning scowl, she gave a soft exasperated sigh, and grasped Landon's arm tighter. "Come, Captain Hart, allow me to show you the way to the ballroom, where the draft is not so cool." She stared pointedly at her parents, and gave them a triumphant smile.

"Keelan!" Dr. Garrison's voice froze her spine. "My darling, you are a vision from heaven!"

Lord, help her.

She tipped her glass and finished the wine in a solid gulp, ignoring the raised brow from Landon. At the moment, she didn't care what he thought of her. Her most immediate mission now was to escape from dancing with the doctor. More importantly, she needed to find a way to speak to him privately. And soon.

She raked a cheerful tone into her voice, "Good evening, Dr. Garrison."

Keeping his eyes fastened upon her face, he plucked her empty glass from her fingers and held it out in Simon's direction. The servant took it without a word.

Dr. Garrison leaned in and whispered, "Please call me Everett, my dear." Then louder, "Come, sweet Keelan, grant me the pleasure of dancing with my betrothed in my arms."

It was hard to swallow the groan. She did her best to keep a bright smile frozen on her face, but her toes cowered in her slippers.

She endured the first two dances of heinous torture. After he tromped on her foot a fourth time, she begged leave to get some air. "Really, Dr. Garrison...Everett... I guess I'm not used to this heat. Allow me to sit a moment and catch my breath."

"Of course, my darling. Rest while I get you a glass of punch."

"You're very kind."

"Not at all, my sweet. Perhaps we could take a stroll outside. It is most beautiful on a night like this, with the full moon."

The stroll would also give her a chance to speak with him

privately. It couldn't come soon enough. The urge to banish her charade grew stronger with each passing second Landon Hart was in the house.

Dr. Garrison made his way toward a buffet laid out with food. Halfway there, a short, stout woman, who was fanning herself madly, heralded him and pointed to a place on her arm. Keelan moved out to the veranda, where she'd have the opportunity to speak with the doctor in a more secluded spot.

If only he wasn't so kind and empathetic, it would be easier. She didn't deserve it, but she hoped one day he'd forgive her and maybe even understand her motives. Having her hand in marriage would never be same as having her heart.

After she accepted Dr. Garrison's hand and presented her proposal for Twin Pines, her father consented to give up the plantation. She was relieved both Jared and Papa understood it would benefit the family better, and even enable her to have a livelihood that could provide for them to a greater degree than country life ever could.

In spite of that, her recent actions still left a bitter ironic taste on her tongue. For all her efforts to prevent walking the same path as her mother, she still fell into the quicksand mire of a life without love.

Keelan would end up exactly like her; she would put all her time and focus into the shop, to distract from the loneliness. She had been foolish to think she could control her life entirely.

She was her mother's daughter, after all.

A young serving girl holding a tray of wine-filled stemware stepped close, and Keelan removed a glass. Perhaps the wine would dull the torment, as well as the pain of her bruised toes.

"Miss Keelan! You look beautiful!"

She turned. A petite blonde woman waved and wove her way toward her.

"Margaret! It's nice to see you again." She managed to smile. Margaret Hampton loved conversation, and if one wanted to know all the happenings in the Lowcountry, one needed only a short chat with Margaret.

Margaret opened her fan and spoke behind it. "What's this I hear about your engagement to the handsome Dr. Garrison? Is it true?"

"Well—" What should she say?

Margaret saved her the decision by jumping ahead. "Wonderful! I can only—"

Margaret froze, and Keelan turned to see what had attracted the young woman's attention so thoroughly, she'd stopped in midsentence.

"That must be the wealthy merchant captain I have heard so much about," Margaret breathed.

Landon was chatting with a stunning woman. Tall and slender, her hair gleamed like blue coal. The sapphire gown sharply contrasted with her ivory skin. Together, they made quite a handsome couple.

Keelan's voice caught in her throat, and she took a quick mouthful of wine to clear it. "Yes, it is. Captain Hart's here at my aunt's invitation," she said.

Margaret's whisper bounced with glee, "I've heard some very interesting things about him. When he was a boy, he emigrated with his family from Ireland, but his parents died on the way over. The ship's captain took him in and raised him as an apprentice of sorts." She paused for effect. "I've also heard the old man once was a pirate, who fell in love with a woman he took captive. He eventually gave up the pirate's life but even now his old ship mates continue to engage him on the open sea, in retaliation for his poorly-timed departure."

O'Brien's uncle Fynn Ahern had been a *pirate*? All the more reason to avoid Landon Hart. "Goodness, Margaret, you do tell the most entertaining stories." Keelan tried to laugh, but it came out stunted.

"These are no stories." Margaret's voice climbed to an excited hiss. "The old captain's nephew and Captain Hart now own an entire fleet of merchant ships. Captain Hart may not have come from old money, Keelan, but I'd wager he's just as rich as any titled lord."

"And pirates still seek him out," she murmured, recalling Landon's partial telling of the tale during the storm. And the solid comfort of his arms. And the heat of his kisses. An odd flutter skittered across her stomach.

Margaret frowned. "I wonder if he remarried."

Keelan choked on a her wine. That young woman really was privy to all *kinds* of information. What else did she know about Landon?

"I was told that while he was at sea." Margaret lowered her voice again, and Keelan had to lean closer to hear. "His wife became pregnant with another man's child, but the pregnancy went bad. Both she and the babe died."

A tight prickly gasp filled her chest. "How terrible," she replied in a hushed tone. Her assumptions couldn't have been more wrong. She felt like a bitter, shallow, shrew.

"Marriage does not suit me..."

Margaret fluttered her fan. "Well, he's done quite well, with the exception of his current choice for a partner."

The lady dancing with Landon was beyond beautiful. Her movements were as fluid as water over polished marble.

"Who is she? We haven't yet been introduced." Keelan couldn't take her eyes off the woman.

Margaret snorted. "Annette Camsby. She tried to sink her claws into the captain a couple of years ago, but he wouldn't let her. She wanted him to sell his shipping company and invest in land, specifically her daddy's failing plantation. He refused and left Charleston. Although, he occasionally returns, or so I've been told."

The woman laughed and pressed her hand to her heart before reaching over to stroke Landon's shoulder in a very familiar manner. If Keelan needed confirmation she'd made the right choice by refusing Landon's offer of marriage, then she certainly had it. She would be a simpleton if she believed he'd bind himself to her if he would rather sail the seas, than marry a woman as alarmingly exquisite as Annette Camsby.

And why marry a man who regularly engaged in hostilities with pirates? How horrible would it be to wait for a husband who never returned and not know whether he'd been killed by brigands, lost at sea or just chose to not come home?

The two conversed as if they were old friends, or lovers. "Mrs. Camsby seems quite comfortable with him."

Margaret harrumphed. "Her late husband left her *very* wealthy. Maybe she's trying to get Captain Hart to reconsider her last offer, now that she's no longer in financial duress."

Keelan felt slightly queasy. Still, she couldn't drag her gaze away as they walked toward an open window, the Widow Camsby's hand resting possessively on Landon's arm. He lowered his ear down to her lips and nodded as she spoke. Keelan found her cousin, standing near one of the food-laden sideboards. Aunt Sarah's fichu had fallen unnoticed, to her elbows. Doreen's arms were crossed as she glared at Annette.

Well, here at last was something on which the two of them could commiserate. Although it pricked her pride to do so, she had to admit she was no less bothered.

"Please excuse me," Margaret said, "I see Mother and Aunt Alice have taken a seat. I am going to see if I can get them anything. I'll be back soon." She gave her a shy sideways glance. "Perhaps you can introduce me to Captain Hart later?"

Absolutely not.

"Of course," Keelan murmured, careful to keep her voice expressionless. For her own piece of mind, she was determined to put as much distance between herself and Landon Hart as possible. In fact, it would probably be best if Margaret couldn't find her after she got her mother and aunt settled.

Keelan took in the activity around the room. Everett was completely surrounded by a cluster of elderly gentlemen and appeared to be involved in a very animated discussion. Doreen had managed to convince some poor young fop to dance. Annette Camsby chatted with several eagerly attentive men whom, like her, found the raven-haired beauty hard to ignore.

Landon was nowhere to be seen. Good, hopefully he left.

A servant wandered past with a carafe.

"Blackberry wine, Miss Grey?"

"Yes. Thank you," she said, allowing the girl to refill her glass. The last thing she wanted to do was watch Landon and Mrs. Camsby waltz again. She sipped the drink and glanced toward the open doors. The gentle whisper of solitude beckoned to her. Perhaps she could wander unseen for a while and enjoy a bit of the moonlit evening in peace. She'd wait for Dr. Garrison to find her in the garden.

She sauntered outside and down the steps. The strains of music from the ballroom drifted with her. She ducked beneath the wisteria blossoms dripping from the arbor and followed the path lined with moon shadows and tiers of herbs, until she reached the small lake. It shimmered in the moonlight, like midnight blue silk sprinkled with diamonds. She recalled her naked swim and how the crisp water had cooled her heated skin, and smiled to herself.

Sleek black locks and steely arms intruded into the memory, followed by hot, hungry kisses. Her breath came out in a puff, and she quickly swallowed another deep sip. When it didn't expel the image, she raised the glass to her lips again. A warm hand closed around hers and gently removed the stem from her grasp.

"Careful, Keelan." Humor laced the resonant timbre of Landon's voice. "Stairs are much harder to navigate when drunk."

CHAPTER 34

A DANCE

Keelan tried to sound disinterested, but her words came out thin, breathy and weak. "Spoken from experience, Captain?"

He gave her a boyish grin, his face savagely handsome. "You could say that."

Landon placed her hand on his arm, solid and warm beneath her palm, slid his other around her ribs and before she could object, they were waltzing in the garden, his fingers scorching her skin. Fragrant blossoms no longer permeated her senses. Instead, the scent of leather, fresh ocean breezes and sandalwood, intoxicating as the blackberry wine filled her to overflowing. The shiver bolting up her spine could be pleasure or unease. Both?

"I don't want to dance with you!" It was a lie, but she'd do better if she listened to her head while it still managed a coherent thought. Her body betrayed her long ago.

Weakling.

Although she stopped and tried to pull away, he trapped her hand against his broad chest, and she wondered what the skin felt like under his shirt.

"Come." Blue eyes brimmed with humor. "At least help mend

my broken heart by dancing one waltz with me before you wed yon gawky heron." He nodded toward the house.

"I can't—" Near panic spasmed in her chest. Absolutely not. "I shouldn't even be alone with you." Let him think it was because she was engaged, rather than the real reason. Rather than admit she had an impossible time thinking clearly when he was close. Or that his touch made her stomach flutter like a newly hatched bird.

Stupid bird.

His right eyebrow jumped up. "One waltz will not harm you, Keelan."

Oh *yes* it will. She slammed her lips together and tried to glare at him, but mirth circled the dimples in his cheeks like whirlpools. It was terribly distracting.

His teeth flashed in the moonlight. "Will you cause a scene at your cousin's ball?" Both inky eyebrows lifted. The answer twinkled in his sapphire eyes.

Yes, she was tempted to say she didn't give a horse's tail if she caused a commotion or not.

"Cause a scene? Here in the garden? Heavens no. I would simply return to the house," she retorted. *If* he released her. And *if* she could get her feet to propel her in that direction. Already warmth crawled through her veins, igniting her blood.

"What makes you think I'll let it be that easy, love?"

He wouldn't dare bring about another scandal.

Her eyes jumped to his, but saw no jest in them. Why waste time considering such a thing? Of course he'd dare. "Haven't you done enough damage?" Her voice sounded reedy and desperate.

His face became shuttered, and his voice dropped to a growl. "Damage? I thought I did you a *favor*. You managed to create a perfect situation where the man your father would've had you wed rejected you, and the man you wanted only had to announce his intent. That was your plan, was it not?" His eyes flashed like blue steel; his words clipped through the night air sharply, like horses' hooves on a paved street. His arms were an iron cage. Had he followed her to the garden to have a row with her?

"Yes. No!" Her insides twisted into a tangled knot, while he spun her words, making her appear mean and devious. His nearness warped her reasoning. The guilt she felt over the effect her actions had on Doreen made everything worse. Or did it clarify things? There'd been no other option that would have helped her attain her objective.

None.

At all.

His hand was turning volcanic. The fire from his palm had to be melting the fabric of her gown. Her breath thickened and became stuck as his gaze shifted from flinty blue to something heated. And lethal.

The hard angles of his jaw relaxed. In an easy silk-coated voice, he murmured, "Were you in your cousin's dress, I would strenuously object to the addition of a shawl, fan, or any other obstacle to my view."

The words barely crawled from her knotted throat. "That's because you are a lecherous rake."

He molded her hand to his chest, she could feel his heartbeat jarring her palm. Or was that her pulse jarring his chest? She studied his ridiculously attractive face and expected again to see mockery, but instead saw something hooded, almost feral lurking in his eyes. Her breath stilled. For a moment, she teetered. Should she flee or allow this to continue? It was fairly harmless, was it not?

That was *not* a clear head talking.

Many words described Landon Hart. *Harmless* wasn't one of them.

His voice rumbled from his chest like a waking volcano. "Relax, it's only a waltz,"

Relax, *ha*. "Fine, then let's get it over with!" she snapped, proud her voice cooperated, unlike her lungs, which were refusing to expand enough.

He sensed her tension so easily. Nothing disguised her frayed nerves. Curse the overpowering effect his very presence had on her peace of mind! Why was she so weak and gullible? She couldn't deny she craved his touch anymore than she loathed the misery its absence would bring later.

As they danced, the distant notes from the strings penetrated her senses and soothed her a little. They glided around the arbor. Their movement had no beginning and no end; it was a constant, fluid motion, moving to the rhythm of the music.

He was quite talented. After being the brunt of Everett's clumsy attempts, it was refreshing to waltz with a partner who seemed to anticipate the next note to float from the string. The night air was bright and alive and in spite of everything, she relaxed in his arms. Gone was the strain from acting her ruse; gone were her fears and concerns. She danced in the moment, and she felt free and safe and vibrant. Landon's long, lean fingers curled around her waist and squeezed gently, almost tenderly, sending that baby bird in her stomach flapping again.

"Dancing is like a passionate kiss," he said, his voice a slightly rasping caress, like callused fingers on sensitive skin. "It's much more pleasurable when you relax, and let the natural movement guide you along, like the kisses we shared."

Just the sound of his voice turned her stomach into lava. "Dancing is nothing at all like kissing, and I don't think you should speak of sharing anything with me." That sounded confidant and commanding, although she was still unable to keep the visions from flooding her senses. Good Lord, she would surely go to hell for all the lies falling from her tongue tonight. She closed her lids, which did nothing to make those sultry images go away. If anything, it nudged her imagination up a tempo.

Humor laced his tone again. "No? Spoken from experience, I gather?"

She pursed her lips. At least she made the attempt to purse them. She wasn't quite sure if she actually succeeded. He was teasing her again. When she let down her guard only a little, he pounced like a panther. Strong, sinuous and sleek. She saw him dripping wet and walking from the lake, with muscled thighs and powerful shoulders that rippled when he moved.

Molten, indigo eyes captured hers and mercilessly refused to release her. In those clear pools was an image of the two of them fused together by a kiss radiating blue heat. Her pulse quickened with the memory. Could he feel it pounding in her fingers? She realized, with some chagrin, he awaited her answer.

"Yes. No. I mean..." her voice trailed off. What was the question? Something about a kiss? Drat that man. Now her cheeks were blazing. "I have kissed plenty of men to know how to kiss." A tiny lie. Just add it to the others.

Tally away.

He leered, as if she'd just shed every last article of clothing. "I seriously doubt that," he said, something like a challenge heating in his eyes.

"Believe what you want, I don't care," she shot back. She almost didn't care. That was fairly close to the truth.

Sort of.

"Show me."

CHAPTER 35

A KISS

"*Show* *me.*"

No two words could have been more destructive to the fragile hold she had on her emotions. Her heart kicked into a more frantic rhythm, slamming against her ribs. "You've stolen enough kisses from me to know. You don't need me to show you anything."

"Oh, but I do." His voice draped over her like blue velvet on naked skin. He gave her a slow mocking leer "You can *respond* to my kiss, but can you initiate the spark? Your mouth is sweet and moist. How could it not be, with lips like these?" His thumb traced her lower lip, it tingled; making it almost too sensitive to touch. "But hear this, my love. It's your passion, spirit and zest for life that I crave to taste, breathe and experience." His gaze fell to her mouth, and she struggled to swallow. "Still, you have much to learn, and I have much I can teach you about the fine art of kissing. And making love."

His last words, spoken lethally soft, jolted her like a lightening strike. The fever abandoned her cheeks and tore down her neck, to crash and swirl deep in her belly.

She tried to sound calmer than she felt. "You must have kissed many, many women to consider yourself so knowledgeable on the subject, you raise it to the glory of an art."

"A few," he replied, apparently enjoying her discomfort. "There is more to it than placing your lips against a stone."

"I have not—" Garrison's kiss snapped her mouth shut.

They glided down the garden path. "Nothing fills the heart like a kiss born from passion and love," he continued, "It's extremely difficult to act as if you're in love, when you're not."

Landon aroused a new worry. When Everett revealed she had already accepted his proposal, did she appear to others as if she was in love? People married without love all the time. Not that it mattered, she would not marry the doctor now. She wouldn't marry anyone. Ever.

"I...was not acting," she scoffed. Nicely said. That didn't even convince *her*.

He leaned forward until his lips almost touched her ear. The light caress of his breath wrapped around her neck, and a shiver slid across her collarbone. "Then, were you acting in the cabin? When you cried out my name after I stroked that sweet, moist spot between your thighs?"

Crazy things were going on in her lower belly. She stared over his shoulder to avoid that sultry cobalt gaze. Places inside her ignited, the intensity driving every drop of moisture from her mouth, pushing it down to her core.

That moment had been haunting her dreams every night. Now she was having trouble controlling her breath. She should be ashamed of allowing him to be so intimate with her.

But she wasn't.

And she didn't regret it, either. No one would ever be able to stoke such fierce desire in her; she didn't regret experiencing it with Landon.

But, this conversation was moving along a dangerous path. She tried to change the direction.

"Love and passion aren't as important as other elements of

marriage. Fidelity. Honor. Trust. Respect. Those traits create the foundation required of a solid union," she countered.

"Commendable attributes." he agreed, squeezing her fingers and brushing them with his lips, hatching a thousand butterflies. "But what good is building a strong base if there is only an empty shell perched upon it?" Landon twirled her around a rose bush. "Love and passion give a marriage substance and purpose. Combined with your keystones of fidelity, honor, trust and respect, no empire could ever possess greater wealth or strength."

Her throat tightened. He didn't sound at all like the scoundrel she'd accused him of being. Did Landon Hart, the man who admitted marriage didn't suit him, truly believe his own words?

Was he simply telling her what she wanted to hear in an attempt to seduce her? He wouldn't assume that since she was already engaged, he could do so with no repercussions, no firm entanglements. Unless he was trying to destroy the betrothal. She was unsure of the answer, but she'd keep her guard up.

His warm breath caressed the tender skin behind her ear, and a jittery tingling moved down her spine. She was weak and vibrant simultaneously. It was a sensation she could have enjoyed, if he was her husband and not a man only concerned with adding her name to his long list of conquests. He played with sugary words and hypnotic touches in ways that made her feel helpless and hungry for more.

In fact, he stirred such a tumultuous whirlwind of emotions, she was like a tiny boat in a storm. Helpless. Adrift.

"What would a man like you know about love?" The knot in her throat doubled and tightened. "Ardor may flow through your veins, your kiss might leave young maidens breathless, but can you love only one woman?" Annette Camsby floated to the forefront of her mind along with the image of them conversing earlier, heads close together, her hand stroking his shoulder like a lover. Landon had appeared as comfortable with that woman as he was here with her. How could she possibly believe she meant anything more to him?

She locked her eyes on his. "Can you stay faithful to your wife when other beautiful women offer themselves to you without demanding the bindings that a marriage vow dictates? Can you love the same woman day after day, year after year?"

Landon's eyes had a fierce light, like a midnight fire. "If she captured my heart and trusted me with hers? Yes."

She laughed her disbelief. "Forgive me if I find your words hard to believe."

"Has Dr. Garrison offered you the same?" Something treacherous gleamed in those smoldering blue eyes, barely shuttered by thick dark lashes, tempting her to fling herself headlong into certain disaster.

"He has offered all I require." Her voice betrayed her flimsy confidence. Stupid voice. Stupid confidence.

"So you do not require to be loved." He twisted her words as easily as string.

"Of...course...I do." For some reason, that response triggered her chest to clench in panic; she wasn't sure why.

"So you love him?"

That's why. It was a trap. She sought to find some threads of truth to mend her irritating conscience. She could love someone without being in love, couldn't she? She repeated Slaney's earlier comment. "Sometimes, love comes later."

His voice was carefully level and soft. "So you are willing to take the chance that it might not? Even though you just admitted you want it?"

Blast. She'd dug herself a hole. She couldn't confirm his statement, because she didn't believe it either. Her own words sounded stoney and false, even to her ears.

What she needed was another change of topic. This exchange was dangerously close to revealing the plan she had recently set into motion before she had the opportunity to end it without causing additional chaos.

The grey and silver tones of the roses blurred. The pressure from his hand had already burned into her waist like a red iron against bare flesh.

She had to get away from him. He made her feel like a flustered little girl. She stopped moving and tried to disengage her fingers, but he was not cooperating.

"Wouldn't you prefer be kissed every day by a man who passionately loves you? Or would you rather kiss someone made of wood?" The corners of his mouth hitched up. "Like your Dr. Barn Door?"

"You are an arrogant..." Her words tripped over her tongue as she wrestled to pry his fingers from her side.

How much did Landon know? Or thought he knew? She spun away from him, away from those eyes that could read her mind easier than a children's reader. Away from the touch that left the scorched imprint of every finger. Away from leather and brandy and Landon's spicy soap.

The heavy, sweet fragrance of magnolia blossoms floated lazily in the night air. Nocturnal creatures added their song to the evening breeze, bringing the night in like a collapsed canopy. The moon was luminous, and her gown glimmered in its light. And things were still spinning even though she'd stopped dancing.

He finally released her. She twirled away and inhaled deeply, swaying with the soft evening air. His presence at her back rippled through her like a physical pulse. His scent taunted her memories. Trapped together while the thunder raged around them, she'd felt both hunted and safe. Then. Now, he was only inches from her and the hair at her nape stood on end.

"You are a vision," The gravelly tone made her entire body hum. "Garrison is a dolt. He has no idea he is betrothed to a goddess. Your skin outshines the moonlight, and you smell sweeter than a jasmine blossom in full bloom." His fingers traced a line up her arm, to her shoulder, heating a trail that made her vibrate. She should protest such boldness, but couldn't bring herself to speak. Or move. She stared at the lake, but saw only Landon's fiery blue gaze, intense and commanding.

"I would love you with the passion you deserve, Keelan. He would never worship you with the devotion I would. He could never sate your hunger or feed your heart as well as I." His fingers skimmed along the back of her neck, making her blood simmer. The tension inside her wanted to fracture and explode like a volcanic fissure.

Despite her desperate attempt to erect a thick emotional barrier to protect herself, an overwhelming need enveloped her. It pulled at her like the moon pulls the tide. His lips brushed her shoulder softly, leaving behind hot impressions on her bare skin. Gooseflesh rose on her arms.

Yes, he spoke honeyed words and made promises she longed to hear, but what about when he boarded his ship and went back out to sea? What then?

The caustic image of Landon waltzing with Annette, her hand on his shoulder, leaning in to whisper something intimate pushed itself into her mind in a bitter rush. How could a man possibly stay loyal when beautiful women practically fell at his feet everywhere he went? He was too handsome, too desirable, too charming. What woman on this earth could ever resist him?

How could she live that kind of life, living alone wondering if her husband was remaining faithful during the months he was at sea?

It was then she realized it wasn't that she didn't think he could love her more than another woman. There was something else standing between them, glaring like a red-eyed demon. It was beyond jealousy.

She didn't *trust* him.

She didn't trust his fidelity. She didn't believe him when he said he thought she was beautiful. She didn't think for a moment that once he seduced her into his bed he would ever want her again.

The craziest thing about it all was that for her, it would be worth the price.

Because, she was in love with him.

Hysterical laughter bubbled in her chest and threatened to escape. All she'd ever be to Captain Landon Hart was a light of love he had one summer in Charleston. He would sail off to the next port and to the next woman to catch his eye and she'd still be here. And her heart would still be irreparably damaged beyond all hope of repair. It already was.

Don't just stand here. Walk away from him.

Walk away.

"Yield to me one last kiss, Keelan."

CHAPTER 36

A VICTORY

The moon could have fallen from the sky, and she would have been less unnerved. She couldn't kiss him! She'd lose whatever tiny grip of control she still possessed.

Swaying slightly, she turned unsteadily to face him again. She'd drunk too much wine. One kiss? It was, in light of everything else, a small price to pay, was it not? Was she ready to abandon her pride completely and allow him to see she'd fallen in love with him? Could she stand to give him the satisfaction that he'd won his foolish game? Did it matter now?

"One kiss for your silence?" Did she just say that? It sounded as if she was actually considering it.

He grasped her shoulders, branding the flesh on her arms, and turned her to face him. "My silence concerning what exactly, love?" A corner of his mouth twitched; eyes flickered with mockery. "Would it be regarding your habit of sparring in boy's clothes in the early morning hours?" He paused and appeared to be pondering a very important thought.

She crossed her arms. "I already paid for that one."

"So you did." He scratched his chin. "Or maybe, 'tis the more treacherous pastime you play with Dr. Garrison's affections." His lips were moving against her temple. "Or Pratt's runaways? Which secret will you silence, dear, sweet Keelan?"

Pratt's runaways? Was he actually attempting to blackmail her? She took an unsteady breath. How could Hart betray Simon and his friends? How could he betray *her*? Her heart pounded in her ears so hard they went numb.

It truly was all a game to him. He had no care for whom it destroyed. Would he really reveal her secrets, or was this simply another ploy? She should call his bluff and make him admit he wouldn't, but it didn't matter now. It was a ruse, a sport. She no longer cared.

Another tiny lie. Maybe she cared a little.

Why couldn't he be honorable, loving, and passionate toward her instead of a duplicitous, scheming, scoundrel? Both versions of Landon Hart warred with each other in her mind. She desperately wanted him to be the former, but was terrified that in reality, he was the latter.

In fact, she was almost convinced of it.

"All of them," she sighed in defeat. "I wish to silence them all."

A victorious light gleamed in his eyes. "Then pay the toll, my love. A kiss." He stepped away and clasped his hands behind his back. "Whenever you are ready, then."

The conceited lout deliberately moved so she would have to approach him! Well, she could be just as sly. He asked for a kiss, but didn't specify any details.

She would beat him at his own game.

She closed the distance between them, placed her hands on his chest, rose up on her toes and plopped a quick kiss on his cheek. *Ha!*

He frowned. "That was not a kiss. It was a re-enactment of a chicken pecking corn."

She smirked and arched a brow. "You said to yield you a kiss, and I have done so. My debts are paid."

He smirked. "Is that why Garrison wishes to take you to wife?

I imagine he must be a simple man with simple needs to require no more than that pathetic version of a kiss. If it's the best you can do, then you are his perfect match."

Walk away.

Chin high, shoulders back.

Walk. Away.

She bristled at the insult and shushed the voice in her head. Stepping forward, she threw her arms around his neck and crushed her lips to his, curving her body into his hard, angular planes. In response, Landon's hands slid down over her waist, feather light, propelling multiple sensations to spiral through her spine.

It wasn't enough.

Her heart clenched with longing. His heady scent threatened to drive away any sanity she had left. She pulled him closer.

The kiss was an exhilarating blend of soft pressure and unyielding strength. Her heart abandoned a rhythmic beat and pounded erratically; her fingers moved to dig into the skin atop his shoulders.

The late spring night, leather, blackberry wine, the whisper of fingertips brushing silk, the velvety strength of his mouth all assaulted her consciousness and melted her knees. Thoughts swirled into a reckless whirlwind. The rigid barrier of indifference she had fought so valiantly to place between them crumbled at her feet.

All the warnings and rules she had given herself, regarding this particular sea captain, had been drowned by a tidal wave of emotion too powerful to stop. Her trepidations were no match for the intoxicating, physical lure of the man himself. She'd been captured by his seductive charm. Tormented by his kisses. Enslaved by the waves of heat his presence stirred in her.

Captured, tormented, enslaved but not loved. Seduced, yes, but not loved. Did she care?

An angry shriek broke through the haze. "Keelan!"

The shocked undercurrent in her cousin's voice hit her like an icy torrent. Startled, she gasped and opened her eyes in time to see Doreen whirl and run back toward the ballroom. Worse still, standing there staring with a deadly snarl on her beautiful face was none other than Annette Camsby.

She shoved against Landon's chest and to her surprise, he immediately released her. Appalled, she pressed her trembling fingers against her swollen lips and stared at him. His expression made her face burn with embarrassment and humiliation.

It was a look of triumph.

He'd won.

CHAPTER 37

A CONFRONTATION

Something was still not right.

Everett Garrison's pain and anger should've diminished somewhat when Keelan agreed to marry him.

Her presence at his side should be giving him peace.

Taking the commodore's daughter should be giving him *peace*.

New wealth in the form of Keelan's inheritance, Twin Pines, should be giving him peace.

He'd expected it to be easy to help Keelan conform, to be more like Rachel.

More docile.

More pliable.

Instead, since Hart showed up, she became more distant over the last few days. She'd taken to spending time in the kitchen house or on rides around the plantation with her maid. He'd never been able to find her alone.

She continued to evade him, just like tonight. He searched the area near the veranda, peeking into corners, and peering at silhouettes in the semi-dark of the moonlight, but didn't see her anywhere. Maybe the garden? Had she already fled to her chamber?

The iron bench wasn't visible from here, but she seemed to favor that spot. He reached into his pocket and caressed Rachel's letter.

Soft, sweet Rachel.

So demure, so willing to please him.

Keelan would learn. He'd help her become the wife Rachel would have been.

He headed toward the steps leading down to the stone path which meandered its way across the back lawn and toward the arbor.

CHOKING BACK A TORTURED SOB, Keelan whirled away from Landon and his victorious smirk and ran.

Arrogant, conceited horse's ass!

Angry tears pricked her eyes and threatened to spill down her cheeks.

She was an idiot. She'd known from the very beginning that he'd do this to her, yet she let it happen.

He toyed with her emotions like a sated cat. Hadn't she predicted it? She'd done her best to guard herself against him, tried to discourage him, but her best was as flimsy as ash.

He was much more experienced at this game. No doubt, he had played it many times before with other less gullible maidens. Fury welled inside her, along with the ever-present embarrassment and humiliation that always followed an encounter with that rogue. Even the cicadas taunted her with their chatter.

Fool! Fool! Fool! Fool!

Under the moonlight, the hedges and shrubs shone a silvery-green, casting ebony shadows. She stopped and sat down hard enough on the metal bench to jolt the breath from her lungs. Hidden by the wisteria vines, she rubbed her temples, willing her ridiculous heart to slow and those stupid butterflies and birds to settle.

She had no one to blame but herself. She had been naïve. He had goaded her into that kiss, and she had fallen right into the diversion. The embarrassment set her face on fire, likely evaporating the tears.

"Miss Keelan? Are you all right?" Dr. Garrison stepped into view.

She tried not to groan aloud. "I'm fine. I think perhaps I drank too much wine," she said lamely, waving a hand in the general direction of the ballroom.

"Apparently, so." There was an icy edge to his voice, "Miss Doreen sought me out with this ridiculous story about you and Hart."

Oh no, there would be *no* discussing Landon Hart.

In fact, she would not even utter his name. Her mortification had reached its zenith, and she was unwilling to revisit it.

Yet, for some odd reason, a giggle escaped, and she batted the air as if swatting a giant fly. "Oh, Everett, it was only a little kiss. He didn't think I knew how, you see, so I showed him I could. It was nothing."

Oh dear, why had she said that?

Everett's jaw dropped. "Nothing?" He sputtered like a soup pot with its lid on, left to boil too long. "Do...do you realize what you've done? It's not decent. You have compromised your reputation! Again! I chose to put aside the ignominious circumstances between yourself and Hart after the storm, because your safety and well-being had been my foremost concern at the time. But I will tolerate no more of it. Your cousin is already telling anyone who will listen that you were acting like some sort of, of... *Jezebel*." His words echoed sharply. "What will people think? We are engaged to be married, and you are kissing another man like a common whore!"

For a moment, she sat in stunned silence. Gentle, serene Everett Garrison now faced her, his face dark and furious.

Jezebel? *Whore?*

She sprung to her feet in outrage; her fists clenched at her sides. "How dare you speak to me that way!" She tried to glare at him, but her vision blurred.

She blinked.

Now there were two Everetts. The ground was uneven and her head was floating.

It would be best to retire now and discuss this in the morning. They needed to have a conversation, but she didn't have the fortitude at the moment. Landon had completely upended her plan and unsettled her nerves too much to concentrate right now.

She whirled away, teetering slightly. She was unsure as to the reason why, but suddenly, she had a strong need to release the guilt plying her conscience.

Hadn't she just decided to postpone this?

Even as her mind silently fumbled to scream an objection, she began to speak, "Everett, reconsider your offer of marriage if you want a wife who loves you, because you should know I do not." She started for the house, then paused and turned back, unsure if she'd spoken clearly enough. "Love you, I mean. *I don't.*"

Time to go to her room before she got herself into any more trouble with her overactive mouth. Kissing, talking, it didn't matter. It always caused problems.

He snatched her wrist and twisted it, yanking her back to him. She cried out in pain, and tried to pull away again, but his grip was cruel and tight. His face darkened and an angry leer sliced his lips open. "I will *not* reconsider."

Keelan's belly gave a sick twist. This man had never shown anger or even frustration toward her in the past. Her own actions were deplorable for a woman engaged, but of course, the wine was mostly to blame. Wicked drink.

"You're hurting my wrist." Her voice shook a little. For the first time since she'd met him, she feared him.

His face flickered and his expression changed to a more neutral one, though his nostrils flared as he spoke. Releasing her, he narrowed his eyes. "I will forgive your little indiscretion. It's obvious the drink addled your mind. Perhaps it's best you retire. We can talk in the morning."

He nervously glanced toward the veranda. "Allow me to escort you to your chamber." He gripped her elbow. "We should go up the rear stair. I'll see you to your room and settled, then I will smooth things over down here with Doreen." He began to steer her to the servants' door.

No. He could not just dismiss her words then lead her away like a misbehaving child. She wasn't going to go with him to her quarters, unescorted either. If Landon could so easily toy with her reputation, she could only imagine the story Garrison would create about his time within the confines of her bedroom. A wedding would definitely occur sooner rather than later. She jerked her arm from his grasp, backing away from him.

"Dr. Garrison." She spoke slowly, both to make sure he understood as well as to prevent slurring too much. "I would prefer to go alone. So please, leave me to suffer the consequences in solitude."

Everett's mouth flattened, gaze turning steely. He stepped nearer, bringing his face close. His eyes had an almost rabid sheen. "You know nothing about suffering the consequences of another's actions," he spat. "So much tragedy has occurred during the last two years in the Grey family, no?"

His ominous tone hit her like a blow to the stomach.

His fingers dug into her arms. "I lost my family too, Keelan. I know the heart wrenching pain caused by such a dreadful event." He shook his agony into her flesh. "Surely you know your father is dying. When he is gone, you'll be entirely alone." He gave her a brief, humorless smile. "Until you become my wife."

She narrowed her eyes, which seemed to clear her vision a bit. "I refuse to be treated like a possession." She shook her head, jaw tight. "I will not permit anyone to decide how I will live my life. You will find, that I do have a say, and I say *no*."

His lips drew back in a snarl. "I will have you, regardless."

It could have been hearing him put a voice to the dark, silent fear roiling in her own mind.

Entirely alone.

Maybe it was Garrison's words, maybe it was Hart's ruthless assault on her pride, or maybe both, that ignited the powder keg in her chest. She balled her fist and punched him in the stomach as hard as she could. He doubled over and gasped for breath, then lifted his head and stared at her, slack-jawed.

A muscle in his cheek twitched and rolled, betraying his effort for control, as he slowly straightened. He spoke through clenched teeth and a frigid hush seeped into his voice while his stare pierced her like a spike. "Your father has apparently neglected his duty to see you properly tutored. Even so, I will maintain my position and accept you as my betrothed. I'll see to it your father's estate and his coffers are well supervised, he owes me that much. I'll make sure your transformation from a wanton young woman to a docile wife is absolute."

His face twisted into shadowed crevices, and he took a step toward her, stalking. "One thing is for certain, my dear, dear Keelan, you *will* learn to treat me with more respect."

A sudden, chilling dread trickled down her spine. She'd obviously pushed him too far. In the past, he had always comported himself in a gentlemanly manner. However, even a man as passive as Everett must have his limits. She did seem to have a talent for testing a man's patience. She started toward the house.

Time to go.

"Do not turn your back on me!" He reached out and grabbed her sleeve. On the edge of panic, she snatched her arm away, and to her horror the seam ripped then separated from her bodice.

Her heel slipped off the garden stone. She teetered for a brief second, then stumbled and fell.

A savage growl broke the quiet night and before she could move, Everett was flying through the air like a spidery rag doll. He crashed into a nearby birdbath. With a muffled groan, he collapsed.

CHAPTER 38

A PROPOSAL

B *last it all.*
Furious, Keelan tried to scramble to her feet, but her legs were entangled in her gown. She'd lost a slipper. A slight headache began to throb behind her eyebrows. A rebellious sob escaped, and she rubbed her eyes with the heels of her palms. What a horrible night.

The cruel scent of sandalwood drifted into her nose just as steely arms lifted her from the ground and placed her gently on the bench. A warm hand replaced her slipper. She opened her eyes.

Sleek and lethal, Landon stood in front of her. His eyes were thunderous, face stony, all marbled planes and angles, every one of them livid.

His voice, although soft and gentle, still vibrated with fury. "Are you hurt?" He scanned her tear-streaked face, eyes softening as he wiped a tear from her jaw.

"This is entirely your fault." She hiccuped. In vain, she attempted to tug her tattered sleeve back into place.

"Yes." He withdrew his handkerchief and dabbed at the trails on her cheeks.

Through the cloth, she muttered, "Why are you here? You won your infernal game, proving that I am weak and stupid around you. What more is there?"

He studied her intently. "There's you."

She turned her face away, but it didn't deter him. He blotted another tear and brushed his fingertips along her jawline. She closed her eyes. Why wouldn't he stop tormenting her?

"Better to admit you don't love Garrison before the wedding, don't you think?" His voice was thick, soothing, almost hypnotic.

"I never loved him, nor did I intend—" She bit her lip, realizing she had let her last secret escape. She huffed a resigned sigh. Her charade had ended; she had nothing to lose by being honest with him now. She fiddled with the torn lace, and plunged on before she dissolved into a soggy, weepy mess.

"My father is still very, very ill and he fears he will die soon. That has led him to take steps to properly secure my future to his satisfaction. I accepted the marriage proposal from Dr. Garrison to ensure I could live in Charleston and run a shop while he runs his practice if all else fails. Truthfully, I planned on delaying the nuptials until Papa was well again, or I turned twenty and one, or found a more suitable solution."

She met Landon's knowing stare, then unable to keep eye contact, dropped her chin and stared at her hands. "But you knew, didn't you?"

"I didn't know for certain until we kissed this evening," he admitted gruffly.

Puzzled, she peered up at his face. "What do you mean?" He was even more handsome in the moonlight, like a carved statue, hard jaw, aquiline nose, eyes like a surging ocean, amazing mouth.

Very talented tongue.

He helped her to her feet. "You can't kiss one man like you just kissed me, when you truly love another," he said, voice remaining low and gravelly. "Nor would you have willingly kissed me if you were in love with him."

A wobbly moan drew their attention to Garrison. Thank God he wasn't dead. He'd raised himself to his hands and knees next to the toppled birdbath. Etiquette dictated she should inquire as to his well-being, but she honestly didn't care.

There. A solid truth.

He tucked a stray curl around her ear before cupping her face, directing her attention back to him. "You don't really love Garrison, do you?" The look on his face made her heart stutter.

The deep pools in his eyes were mesmerizing. "Nay," she said softly. "I do not love him." She closed her lids, the rest shouting in her head. I love *you*.

He tipped up her chin drawing her eyes back to his, voice dropping to a ragged whisper, "What about me, Keelan? Will you deny wanting to be with me, even when your lips tell me otherwise?"

Did he jest? Did it matter to him what she desired?

Didn't he realize he had conquered her weeks ago?

He trespassed upon her dreams at night and seized control of her thoughts during the day to the point of dangerous distraction. Sure, she tried to convince herself for days it was all simply a girlish fascination and lust for adventure, not actual feelings for him. However, would she want Dr. Garrison were he in this captain's shoes? No, she wouldn't.

She flicked a sideways glance to the birdbath. The doctor was gone. Good. With any luck, she'd be able to avoid him the rest of the evening.

Her heart was already too mangled to bother protecting it anymore. It was time to shrug off her pride for once and be honest. Her voice was no more than a wisp of air. "I can't deny that I wish to be with you."

Potent desire swirled in his azure eyes. "I have wanted you from the moment I first kissed you." He stroked the back of his fingers down her cheek and along her jaw. A heated shiver followed their path.

She let out a small sigh. "It's not the wanting and it's not the passion, Landon." His eyes clouded with confusion and she looked away.

Now he was torturing her in a different manner. Forcing her to put words to her emotions? He might as well strip her bare, and make her say it in front of the entire city of Charleston. "It might sound petty and vain to your ears but I can't—I won't—marry a man who beds other women or has mistresses in every port town. I'm not willing to live that life. I'm prideful, I know but—"

Keelan's breath caught as he silenced her with a single finger on her lips. He lowered his head. "Sweet, sweet Keelan, I want no one but you," he murmured against her mouth. "*Ever.*" His lips brushed against hers, causing her heart to give a hopeful lurch. This time, the caress contained such tenderness her tears flowed anew. Time stopped as he slowly claimed her mouth. She couldn't move, nor did she want to.

He finally broke the kiss and took both of her hands in his. She couldn't tear her gaze from his now if her life depended on it. The cobalt stare deepened. "Even when you chose another, I cursed myself for allowing the opportunity to have you slip away. I resolved that before the week was out, I would return for you and ask you to break your engagement and choose me instead." Voice husky with emotion, he urged, "Join me, Keelan. Leave behind your secrets and schemes and let me show you what it's like to be loved and worshipped for the woman you are."

She sucked in a frail, reedy breath. How cruel of him to say something so beautiful to her. This time, she didn't doubt his words or intentions. In his crystalline irises she saw nothing but a burning intensity, flaring with determination.

Emotion roughened his voice. "You do want me, want to be *with* me, don't you, love?"

How could she not? His thumb was making distracting circles on the top of her hand. "Desiring you, being with you, has never been a problem, Landon." His expression shifted. Guarded, anxious. She reached up and touched her palm to his cheek. "Loving you is the easy part."

There. She said it.

It was painful, but now it was out. Her heart was leaden, thick with sorrow, already grieving for something she never had in the first place. "The problem is the torment you'd cause with every departure." She gestured weakly toward the house and Annette Camsby. "It's the beautiful women who are naturally drawn to your charm and handsome smile and *you*." Her heart had been scraped raw; she had nothing more to protect, so she stumbled on. "I could never stand to be away from you so long, and the distance will always prevent me from completely trusting your fidelity."

"I know." His face softened even as something primal flashed in his eyes. "But, Keelan, love, I promise—"

She hushed him with a finger on his mouth. "Don't make promises you can't keep." She lowered her hand and turned her face away. In the light of the moon, the wisteria blossoms looked like drops of silver cascading from the vines. She didn't trust Landon and that hurt him, which made her hurt for him, but it didn't change anything between them.

Passion coated Landon's voice, making it husky and raw. "You once told me you'd never want a man who comes home for only a few weeks time."

She nodded.

"Do you recall what I said in response?" He wiped away a tear with a callused thumb. "I told you that any man who would leave you for even an hour was a fool." He cradled her face in both hands, storm cloud blue eyes drank in her features like he was memorizing every facet. "I am many things, but I'm not a fool."

For a moment, it was impossible to breathe. Her heart slammed into her ribs. "What are you saying?" It would be foolish to read a message in his words that wasn't there. Hope surged.

Would he do that for her? Would he leave his seafaring life behind? She could never ask such a thing. He loved the sea. Never would she ask him to abandon the source of his joy for her. But what if he chose it of his own volition? "Are you staying in Charleston?"

He shook his head, sending her world plummeting to shatter on the jagged rocks of disappointment. "I cannot. I have responsibilities and obligations to a great many people who count on me."

Her heart constricted painfully. "I would never ask you to abandon them."

He gave her a slow, painful smile. "Sweet, brave honorable Keelan. That is one of the things that pulls me to you." Heated blue eyes held hers with a charged intensity that made it impossible for her to even blink. "Keelan, I need you. I can't imagine setting the sails without you by my side. You've stolen my heart, lass."

By his side? "Do you mean—" Her voice came out thin, tremulous. She searched his eyes for any trepidation. Only warm conviction and a promise of fire swirled in his gaze. "Are you saying you want me to go *with you*?"

The fire flamed, brightened. He dragged his fingertips down her throat then rested his hand over her heart. "I'll always crave that reckless courage and untamable spirit in here. I can't live without them. I want you beside me every day for the rest of my life."

Every day.

A surge of pure joy cascaded down her ribcage, healing her heart and sending those birds and butterflies on a wild, gleeful flight.

He took both her hands in his. "Keelan, love, leave behind your schemes and plots. Break off your engagement with Garrison and marry me instead. Come with me now, tonight."

God, yes.

She flung her arms around his neck earning a satisfied growl from him. Here was a solution that hadn't occurred to her. To be able to both love a man of the sea and never be parted. It was *perfect*.

"Oh, Landon yes! I will marry you."

He crushed her mouth with his. From their first meeting, she was drawn to this man in a way she couldn't explain. It was as if, when she breathed, his essence flowed into her chest and surged through her veins. It permeated her being, invaded her mind, surrounded her heart, and enveloped her soul. Simply being next to him energized her and brought her senses sharply into focus. She craved the strength and freedom and vitality he stirred in her. Her mind stilled even as her heart soared to the heavens and time hung suspended in a mad twirl among the clouds.

Landon's voice rasped low and gravelly in her ear. "My light, my love, my beautiful tempest, I shall show you the world."

THE END.

TALES HAVE BEEN TOLD of events in Charleston in the waning days of July 1811 that set the course for the destruction of Twin Pines and the decline of the neighboring plantation owned by Leon Pratt. There were whispers of manipulations by a pirate to draw certain merchant captains into positions of weakness and easy plunder. Captain Gampo's spies were everywhere, and word was that he had targeted Hart's merchant fleet as his next prize.

FOLLOW Keelan Grey and Landon Hart's journey in The Heart of a Siren the second book in The Hearts of Adventure Sweet Romance Series.

Want it for FREE? Tap or type this into your browser:

https://BookHip.com/LBMLFDZ
Or, sign up for new release email alerts on Chloe's website: www.chloeflowers.com

THE HEART of a Siren

A DEATHBED CONFESSION.
A dark plot of revenge.
Enemies close in.
Will her charade be uncovered?

HER LIFE DEPENDS on her playing the part of a galley boy. She must rely on her wits and skill with a blade to both survive and defend the man she loves.

He has secret cargo to deliver, but when pirates kidnap the impetuous beauty who claims his heart, his plans go awry. Rescuing her turns out to be the easy part.

Then she disappears.

Has he lost her forever?

If you enjoy reading about strong heroines, charming smugglers and romance mixed with action, intrigue and a few laughs you'll love this series! Start the adventure today.

SNEAK PEAK

THE HEART OF A SIREN

BOOK 2

CHAPTER 1
THE PERFECT CRIME

The Heart of a Siren

CHAPTER One

CHARLESTON, South Carolina
June 1811

IF THEY WERE GOING to steal it, tonight would be the perfect time. The pirates watched.

And waited.

The moon was nothing more than a sliver in the sky, leaving the night almost as dark as pitch. A single sentry strolled along the street in front of the warehouse. He passed the main doors and continued until he reached the far corner. He yawned, stretching his arms out wide. Removing his floppy hat, he scratched his head vigorously and then jammed the hat back on.

After a lazy glance up and down the street, he pulled a bottle from his pocket and took a swig before he leaned against the wall and yawned again.

A dog barked in the distance, provoking a shouted curse from one of the city's sleepy residents. The sentry sank to his haunches, tipped the bottle to his mouth and then rested his head against the bricks behind him. Once more he looked around. Finally, with a bored sigh, he sat on the ground and placed his bottle within reach before resting his arms on his knees. Within minutes, his head slumped to his forearms. The gentle sea swayed against the pilings with the easy rhythm of a rocking chair. The street was quiet except for the gently breaking waves and the soft snoring of the sentry.

Drago Viteri Gamponetti, Gampo to his men, leaned around the corner and gestured to a pair of wagons waiting behind him. A few men slipped down to lead the teams forward. A loud 'clop' on the cobblestones made everyone freeze in stunned silence.

"One of the mufflings has fallen off," whispered a driver.

"Crowe, you'd best check them all before we head on," he hissed. "And check all the wheels!"

"Aye, Cap'n Gampo, sir." Crowe muttered, as he scampered hastily about doing as he was told. All metal parts should still be wrapped in strips of dark cloth to keep them from jingling with the horses' movements. He ran his hands over the strips of oiled leather covering each wheel. As soon as everything was secure, Crowe motioned for all to move out. The caravan stopped near the warehouse doors.

With the stealth of a shadow, Gampo descended from the lead wagon. Producing a key, he placed it in the lock and turned it until it gave a dull 'click.' After a quick glance toward the end of the building and the sleeping sentry, he pulled a glass bottle from his pocket and squatted by the door hinges, then removed the cork with his teeth. After the hinges had been fully doused with the oil, he stepped back and gently pulled one of the doors open a bit and then closed it again, testing. He repeated this procedure several more times. Satisfied he'd eliminated any squeaks, he opened both doors wide.

One of the men gestured toward the snoring sentry near the corner. Gampo studied the man, noted the whiskey bottle next to him and gave a slight shake of his head. The other shrugged, stepped down and grabbed the halter of one of the horses, then led it inside. Gampo followed and pulled the doors shut.

Once inside the warehouse, the men remained motionless while Gampo struck a match to the candle wedged between the boards of the wagon seats.

"Take the blankets and cover the windows facing the street," he directed in a dry whisper. "Once they're secure, light your lanterns and get to work."

"Aye, Cap'n."

The men went about doing what he'd ordered. They all were well aware there was no room for error. Failing to execute even one small detail could get them caught. Getting caught would get them hanged. It gave the men strong impetus to do the job correctly.

An hour later the wagons were loaded with casks of brandy and whiskey, rolls of silk fabric, boxes of spices, ammunition and countless other treasures from across the sea. They snuffed out the lanterns and removed the blankets from the windows. Gampo was the last to exit. The sentry hadn't moved. He chucked to himself. The poor tar would have a great deal of explaining to do when his employer arrived in the morning. Still smiling, he reached into his pocket, pulled out the key and locked the warehouse.

That ought to give 'im something to think about.

THE SENTRY SHIFTED SLIGHTLY. Steel blue eyes glinted from under the rim of his hat as he watched the wagons pull away.

After giving a slight nod to the roof of the boarding house across the street, an oil lamp flared in answer. Landon Hart rose and headed in the direction taken by the wagons seconds before.

"THEY TURNED east down the next street," Landon whispered to his friend Captain Conal O'Brien, as they followed the path of the thieves, staying near the darker shadows. "They're heading in the direction of the warehouses we scouted earlier."

Conal nodded. "Hopefully they take it to the one containing the rest of our cargo. It'll be harder to find the first half if they put this load in a different place."

It was a risky venture, but the only way to find out where their goods were taken was to leave the rest vulnerable. Conal had bragged at the pub near the docks that they had rented the most secure warehouse in the city and had complete confidence in the quality of the locks. They were so convinced, he'd boasted only one man was needed to guard the lot.

The thieves swallowed the bait, and now Landon had his hook embedded deeply.

An ugly image of Keelan in the brutal arms of one of those leering pirates nudged its way to the forefront of Landon's daydreams. He couldn't get the fiery-haired vixen out of his mind. His chest felt twice its size. The world around him settled. Keelan was *his*. He couldn't think of a better way to live out his days aboard the *Desire* than with Keelan by his side.

This was no time to be preoccupied with thoughts of a woman, but this wasn't just any woman, it was his heart, his love. It was difficult to avoid thinking about how sweet her mouth tasted or how she smelled of jasmine and sunshine...

Stop it.

An entanglement was the last thing he'd wanted when they made port in Charleston. He and Conal had suffered a major loss,

Conal's Uncle Fynn at the hands of Gampo. Bloody, ruthless pirate.

Fynn planned a trade route to include a stopover in Charleston so he could meet with Commodore George Grey, who'd turned out to be Keelan's father. Fynn had been very secretive about the reasons why he wanted to meet with the commodore. So, following the run-in with Gampo, they tucked their ships in dry dock for repairs. Landon and Conal kept Fynn's mysterious meeting out of curiosity more than anything.

While visiting Twin Pines plantation, he'd met Keelan, who was masquerading as a boy and dueling with swords with her father's valet. It was only after he'd had given her a brief lesson in knife throwing he'd learned Keelan was actually a young lady. Conal found it highly amusing and had retold the story several times at The Whistling Pig Tavern, where they'd rented rooms.

What Conal hadn't seen occurred later the same morning. Landon had caught Keelan eavesdropping from the depths of the garden bushes. At the time, he didn't know she was the commodore's daughter. He saw her as a curiosity. Up close, she was more than that. She was smooth and sleek with the quickness of a cat and the curves of a woman.

Eyes wide like a startled doe and lush lips parted in surprise, she'd have bolted if her hair hadn't been severely tangled in the branches. How could any normal man possibly *resist* the opportunity to kiss her? So he did.

She froze in shock at first, of course, but after a moment her lips softened. His boyish prank soon became something over which he nearly lost control, especially when he pressed his hips against hers and instead of pushing him away, she slid her hands over his forearms and pulled him closer.

Enough! Focus on the task at hand. Retrieve the stolen cargo without getting killed.

Then, he'd locate Keelan and find out why she had not yet arrived. Less than a week ago, she'd promised to sail away with him on the *Desire*. The Blue Peter was flying above his top gallants, signaling the ship was preparing to sail. She should have already arrived.

Unless... she'd changed her mind. Life on the sea could be hazardous and hard.

It could also be invigorating and prosperous.

Running away with him was a risk for Keelan. She'd have to leave behind the shelter of what little family she had left: an uncle, aunt and cousin, as well as the possibility of marriage. Dr. Garrison had already asked for her hand. Her uncle would have her marry Pratt, a wealthy plantation owner old enough to be her father.

To accompany Landon on the *Desire*, she would have to accept that there'd be a certain degree of uncertainty with each dawning day. Danger presented itself in many forms: British warships, pirates, privateers and tempests. Had she changed her mind and decided to stay within the protective embrace of the Charleston Lowcountry? Had Garrison convinced her that she'd be better off married to him, a country doctor, rather than a merchant ship captain?

Stop.

There was work to be done.

Landon pulled a bottle from his pocket and took a mouthful of the amber liquid. He sloshed it around, then spit it into his hands and rubbed it on his face and shirt. He handed the bottle to his friend.

"Seems a shame to waste it," Conal muttered sadly, as he repeated the same procedure.

Landon grinned. "Leave it to an Irishman to mourn the loss of a mouthful of whiskey."

"Look who's talkin'."

Landon threw his arm over Conal's shoulders. "Let's go."

The two men staggered down the alley.

Conal broke into song:

Oh, my wee lass is a fine, young lass if ever a lass there be...
Her bosom's as big as a bowl of figs
Hips broader than a wil... (burp)... low tree...
Oh, my wee lass is a fine young lass I hold in high regard,
Although she uses lard, her bannocks are marred,
'Cause they're shaped like me head... and just as hard!

They burst into bawdy laughter and stumbled past the first warehouse with no incident. However, as they passed the entrance to the second building, a wide bulk blocked their path.

"'Hoy there, mates. Where're ye headin'?"

Landon and Conal halted, each swaying slightly.

"Why, we be headin' to Miz LeBlanc's housh, my big man," Conal slurred. "Gonna bed me a strong Irish lash. Best in Charson. Char-lesson." He shook his head numbly. "Town," he finally stated firmly.

Landon jiggled the bottle enticingly. "Ha' yersef a slosh and join us, man." He thrust the bottle at the burly guard. "But we git firs' choice of the wenches, since it's our idea."

The man frowned and shook his head. "Ye couple of drunken sots can't find yer way to a wench if ye was locked in a room full of 'em. Madame LeBlanc's be two blocks west of here."

"Two more blocks, ye say? Wish way is west?" Landon scowled and squinted over the tar's shoulder. The windows were covered, but there was a sliver of light shining from the side of one, along with a bright red bolt of fabric. *His* silk, he'd wager.

Conal made an exaggerated turn toward his friend. "Did not the wench say three streets north and two streets east?" he said with arms crossed and fingers jutting into the air.

"Aye. She said two streets east and three streets south," Landon bobbed his head then staggered a couple dizzy steps sideways.

"Ha' we been goin' east or wes'?"

The warehouse guard rolled his eyes. "Listen lads," he said impatiently, pointing back up the alley. "Turn yer arses around and go two blocks that way and turn left." He waved his left arm and pointed. "Madam LeBlanc's be the white house with the red front door. Ye can't miss it."

"Two up then left ye say?" Landon repeated, blinking.

"Yes, man. LEFT. Turn LEFT," the sentry confirmed in an exasperated tone as he batted his hand to the left yet again.

Conal brightened. "Oh, well then. It's not sa far from here. We thank ye verra mush, me good man." He clapped the man on the back and nearly fell down.

Landon made a show of helping Conal regain his balance, then wrapped his arm over his friend's shoulders and spun him around. "Let's be off then. Ahead and to the lef'!"

"The left!"

Conal thumped Landon on the back and pointed up the street. "To the wenches!"

"The wenches!"

They staggered a few steps before pivoting around again to face the surly guard.

"Ye sure ye won't join us for a romp?" Conal shouted, although he was only ten feet away.

The man gave a wave and shook his head. "Nay lads, I'm workin' this night. Have a warehouse to guard." He pulled aside his vest to show the handle of a pistol sticking out of his waistband. "Ye go on."

"Suit yershelf," Landon slurred. They swung back around and shuffled away.

The guard chuckled as the drunkards staggered down the alley and paused a moment before making a right turn. Leaning against the warehouse door, he gave a dry laugh, shaking his head. "Ye'll not find a lass this night, lads."

CHAPTER 2
A PLOT

D r. Everett Garrison stumbled into the foyer of Twin Pines
and up the front stairs. It was hard to focus, and his head
ached with fury. Keelan's betrayal and Hart's interference roiled in
his gut. The events at the ball a few nights ago necessitated an
adjustment. He had planned to finish off Commodore Grey *after*
he wed his daughter, but the haughty wench made it necessary to
alter the timing. Keelan was his! He'd not allow Hart to steal her
away.

Two years ago Commodore Grey sealed his own fate when he
sunk the ship carrying Everett's family and beloved fiancée,
Rachel. The memory made him trip up the last step.

Rachel.

So loving, so devoted, kind, and gentle. In his dreams, he still
heard her whispered promises...to love him forever, and give him
a family. Children. Their children. Now, without her, he was a
spinning compass with no true north.

What else could he do?

What else would ease his despair?

He owed her more. She deserved more. Rachel should be
avenged.

Don't fret, Rachel, my love. The result will be the same. The commodore will resign his life racked in pain.

Vengeance would release his mind from the torment of her absence. It had to. It was all he could think about. Rachel came to him at night, crying in despair for the children she would never have. Her tears filled an ocean, rising up above her ankles to her waist, and neck; it swallowed her down into its depths, her mouth open, her arms wide...pleading...sinking.

It took considerable willpower to restrain himself from simply killing the commodore and be done with it. However, the man who murdered his family and his love didn't deserve a quick pain-less death. The gallows were too good for him, and while Everett was furious at the time, now he was glad the idiot was rescued and shipped off to America. He had time to coordinate and execute a slow, agonizing poisoning coupled with sharp, steady grief. One murder at a time.

Justice.

Sweet Rachel would have her revenge.

Hoping each death would chip away at the painful stone encasing his heart, he vowed to eliminate Commodore Grey's family members one by one. It was easy to spook the well-bred, but spirited horses pulling the commodore's carriage. The acci-dent was spectacular; the wife died instantly.

Excellent news arrived earlier this week. He received word the assassin he hired in London recently succeeded in eliminating the eldest brother, and that information lightened Everett's mood considerably.

Keelan was a jewel. Beautiful and kind, she'd make a suitable wife, after he polished her a little. He would teach her how to be more like Rachel...daintier...softer...reticent.

Obedient.

She would put his needs and desires before her own and see to his comfort. She would give him children. She would commit her life to making him happy. A fitting patch for the gaping hole the commodore tore open.

Keelan could never replace Rachel.

Never.

But he'd make sure she'd come very close.

Like a clay mold.

A replica.

She would learn how to be more like his Rachel. Then his life would be fulfilled and whole again. The dark, sad days churning with wretched loss would be behind him, forgotten. The world would be as it should be once again.

But Keelan must love him. She must love him as Rachel loved him.

It was bothersome to hear her say she didn't. That would change. He developed a plan to fix that element.

This meant he required the pirate Gampo's assistance, again.

Buy The Heart of a Siren, Book 2

MORE BOOKS BY CHLOE FLOWERS

THE HEART OF A SIREN

The Hearts of Adventure Sweet Romance Series

Book 2

A DEATHBED CONFESSION.

A DARK PLOT OF REVENGE.

A BAND OF TICKED OFF PIRATES.

WHAT ELSE COULD POSSIBLY GO WRONG?

*NOTE: This is the *sweet version* of the novel *If You Give a Rake a Reason*, (Book 2 of *Pirates & Petticoats Series* By Chloe Flowers).

A deathbed confession plunges Keelan Grey into a dark plot of deception and revenge. As enemies close in, she is forced to act a charade and soon her life depends on her playing the part. Now with the mystery of her true identity to be solved, she must rely on her wits and skill with a blade to both survive and defend the man she loves.

Smuggler and ship's captain Landon Hart has secret cargo to deliver up north, but when pirates kidnap the impetuous beauty who stole his heart, he prepares for battle. Rescuing her turns out to be the easy part. With a bounty on her head that has too many watchers out looking for her, keeping an eye on her seems like a good plan.

Until she disappears.

If you enjoy reading about strong heroines, charming smugglers and romance mixed with action, intrigue and a few laughs you'll love this series!

THE HEART OF A BRIDE

The Hearts of Adventure Sweet Romance Series

Book 3

REMEMBER ME...

HIS MEMORY OF HER IS GONE.

BOUNTY HUNTERS ARE CLOSING IN.

HER FIGHT FOR HIS LOVE SOON TURNS

INTO A FIGHT FOR HIS LIFE.

*NOTE: This is the *sweet version* of the novel *If You Give a Hellion Your Heart*, (Book 3 of *Pirates & Petticoats Series* By Chloe Flowers).

An accident throws him back five years into his past turning his new wife into a complete stranger.

Worse, a series of catastrophic events has Landon accusing Keelan of conspiracy and betrayal. When each explanation sounds more and more outlandish, her hope for Landon to remember their love becomes more and more futile. Bounty hunters are closing in and a nefarious landowner has discovered Landon's secret identity. More than ever Keelan needs Landon on her side if she's going to save both their lives.

Can she persuade him to trust her? Will he remember his love for her before it's too late?

If you love romance swirled with adventure and intrigue, you'll love reading about Landon and Keelan's road to their happily ever after, because true love always finds a way.

THE HEART OF A PIRATE

The Hearts of Adventure Sweet Romance Series

Book 4

HER TWIN SIBLINGS HAVE BEEN KIDNAPPED.

THE RANSOM IS A SHIP CALLED THE SEEKER.

SHE'S NOT A REAL PIRATE.

BUT THEIR LIVES DEPEND ON

HER PLAYING THE PART.

*NOTE: This is the *sweet version* of the novel *If You Give a Pirate a Treasure*, (Book 4 of *Pirates & Petticoats Series* By Chloe Flowers).

Captain Conal O'Brien's ship is overrun by the most unlikely band of pirates to sail the seas. When he discovers their true objective, he develops a scheme of his own. But these nutty brigands aren't who they seem to be, and if Conal's not careful, he's going to lose his heart as well as his ship to a lady pirate determined to possess both.

Stevie Sauvage is on a quest to find a hidden family treasure. When her eight-year-old twin siblings are kidnapped by the pirate, Captain Gampo, and the ransom demand is a merchant ship, she must find the courage to conquer her fears and fight for those she loves before time runs out for the twins.

The Heart of a Pirate is a high seas, historical, pirate romance filled with action and adventure, mystery and intrigue, and a quest for hidden treasure (with a few laughs along the way).

What readers have to say:

This storyline itself was well thought out and engaging. I have read a fair few "pirate romances," and I have to say that (this book) is up there with the best. FANTASTIC READ!!

I thoroughly enjoyed (the book), and I look forward to reading more books from this author. Well done, Chloe Flowers!

I Highly Recommend.

~ Amazon Review

THE HEART OF A SPY

The Hearts of Adventure Sweet Romance Series

Book 5

HE STEALS FOR THE FRENCH CROWN.

SHE HEALS FOR THE CATHOLIC CHURCH.

HE WILL HEAL HER HEART.

SHE WILL STEAL HIS.

*NOTE: This is the *sweet version* of the novel *If You Give a Spy a Scheme*, (Book 5 of *Pirates & Petticoats Series* By Chloe Flowers).

"Dramatic, engrossing, suspenseful, exciting."

French Privateer and former pirate, Captain Drago Gamponetti is given one final mission from his employer, the king of France: reclaim religious relics from a New Orleans cathedral. Trouble begins when he's forced by a mysterious, veiled, novitiate nun to swear on the Bible to protect the very items he was instructed to steal.

Church healer, Eva Trudeau hides more than her face behind the veil. The convent has been her safe haven since she crawled, beaten and bloody, to its door nine years ago. When an old enemy re-surfaces and threatens to drag her back into the dark underworld from where she'd escaped, both she and her dark pirate captain stand to lose everything they've fought so hard to protect...including each other.

What readers have to say:

Set against the backdrop of the famous Battle of New Orleans, This story will have you turning pages into the wee hours of the night. If you love pirates, history, humor and a bit of romance you will love this newly released book by Chloe

Flowers. The author has a way with historical fiction that enthralls and entertains.

BRIDAL VEIL FALLS

THE TOWN OF HAPPILY EVER AFTERS

COMING SOON: A NEW SWEET CONTEMPORARY SMALL TOWN ROMANCE SERIES SURE TO CAPTURE YOUR HEART AND TICKLE YOUR FUNNY BONE.

Chloe's Website: www.chloeflowers.com

ABOUT CHLOE

CHLOE SUPPORTS THE NATIONAL BREAST CANCER FOUNDATION.

Chloe Flowers is an award-winning author and the recipient of the University of Akron, Wayne College *2018 Writer of the Year* Award. She writes small town contemporary women's fiction, and historical women's action and adventure romance novels about scoundrels, pirates, and spunky, independent heroines.

Chloe keeps bees, and identifies her hives by the different flowers she paints on them. Her pets have always been named after her favorite characters or action heroes: Indiana, Luke, Gimli, Thelma, Rocket, Al Giordino, Severus, Mushu, Mérida, Jack...Dead Pool (he's a goldfish).

Chloe's biggest fault is the apparent inability to say "no" whether it's in response to a call for aid or a double-dog-dare to hike home through 30 acres of a snow-covered forest at midnight...during a full moon. It was early morning during said adventure when she came upon a group of sheriff's deputies searching for a lost girl. So, of course she offered to help (turns out, they were searching for her).

She is a member of the Romance Writers of America, Northeast Ohio Romance Writers and RWA Contemporary Romance Writers, The Beau Monde Romance Writers group, where she served as secretary 2017-2019.

She has given workshops and presentations on creating a critique group, how to provide effective critiques, story structure, marketing and self-publishing lessons to writers groups, library patrons and school children.

Chloe has a weakness for good red wine, Calvin & Hobbes comics, pie, dark chocolate and brown-eyed guys with beards, which is probably why she digs pirates, men in uniform and treasure hunters and writes about action and adventure and of course romance, which is the greatest adventure of all.

RECIPES

SCONES

COMBINE:

3 cups of Flour
4 T. Sugar
1 T. Baking Powder
1/2 tsp Salt
Cut in 3/4 cup of Butter with 2 knives used scissor-fashion
until you have coarse crumbs

Separate 1 large egg, and put the yolk into 1 cup of milk and then stir it into the crumbs until just mixed.

Separate dough in half and put one half on each end of a baking sheet. Using your hands pat each into a circle about 7 inches round.

With a floured knife, cut each circle into 6 wedges, but do not separate them.

Beat the egg white with a fork and brush the tops of the dough rounds.

Options: gently press raisins, dried cranberries, raw pumpkin seeds, or chocolate chunks onto the tops and bake 25 minutes at 400 degrees.

BANNOCKS

(Originally a Scottish bread) evolved to this recipe in the low country where corn meal was more plentiful than oats:

Boil 1 pint of milk and whisk in 1 pint of Indian Corn Meal. (Yep-use the same container to measure)
Beat well the yolks of 4 eggs with 1 pint of cold milk.
Add the 4 egg whites.
Add 1 tsp baking soda.
Add 1/2 tsp salt

Bake.

Yup. That's the recipe. I did some experimenting, and found that if you make 1/2 inch thick, round, scone-like patties, about the size of a dessert plate, and place on a cookie sheet and bake at 350 for about 12 minutes they turned out fine. Traditionally, you would grease a cast iron skillet and cook on the stovetop. 15 minutes for the first side, about 10-12 on the other side.

* If you want a more *traditional* Scottish Bannock, then you need a recipe that calls for oat flour or barley flour. I found a terrific one developed by chef Theresa Carle-Sanders. On her blog "Outlander's Kitchen," she presents historical and character-inspired recipes from the fictional world created by Diana Gabaldon,

author of *The Outlander* series. It's *brilliant*. I found one similar to it on another recipe site and tweaked it a bit until I came up with the one below. I have made flaky southern biscuits for years, but I have to say, the oat flour keeps the bannock moist without falling apart. I like it better that a regular biscuit, plus they are good even when they're cold!

TRADITIONAL SCOTTISH BANNOCKS

Yield: 12-18

Preheat oven to 400° F.

2 Cups All-Purpose Flour
1 Cup Oat flour (or you can use old-fashioned or quick oats-just pulse them in a food processor or blender until fine)
2 Tsp Baking Powder
1 Tsp Baking Soda
1 tablespoon Sugar
½ tsp. Salt
½ cup of cold Butter, cut into small pieces
¾ Cup Cold Milk
½ Cup Greek Yogurt

Combine all dry ingredients in a large bowl and mix well. Cut cold butter pieces into dry ingredients and mix well. I like to use a pastry cutter.

Stir together milk and yogurt. Add to dry ingredients and stir with wooden spoon to make a sticky dough.

Turn onto a floured counter and sprinkle with more flour. Knead dough lightly 5 or 6 times, working in additional flour, so that dough is no longer sticky

Roll about ½" thick. Use a biscuit or a 2" square cutter. You can also use a floured butcher knife and cut squares with it. Don't forget to keep dusting it with flour before you cut. Depending on the size of the square, you should get at least 12-18.

I usually use parchment paper instead of greasing a cookie sheet, but either works. Bake until just golden around the corners, about 15 minutes. Cool on a wire rack for a few minutes before serving.

Serve warm with butter, honey, or jam. For a more savory version, add 1/2 cup of shredded cheddar cheese in with the dry ingredients and serve with meats or soups.